IFWG AUSTRALIA DARK PHASES TITLES

Peripheral Visions (Robert Hood, 2015)
The Grief Hole (Kaaron Warren, 2016)
Cthulhu Deep Down Under Vol 1 (2017)
Cthulhu Deep Down Under Vol 2 (2018)
Cthulhu: Land of the Long White Cloud (2018)
The Crying Forest (Venero Armano, 2020)
Cthulhu Deep Down Under Vol 3 (2021)
Spawn: Weird Horror Tales About Pregnancy,
        Birth And Babies (2021)

CTHULHU DEEP DOWN UNDER

VOLUME 3

EDITED BY

STEVE PROPOSCH, CHRISTOPHER SEQUEIRA,
AND BRYCE STEVENS

INTRODUCTION BY
CAT RAMBO

AFTERWORD BY
JACK DANN

A DARK PHASES TITLE

Cthulhu Deep Down Under Volume 3

All Rights Reserved

ISBN-13: 978-1-925956-64-1

Anthology Concept Copyright ©2017 Steve Proposch, Christopher Sequeira & Bryce Stevens

V1.0

All contributions (story, or introduction or afterword) to this anthology are copyright ©2021 the authors of each contribution, with the exception of 'They Are Impatient' by Maurice Xanthos first published in Cthulhu Deep Down Under limited run publication (Horror Australis, 2015) edited by Steve Proposch, Christopher Sequeira and Bryce Stevens.

Frontispiece art ('Elder Things') by Michael Cunliffe; back art ('They Are Impatient') by J. Scherpenhuizen.

Cover backdrop image: permission granted for its use by Silky Oaks Lodge, Daintree Rainforest. Cover art and design by Steve Santiago.

Printed in Palatino Linotype and Bebas Neue.

IFWG Publishing International
Gold Coast

www.ifwgpublishing.com

This collection is dedicated to three wonderful horror anthologists who have greatly inspired the three of us: Ellen Datlow, Stephen Jones, and the late Martin Greenberg.

TABLE OF CONTENTS

INTRODUCTION

WHY I WILL ALWAYS LOVE (AND FEAR) THE WORLDS CREATED BY H.P. LOVECRAFT

CAT RAMBO

I was a voracious reader as a child and, after I'd made my way through most of the fiction in the children's room of our local library and had moved on to folklore and mythology as the next best thing, a decision was made among the adults in my life to give me access to the rest of the library. This was the norm at home already, where no bookcase was forbidden, but there was a certain gravitas had in being able to go down and pick out books from the much larger and grander first floor. The fantasy and science fiction section, my first stopping point, was at that time a handful of shelves set below one of the east-side windows. There was a set of H. P. Lovecraft's short stories, a multi-volume set, and whichever volume I grabbed during that initial foray contained *The Dreams in the Witch House*.

The witch's familiar from the story, Brown Jenkin, gave me nightmares for at least a week, and remains hanging in my own personal closet of terrors. Adding to the fright was the fact that I couldn't ask any adults for advice, lest the verdict be that my access to those books be removed. I knew, even then, I'd been hooked by the worlds they contained, including the Cthulhu mythos, which I'd revisit not just in the forms put forth by Lovecraft, but by his successors: Clark Ashton Smith, Robert Bloch, Ramsey Campbell, Brian Lumley, and then in game form, with *Call of Cthulhu*.

I ran a *Call of Cthulhu* game for multiple years and still remember particular moments with glee and fondness. And I kept reading in it, seeing new writer after new writer celebrating the universe where Cthulhu waits dreaming, drawn to its mysterious and sublime terrors, its caverns and mountains, and the horrific creatures that inhabit it.

The worlds are bleak, where unspeakable horrors lurk. Perhaps part of their appeal is that they embody the modern fears that creep around our own souls. Certainly they show us a side of what Lovecraft feared and hated; which poses another challenge—how to draw on that material without drawing on the racism and classism that underlay such images as the degraded denizens of Red Hook, dedicated to ancient and unappeasable gods, or the almost unintelligible locals in *The Color Out of Space*? How do we reach through Lovecraft's filters to the terror beyond, that fear of the unknown that we carry deep in our brains, handed down by generation after generation? This is a challenge that all of the writers contained in this anthology have risen to.

These stories—following in the footsteps of two excellent predecessors—bring the Cthulhu mythos to vivid life in Australia, placing it in locations across the country's varied landscape and even the waters nearby. There are stories set in the modern day, where technology allows the intrepid to explore new depths below the earth's surface and the ocean's waves. Others take place in more urban modern jungles, such as nightclubs, or hospitals. Some mingle the soul-eroding moments of mundane life—of caring for a parent whose mind is failing—with the soul-flaying terror lurking in a piece of art. Others see a far flung future, where children are forced into a struggle not just for subsistence, but life, with death baying at their heels in the form of unearthly hounds. Others fall back to the end of existence itself, showing us the last moments of humans trying to connect and assemble meaning from each other in the face of worlds being gradually extinguished.

What does it mean to story-tell now, at a time when we see implacable elemental forces working in our own world: fires ravaging Australia, earthquakes twisting the earth's spine, plague shutting down travel and socialising? These are stories of what people do in the face of an uncaring universe, how we band together to take on the worst that life can give us. They are moments where the impossible confronts us, and we do what humans have always done in the face of such tribulation: we say "huh, that's weird" or "oh, that's sad" or "man, that's tough" then we readjust ourselves, we cry, or we swear, or we vent our anger, and then we continue on with life and its daily priorities.

Enjoy these stories. They're stories of humans confronting monsters and unreal, alien landscapes, and yet, like so many of the stories written within Lovecraft's incredible, ever-expanding universe, they are almost unbearably real.

ALL THE LONG WAY DOWN

ALF SIMPSON

I wouldn't be too quick to believe what you've heard about the Ellie Dawes thing, because what you've heard is that we never found the body. That's the official story—meaning, that's what we told her family—but it's not exactly true. It's more that as a father, or a mother, or brother, there are certain things you just don't need to hear. Certain things that make it worse, right when you thought it was the worst it could ever be.

It's true about the rip. And it's true that, maybe if we'd been a bit quicker, we could've got the boat out to her in time. But that's always true. You could always have been quicker. Surf lifesavers patrol almost five hundred beaches around the country, but rips still take about nineteen lives a year. And people go: "Oh, yeah, but that's mostly tourists and people who don't know what they're doing." But they're wrong. It's mostly Australians, mostly young guys, and most of them are decent swimmers. Two out of three people who think they can spot a rip can't.

Learmonth Point is just a little way north of Sydney. It's not a popular enough beach that you'd have heard of it, but it's got a big surfing crowd. There's an SLS clubhouse there, usually pretty empty, and an observation tower. During the week, we'll have two or three lifeguards patrolling, more on weekends and public holidays. On the good days we don't do much. We get the flags set up, and people tend to try and stick between them. Sometimes they'll swim a little way out trying to catch a wave, or they'll catch a wave and it'll carry them wide, but most of them are smart enough to paddle back in when that happens.

This was a Saturday, so there were four of us on duty—Darren and Sam on the sand, me and Jane in the tower. Things had been pretty quiet so far. It was almost four o'clock now, and a lot of the surfers had already swum in and were packing their gear. I was watching a couple of guys who'd been getting a bit too close to the rocks when Jane put down her binoculars.

"She's in a rip," she said.

I brought up my own binoculars. There was a young woman in the water, a good way outside the flags, clutching her board to stay afloat. Ellie Dawes, twenty-one years old. She was on a weekend trip up from Sydney, where she'd been studying history and French at UNSW. She had family in Melbourne, and a long-term boyfriend. I didn't know any of this then.

We moved fast, although no one was panicking. Why would we? She had her board. It'd keep her afloat for as long as she needed. And she wasn't struggling, either, so she obviously had some idea about what was going on. A lot of rips will take you back to shore if you let them. Or you can go parallel to the beach and try to reach the breaking waves. Just as long as you're not fighting the current. Exhaustion is what'll get you killed.

I radioed the others and they got the boat in the water and started making their way out. Ellie was probably a hundred metres offshore now. She'd been a long way out already, and she was moving fast. And then she was moving *really* fast.

"Shit," said Jane. "Look how quick she's going."

"She's got the board," I said. "They'll get to her."

Jane had her binoculars back up. "She's accelerating, Tim. Like, she's actually picking up speed."

"As long as she holds onto—"

And then she went under. Board and all.

Rip currents don't do that. They're strongest on the surface, and they don't suck people down. For a moment I was thinking a shark had taken her, but we would've seen it. Or the guys in the boat would've seen it. Or seen her. She couldn't have just disappeared.

"She's under!" the radio crackled. "I've lost her!"

The boat crew were out there by now. At the place where she'd gone down.

"Got anything?"

"No good. I'm jumping in."

We watched one of them, Sam, dive out of the rescue boat. She didn't come up for a few seconds, and I had this flash of panic where I thought she'd been dragged down, too. But then she broke the surface, and, after another couple of seconds, Darren radioed back.

"Sam says something's kicked up a whole heap of sand. She can't see anything."

"What about the board? The board would've floated back up." And if she'd had the wrist-strap on, she'd have come with it, maybe. Though perhaps that was hoping for too much.

Jane was already talking to Emergency Search and Rescue. "Fifteen minutes," she said to me.

Which was too long. Once you're under, you've got about sixty seconds until your body forces you to inhale water. Then it's minutes. We might already be looking for a body. We might've just watched a woman die.

"I'll grab the other boat," said Jane. "She might've been dragged back by the rip. Maybe she's still okay. We should search either way."

"Yeah," I said. "Good thinking."

The radio squawked again. "Tim, Jane." Darren's voice. "We've got something."

"Is it her?" I asked, dreading all of the answers to that question.

"No, but it's…The sand's cleared and we can see…Screw it, you're going to have to come out and look at this."

I didn't quite catch his tone—the meaning in it. I was following Jane, then I was helping her launch the boat, but I was also somewhere else. As the senior lifeguard on duty, whatever else happened today, I was soon going to be making a call to Ellie Dawes's family and telling them that their daughter was gone. Missing or dead. It was a call I'd had to make twice before, to other parents and brothers and sisters and lovers, and I still made it sometimes in my dreams.

It wasn't their voices I heard, but the silence. The moment after I'd said what I needed to say, and was simply waiting for the impossible to resolve. I say simply, because grief is simple. Blunt and ruinous.

And that was it, I think. That was why, in the end, I decided to tell them only half the story. The official version. That, and many other things. There's an argument, and I'm not dismissing it outright, that they deserved the truth. For their grief. For their peace of mind. But there was no peace in this. And there are some things that no one deserves to know. Not really.

Because I couldn't have said that. I couldn't have endured that silence while they attempted to understand what I was telling them: yes, we knew exactly where their daughter's body was, and no, we weren't going to bring her back. We weren't even going to try.

Sam was back in the water by the time we got out there. Jane looked around at the shore as we pulled up to the other boat.

"This is crazy," she said. "We've got to be half a kilometre out."

A rip current generally doesn't run much further back than the breakers. That's what a rip is—excess water from the breaking waves running back into the ocean. The only explanation I could think of was that Ellie had been unlucky enough to ride the rip current directly into the path of another, apparently even stronger current. Though what might've made that other current, I couldn't imagine.

Sam was diving below us. She wasn't going all the way down—it was seven metres deep here—just trying to get a better look.

And it was obvious what she was looking at, because the rest of us were looking at it too. Darren and me silent. Jane quietly swearing.

"What is that?" I asked.

"Cave," said Darren. "We reckon."

The wrong word. Caves are natural formations. Cracks and erosions between plates of rock. This was a hole. A gap. A place where the sea floor should have been, and wasn't. Almost perfectly round, and you could've driven your car down it. A tunnel. I didn't like that word either. Tunnel suggested connections. A junction. A light at the end. I didn't want to know.

"Sam's trying to see if there's anything." Darren was saying. "Bits from the board, or…"

Jane was shaking her head. "She can't be down there," she said. "No way. How? She was holding a surfboard. Even if…" Her voice had a numbness to it. And a hint of longing. Any other explanation. Please, god.

"There's nowhere else," I said, feeling it as well. "This is where she went down."

Sam came back up, spitting water. "It's deep," she said. "Seriously deep. I can't see anything."

"This is insane," said Jane. "We would've been told if something like this was here. We would've *seen* it. Where the fuck did it come from?"

"There's debris." Sam was climbing back into the boat with Darren. "Broken rock and stuff around the edges. I'm thinking maybe it's just opened up."

A cave-in, of a kind. A chamber of rock buried for years, maybe centuries, suddenly cracking open. The water rushing in, sucking down, down into the deep. The plug pulled from a giant tub. What were the odds of being out there, right next to it, at the moment it happened? Slim, but not slim enough.

"You think that's it?" I asked. "The floor—roof—broke, and it sucked her in?"

"I'm positive," Sam said, pulling her swim cap off. "She vanished, Tim. She just straight up disappeared. She's got to be in there."

And, by now, almost certainly dead. Closing in on twelve minutes underwater. We stared into the hole, each of us sinking down. Swimming, struggling for the surface, only to find ourselves going *backwards*. Sliding down a slope in a nightmare. Mouths locked against the pressure while our throats pumped for air. That impossible choice between endings. And the dark. That deep dark.

"Fuck," said Jane.

"Search and Rescue's here," said Darren.

"Fuck," said Jane again. A sob.

The rescue diver went as far as the entrance, then came straight back up.

"Fuck that," I heard him saying to his team. "Dropped a flare, and it's still fucking falling. Thing's got to be more than fifty metres deep. There's no way in hell."

There were more boats in the water, vehicles on the beach. The rescue team got us to patrol the shoreline. We weren't going to find her, and everyone knew it, but it felt like something. It was better than staring into that hole, drifting above it. Less helpless.

It got dark, and the searchlights came on. A police helicopter made a few passes over the course of an hour, then had to pull out to refuel. The boats stayed longer. Cones of light out on the water, scanning at first, then all gradually circling around to the same point. Down. Enough light to see the darkness. And even then, only the edge of it.

We knew Ellie's name by now. One of the searchers had found her car in the parking area, and tracked the plates to her father in Melbourne. I'd made the call from the tower. Listened to that awful silence. Heard the disbelief in the background, then the crying. And at the end he'd said thank you, thank you for telling me, his voice blank with hate. I hadn't killed Ellie, but I'd brought them her death. I put the phone down, shaking.

Jane poured me tea from her thermos. "You okay?"

"No."

"Are they coming up, the parents?"

I rubbed my eyes. Lights on the water. "I think they will, yeah."

"We're not going to show them the…?"

"Would you want to see it?"

She sat back. Screwed the cap on. "If it was my family down there, then yes, I would."

"Why?"

"Because I'd hate not knowing. I'd hate even *feeling* like I didn't know."

"Even if there was nothing you could do?"

"There'd be something. Even just being there. Even just imagining it, with all the facts. Just *looking*." Her gaze had travelled to one of the vans on the beach. The rescue diver was packing his gear into the back.

"You can't blame him," I said. "It's a crazy risk to take, just to recover a body."

"He didn't even go inside."

"He doesn't know what's down there. No map, no light. It might not even be stable."

"You think I'm being harsh?"

"A bit."

"Well, fuck you. I'm not." She drank her own tea, cradling the mug in both hands. "We were thinking of heading back soon. Sam's place. It's closest." A searchlight passed over us. "You should come—try to get some sleep."

Sleep wasn't going to happen for any of us tonight, I thought. But it would be good to be with friends. I stared out at the water.

"Come on," said Jane, standing up, her hand on my shoulder. "They don't need us anymore."

And it ended, that never-ending night. And we did sleep, all of us, sometime between then and dawn, spread out in blankets and sleeping bags around Sam's coffee table and across her sofa. Needing each other in the way you need people in the dark. Their presence. Their nearness.

The search continued for a week, and we helped where we could. They brought in a few professional cave divers, who made a short foray into the hole, but came up empty-handed. "It just keeps going down," were the words. After that, they gave it a shot with a submersible drone. This bottomed out at around a hundred metres, as far as the remote connection would hold. And still nothing. It just kept going down.

A geologist came out to look at the site. His explanation for the cave's existence consisted mostly of jargon about water tables and limestone erosion, but was also littered with 'shouldn't be' and 'shouldn't have'. Shouldn't be that deep. Shouldn't have formed the way it had. Shouldn't be there at all, but was. He didn't say he was baffled, and he didn't need to.

Meanwhile, the news had spread and the mourners had come. Ellie's family. Her friends. Surfers who'd been there that day. Candles and wreaths in the water. Darren and Sam brought flowers. Jane helped toss them into the waves. I stayed in the tower, watching. A tide of tears and petals.

And then, a few days later, it was finished. The rescue, turned recovery, had been called off. The waves had washed away the wreaths. The surfers had come back. The only difference was the sign we'd put up on the beach—a warning to keep away from the cave. Not that anyone needed it. A few more divers came by— thrill-seekers, this time—but only made it just past the entrance before deciding to turn back. I caught them in the car park and asked them why.

"I don't know," one of them said, towelling her hair. "We got maybe ten metres in and I started feeling really weird."

"Like narcosis?" I asked.

"Yeah, that's what I thought at first, but we weren't that deep. I've been narked before, too, and this was new. More intense. Real call-to-the-void shit, y'know? I wanted to swim down. More than wanted to. I started thinking I'd die if I didn't. Then Matt grabbed my foot—I'd just started going for it. So, yeah, we came back up."

The rescue divers had mentioned something similar. At least, the ones who'd agreed to go in. A few, like the first, had simply refused. The others had found themselves gripped by that same desire to swim down.

It wasn't unusual. Breathing compressed air at depth messes with your head. Past thirty metres or so, the air in your tank literally becomes toxic, causing what's called nitrogen narcosis. It creates a sense of drunken euphoria, sometimes dread, and makes it difficult to focus. Divers can become wildly overconfident, forget to check their air supply, or confuse down for up. It gets worse as you go deeper.

But the others had all said, too, that this wasn't like anything they'd felt before. These were all experienced divers. They did this for a living. They knew what narcosis was and they knew that this was different. Something about the hole had drawn them in, or pushed them away.

I went back to the tower to find Jane with her binoculars raised. It was just the two of us today. There were four surfers out on the waves, but she wasn't looking at them.

"What's up?" I asked.

"See that guy? Down by the water?"

I did. And I definitely didn't need binoculars. "Yeah…"

"What would you say he was doing?"

He was short and bearded. Greyish hair under a bucket hat. Maybe early fifties. He had a jacket on, and shorts, but bare legs and feet. I would've picked him as a fisherman, except for the fact he didn't have a rod or any equipment. He was carrying a small basket; at this distance, I couldn't tell what was in it.

"Beachcombing," I guessed.

"Yeah. Except he's not picking up shells. Or sponges. Or anything, really."

"How long have you been watching him?"

"Today, only an hour or so."

I didn't like the way she said that. "And yesterday?"

"All day. And the day before that. And before that. He's been here every day since the memorial. That's when I saw him first."

"So he's a relative of Ellie's, you think?"

"Did you speak to her family at all?"

"No."

"Well I did. He doesn't look a thing like them."

"That doesn't prove anything." I was starting to feel uncomfortable. We were very visible in the tower, and it wouldn't be hard to tell where Jane was pointing her binoculars, if the man happened to glance up. "Should you really be doing that?"

"Doing what? It's my job to watch people. Our job."

"Not like this. This feels like spying."

"Nearly a week he's been doing this, and he hasn't put a single fucking shell in that basket. Not one. You want to know what he's picking up? Junk. Glass, bits of rubbish, and anything— absolutely anything—that looks like metal or plastic."

I had to laugh. "Seriously? He's Clean Up Australia or something. Doing his bit for the environment. We should be out there helping him."

"He doesn't pick up paper. I've seen him walk past heaps of wrappers and stuff." She lowered the binoculars, finally. "He's looking for something specific."

I shrugged. She was waiting for the question. "Like what?"

"Ellie surfed with a camera on her board—a GoPro. She used to put the videos on Facebook."

"How'd you know that?"

"I met her brother. He came up to me at the vigil, took me aside." She took a shaky breath. "He told me, if the board washed up, and if the camera was still on it, he wanted me to wreck it. Not return it. Not see if it still worked. Not even check what was on it. Just smash it to bits. He made me swear. Because he never wants his parents to have to watch their daughter drown."

She nodded at the man on the beach. "He was listening. I'm sure of it. I remember his face. He's a journalist, or something. Or he's got a website, or works for one. He reckons if he can get hold of that video, he's got the post of his life—and, given how utterly fucked-up the internet is, he's probably right."

"I mean, what are you going to do?" I asked. "You can't just walk up and take his stuff."

"It's not his, and I absolutely can. I'll whack the shit out of him if I have to. And you'll help me."

"Jane—"

"No. Don't even try it. If he finds that camera, we get it off him. How fucking awful would that be? Watching your kid die on Facebook? Having the whole world watch it?"

She wasn't wrong, though I still didn't see how, if he did find the camera, we were going to take it from him. Two lifeguards attacking and robbing a fifty-year-old wasn't going to go over well, no matter how we justified it.

"Maybe we should talk to him?" I suggested.

Jane didn't answer for a while. "I don't know. These guys don't really have a conscience about this sort of stuff."

"Could it hurt, though?"

"Yeah, actually. I think it could. If he knows we're after it too, he'll be careful. So maybe he sees it, but doesn't pick it up—kicks sand over it or something and comes back to grab it at night. He might not be that clever, but still."

"So what do we do?"

"We find it first."

She looked at me, then, and I realised she was asking a question. She was standing slightly off-centre, binoculars clutched above her heart. Everything about her was furious and desperate.

"Okay," I said. "We find it first."

We came back at night, when the tide was high, with torches to help us search. The wind off the sea was cold, and there was a hint of rain beneath the salt, so we'd each brought a jacket. Jane had also managed to rent a pair of metal detectors—cheap ones, but they'd make things a lot easier. I suggested we work our way out from the tower, but she had a different idea.

"He started at the south end," she said, indicating with her torch. "First day, he went all the way up and down—a quick pass, to see if it was just lying there. But the last couple, he's been thorough: turning stuff over, digging around. So if we assume that he hasn't missed it, and I think we can, then our best bet is to start from where he left off. So, here."

She led me to a space on the sand. "Maybe you go up the other end, to the rocks," she said. "And we work towards each other."

"Okay," I said. "Call if you find anything interesting."

"You too. And be careful."

I turned to look at her. "Of what?"

She hesitated, caught for a moment. As if she'd said something she'd only meant to think. "I don't know, okay. Just be fucking careful."

I made my way up to the rocks at the north end and started sweeping the detector about. I got a few pings early, but turned up only rubbish and the occasional coin. After a few minutes of this, I had a neat little collection of useless metal objects. I could make out Jane's shadow further down the beach. She didn't seem to be having much luck either. I waved my torch at her questioningly.

"Nothing yet," she called, and we resumed searching.

I wasn't convinced we'd find the camera. I wasn't convinced it was even out here. It had been attached to the board, and designed to stay there despite waves and wipe-outs, so I couldn't see how it would have simply come loose. And there'd been no more sign of the board than of Ellie. She'd carried it with her into the cave. Perhaps clinging to it in the hope it would bring her up.

I wondered if the camera had recorded sound. If we found it tonight, would we hear her voice? The first people to hear the last things she'd said? Had she been frightened? Calm? Maybe neither. Maybe just oblivious, or simply confused.

And would the recording continue underwater? Would we hear her start to panic, perhaps fatally? Thrashing for motion, frantic bubbles loping from her nose and mouth. She couldn't have understood, in that instant, just how precious they were.

And finally, would we see where she had come to rest? Was it possible the camera had been jarred loose when she struck the bottom of that pit? It was small. Buoyant. It could have floated back out. Would we see what she had seen as she drowned?

No. She'd had no light. The recording would show only darkness after she passed the entrance. And anyway, our plan was to destroy it.

I kept searching. Once or twice I looked up to see Jane crouching down on the sand, but when I flashed my torch at her, she always waved back a negative. I kept going until she called over to me.

"Check it out!"

She was pointing at the shallows. The water crawling up the beach had taken on a strange shimmer. Blue flecks of light were swirling in the waves. I hurried over to her.

"Bioluminescence," she said breathlessly. "Look at it."

I'd seen pictures of it before. I'd been to see it myself, in fact, down at Jervis Bay. Millions of tiny bright animals, reacting to motion, lighting the sea a brilliant, unearthly blue. Stars beneath the surface.

"It's incredible," said Jane. "I don't think it's ever happened here before. How lucky are we?"

We stood and watched it for a time. The waves igniting as they crested. Bright splashes on the rocks. Jane's silhouette before the neon water. Her hair spilling over her collar, the strands at the edge turned butterfly-blue. It was beautiful and wonderful, and for some reason I couldn't relax.

Jane brushed sand off her fingers, transferred her detector to her other hand. "Look over there," she said. "See it? Look how bright it is!"

I think she realised what she was pointing at, then.

The place where Ellie Dawes had gone down was alive with light. Riddled with it. Sparkling rashes in the water. Somewhere beneath it all was the cave that held her corpse. The cave that sucked in divers' minds, or retched them back out.

And now the sparkles seemed wrong, and watching them made my eyes itch. Visions of them burrowing into Ellie's body. Her mouth, her eyes. Bright parasites. A girl, organs bloating luminous through her skin. A girl diseased with light.

"Oh shit," whispered Jane. "Do you think that's where they're coming from?"

"Yes." There was no question about it.

"Would that even work? How would that work?"

"Maybe they were always down there. Could be a whole ecosystem." I paused. "Are we supposed to tell someone? CSIRO or somebody?"

Jane looked at me. "Do you think we should?"

"No. The less people that fuck around with that cave, the happier I'll be. They can find out from someone else."

"Okay then," she said, and checked her watch. "Two a.m. Ready to call it?"

I nodded and followed her back up the beach. I was trying not to look at the water now. Trying to avoid the light. We hadn't found the camera, but I was glad she'd chosen to leave. Glad, too, that on the drive home, she didn't voice the question I knew was in her mind.

A billion microscopic animals had been living in that cave.

What else could be living down there?

We searched again the next two nights, but faster, and less thoroughly. The bioluminescence had begun to attract small groups of night-time beachgoers, and we were worried that the bearded man might show up alongside them. We searched as best we could without making ourselves too obvious, and Jane eventually decided the camera wasn't here after all.

"I doubt it even came off the board," she said to me. "And it could have washed up anywhere."

"So it's gone?"

"I think so. Hopefully."

The bearded man didn't seem to think so. We saw him later that day, combing the beach from where he'd left off. He'd been all the way up once already, and was now working his way back.

"Fuck him," said Jane. "He can search forever if he wants to."

There were only a few surfers out today. I left the tower at one and went to eat lunch on the beach—a ham sandwich with cheese and egg that I'd picked up from a deli near my house. I gazed out past the breakers, to the place where the cave was. The bioluminescent plankton were invisible by day, but I still had the impression that the water above the site was of a slightly different hue to the surrounding ocean.

Jane was probably right about the camera. Still, it surprised me just how quick she'd been to give up the search. There was always the chance that it could surface somewhere. Perhaps the board would start to deteriorate and float free, and the camera would wind up at some spot along the coast. Even then, it was unlikely to be found, but I couldn't see Jane sitting well with that possibility. She'd want to know. She'd want to have seen it herself.

"Excuse me," said a voice nearby.

I looked up to see the bearded man standing over me. He was wearing his bucket hat, though his face was slightly sunburnt beneath it—patches of redness on his nose and cheeks. He gestured to a spot on the sand. "Mind if I join you?"

I shrugged and nodded, and he sat down.

"You're one of the lifeguards," he said.

It wasn't a question—I was wearing my bright yellow uniform shirt. "Yeah," I said. "Just taking a break."

"Were you here when that poor girl drowned?"

"I was, yeah. Did you know her?"

He shook his head. "No. I just thought it was very sad. But she's in a better place now."

A cave in the sea, my mind went. But I nodded again all the same. "I hope so."

"Do you have a god?" the man asked.

It was a weird question, out of the blue. But I looked the man over for a few seconds, and started to see him differently. It was easy to picture him leading the service at a little chapel somewhere, or sorting clothes for charity, and maybe still doing a bit of fishing on the weekends. Perhaps not a journalist, but a priest of some sort. The longer I looked at him, the more it seemed to fit.

He was waiting for me to answer. His eyes were very blue.

"I'm not religious," I said. "If that's what you're asking."

He nodded. I think he'd expected that response. "It was almost that, yes. What I was actually asking is whether you were a believer—whether or not you had faith."

I didn't quite follow. "Faith in a god? Or..."

"In anything, really. Faith in yourself. Faith in nature. Faith in people."

"I mean...I guess I do. Doesn't everyone?"

"Exactly." He gave a small smile. "I'd like to think so. Can I ask you something?"

"Uh, sure."

"Did you find it?"

There was a very long silence. "Find what?"

"We've all been looking for the same thing. You and me and your friend. I haven't managed to find it, I was wondering if you had."

"It's not yours," I said, after a minute. "Why do you want it?"

"Why do you?"

"We're going to destroy the video. So her family never has to see it. So no one does."

He sat with that for a time. "I see," he said. "That's a very noble purpose. I can see why you'd want to make sure of that. Can I ask a favour, then?"

I said nothing. He went on anyway.

"I would be very grateful if you'd let me see the tape. I'd only need to watch it once. But I'd like to see it, before you destroy it forever."

"No." I said, then: "Why?"

He chewed a piece of his beard. "Would it be enough to say that I have faith in what it would show me?"

"The whole point is to stop people seeing it. It's none of their business. Or yours."

The man sighed. "Very well," he said. "I didn't really think you'd say yes. I do understand, believe me." He shifted on the sand. "I'd like to ask something else, then, if that's all right by you."

"If it's about the camera—"

"Hear me out. The decision's still up to you, of course. And I imagine you won't change your mind. But I think, before you do it, you should watch it yourself. I think you should know what you're destroying."

"I already do. It's Ellie Dawes dying."

"The last moments of her life, yes. Someone should see them. Don't you think you owe her that?"

I'd had enough. I started to stand up. "Just what do you think's on this tape? What do you think I'm going to see?"

He paused, making a decision about something. "I own a map," he said. "It's a very old copy of a vastly older original, written in a language that is no longer spoken or read. Trying to decipher it has become a bit of a hobby for me."

"A map of what?"

"Well, that's just it, isn't it? No continents. No recognisable land masses. Just words, located only in relation to other words. Sounds difficult, doesn't it? You have no idea."

"Why are you telling me this?"

"Because—if I'm right—that cave you found out there, the cave where that girl died, is marked on my map. Marked by a single word. Would you like to know what it says?"

He waited for a response I didn't make.

"We're talking a few thousand years of translation," he said. "But I've gone through several sources, several times, and the closest word they've come up with is *exit*."

I struggled to put all this together. One thing stuck. "So you knew it was there, and you didn't tell anyone."

"Oh, absolutely not. Two-hundred-million years of tectonic motion between then and now. It could have been anywhere else. It should have been, in fact. But no, it's exactly where it's supposed to be. And you have to ask yourself *how*, don't you? Did the cave stay where it was, or did the cartographer predict its movement? Or—and here's one I particularly like—did the cave move to be where the map said it would be?"

"That's impossible."

"Ah, well, there's that faith I was talking about. I would hold onto that, but lightly. You'll want to let it go soon enough. It will be necessary, even."

"Now you're just talking shit."

"Call it the privilege of the elderly. I asked if you had a god. What you will find, very shortly, is that you do have one—in fact, you have several—and that these gods exist not because of your faith, but despite it. This will not make sense to you now. It will begin to make sense later, but by the time you are able to fully comprehend it, you will be blissfully and radiantly mad."

I was leaving by now. "Sure. Whatever. Good luck with all that."

"Tell her to watch it before she destroys it. Both of you should."

"It's gone, okay?" I snapped. "The camera's gone, so you can forget the whole fucking thing. It never came out of the hole."

He looked momentarily distressed, then broke into a broad smile. He had too many teeth. Maybe I made that up.

"Oh, good," he said. "I'm so glad to hear that."

It started raining later that week, and the wind turned arctic. All except the most hardcore surfers packed their stuff and went to find somewhere to warm up. We had to make do with jackets over our uniforms. I spent as much time in the tower as possible, and when it was my turn to patrol, I took to jogging up and down the beach to keep myself from freezing.

I didn't see the man again. He'd decided that whatever he was after wasn't here, or that he wasn't going to get it. I still found myself checking the sand for anything that might've washed up. But, aside from the usual heap of cans and plastic and Freddo wrappers, there was nothing on the beach that shouldn't have been there.

The bioluminescence had receded, too. The sea no longer lit up at night, and the beach was deserted after sunset. A follow-up story had been published concerning Ellie's death, and the brave lifeguards who'd risked themselves to save her. It was described as an attempted rescue, not a failed one. But that passed as well, and I slowly convinced myself things were returning to normal. Maybe they would have, if I'd never seen him smile.

It bothered me. More than the fact that there'd been something unnameably *wrong* about it, it bothered me that he'd done it at all.

I knew from all his talk about faith and gods that he was delusional in some way, but that sudden transformation seemed to seal it. He'd been intent on finding the camera, like we had, and insistent that *someone* should see what was on it. And then, the moment I'd told him there was no hope, he'd smiled. Like he was relieved. Like I'd released him from something.

I hadn't told Jane about any of this. She'd called in the day before, sounding like her nose was filled with Play-Doh, to report that she had the worst cold in history and would be taking a few days off. I thought about going to visit her, but decided it could wait. At least while she was still contagious.

Sam came into the tower. She hated the cold, and she'd swaddled herself in a blanket she'd brought from home, clutching it together with one hand.

"Oof, that's better," she said as she stepped inside. "It's bitter out there. My nose is going pink." She rubbed at it with her free hand. "Can I take a tower shift for a bit?"

It was just me and her this afternoon. Technically, one of us should be on patrol, but there was literally nobody on the beach.

"May as well." I pulled out the other chair for her.

"Awesome. Amazing. You, sir, have just netted yourself a five-out-of-five manager effectiveness evaluation from this minion."

"You're not a minion."

She did her best goblin voice. "Of course not, master."

We talked for a bit, but gradually the brightness went out of her. Then we were quiet for a while.

"How're you holding up?" I asked.

She tensed slightly, like she'd been expecting me to ask. "Oh, well. You know. It's gotten better. I mean, you don't really get over it, but also you do. You kinda have to." She paused. "It was the first time for me. I don't know if you knew that."

"Have you been talking to anyone?"

"Yeah. It's really good. And I've worked out a bunch of other stuff I never even knew I had, so there's that. But..." She chewed her lip. "I mean, I suppose now's as good a time as any. The person I'm seeing—I guess you'd call her my therapist, or whatever—she was saying that if I'm going to keep doing this, I have to get my head around something big."

"Which is?"

"That Ellie won't be the last. That it'll happen again. And I'll be right there, but I'll have to make a call, like I did with her." She pulled the blanket tighter, hiked it over her shoulders. "See, when she went down, I thought I saw her. There was sand and everything, but the water was clear, and I saw her. And after I jumped in, I still had this idea of where she was. And I knew I could make it, and I did. But she wasn't there. And so I thought, maybe just a bit deeper, maybe just a bit further down, and I can grab her. And at some point I realised I was way too far under, and that I had this call to make: her or me?"

She was looking at the ocean now, eyes unfocussed. "It sounds super-dumb, right? Because it's not even a choice. I can't bring her back up if I've drowned. But that was what it felt like—like if I started swimming back to the surface, then I was condemning her. Choosing for her to die and me to live. I don't know if that makes any sense."

"It does. Completely."

"Okay. So I take it you know what's next?"

"You want to quit."

She nodded. "Yep. Probably a month. Sorry."

"You've got something lined up?"

"Not really. But I'll manage."

"It'll suck to see you go. Like, really suck."

She gave a small smile. "Course it will, it's me."

"Have you told the others yet? Would you like me to—?"

"No, no. It's fine. They know. I told Jane when I saw her yesterday, and I called Darren this morning—mostly to give him crap about leaving the boat untied, but it sort of came out... What's the matter?"

I was sitting up, gripping the chair. That had to be wrong.

"What's this about the boat?" I asked first.

Sam put a hand to her mouth. "Oh shit. I wasn't supposed to say anything. You can't be mad at Darren, okay? I told him I wouldn't—"

"Sam."

"Okay, okay. I found one of the boats in the shallows this morning, just drifting in. Darren said he thought he'd pulled it up the beach, but the tide must've grabbed it. He was really upset. I promised not to tell you."

"And you said you saw Jane *yesterday*?"

She blinked. "What? Yeah. I came in to grab some of my gear and she was in the clubhouse."

"Doing what?"

"I don't know, something on the laptop. Tim, what's going on?"

"What time did you see her?"

She looked frightened now. "I...Like nine or ten, maybe? Tim, seriously—"

I checked the log in my phone. Jane had called me at eight thirty. She'd said she was sick. She'd even sounded sick. Then she'd come here.

"It's okay," I said, deceiving no one. "I just…I thought she was meant to be somewhere else."

"You're being really weird about it."

"I know. I'm sorry. Do you…Could you see what she was doing on the laptop? Or, if you had to guess?"

Sam shook her head and shrugged. "I didn't see the screen. She had headphones in, I sort of remember that. So maybe she was listening to music or watching a video or something. Do you want to tell me why this is such a big deal?"

"She found it," I said. "Jesus Christ, she found it."

"Tim?"

But I was already moving.

Why would you smile?

Let's say you were searching for something. Maybe you even had a map—a mad, indecipherable map that your family had passed down generation by generation, until it finally reached you. And maybe you somehow figured it out, and you went to that location—or maybe many locations, maybe there was more than one—and you searched, but never found anything.

Now you hear a story on the news. A woman's died in the water, her body's missing, possibly trapped in a cave. And now you think that this cave could be one of the spots on your map, and you roll up to take a look. But the entrance is underwater. Even experienced divers are having trouble getting in. You haven't got the training or the equipment.

And maybe you don't even want to go inside. Maybe you just want to *see* inside, to know what's in there. Perhaps it doesn't even have to be you: perhaps it's enough that someone else sees, enough that they bring that knowledge out with them, where you can get at it.

Then you learn the woman had a camera on her board. That there might be a video of whatever happened to her—of whatever's inside the cave. You search for it. You don't find it. You ask someone, and they tell you it's gone. The thing you've been after for years. Lost forever.

And you fucking smile.

The clubhouse reeked of seaweed, and all the surfaces were covered with sand. I went around the counter and checked the shelves beneath. The laptop was there—Darren's old one that we all shared between us. On top was a USB stick. I grabbed both and went to a nearby table, brushing the sand off and pulling up a plastic chair.

He'd smiled because he'd known something. He'd come to me, asking if I'd found the camera, and, for a long time, I hadn't said no. Then he'd asked me to watch it. Then he'd said *tell her to watch it*. Then I'd told him it was lost, and he'd smiled.

Because he'd seen her. Probably that very first night, he'd seen her pick it up and pocket it. And he knew that the only reason she wouldn't have told me would be because she'd changed her plan. So he'd known, right then, that it wasn't lost, and that it wasn't destroyed, and that Jane was going to watch it, if she hadn't already.

And now she was missing, and Sam had found a boat drifting in the shallows.

I flipped the laptop open and waited for it to wake itself up. I plugged the USB in and opened it. There was one file, the name just a string of numbers. A video. The video. I clicked on it, then hit pause immediately.

I couldn't watch this, but I had to watch this. Whatever Jane's plan, whatever she was doing now, it was tied to this video. I needed to see what she'd seen. I let it play.

A young woman. Blonde hair dull with salt and water. Freckles spread across her nose. She was paddling out, duck-diving the occasional wave, the camera centimetres from her chin. Hello, Ellie. Rest in peace.

She stood up to catch a wave. Rode it in. There were several minutes of her paddling, standing up, wiping out. She laughed when she caught the waves, and she laughed when she fell off. And she always paddled out to find the next one. I watched all of it. I didn't want to skip ahead in case I missed something.

Then she was in the rip, lying flat on her board and looking towards the shore. Somewhere off screen, Jane and I were watching from the tower as the current dragged her out to sea.

She looked worried, but not panicked. I could hear water. I could hear her breathing. Then I heard something else: a cracking, grinding sound from below the surface. Rock coming apart.

Ellie heard it too. Her head whirled around, and she bent to look over the edges of her board. When she came back up, she was pale. She started paddling. Her mouth opened to yell, and she was under.

The footage became bubbles and swirling sand. I could hear the sounds of Ellie thrashing. Whimpered half-cries under the water. I had to turn it down a bit. Then the screen started to darken. Deep green-blue into black. Still the sounds of thrashing. Bubbles. It felt like hours before it stopped, but then it did. And it had been less than sixty seconds.

There was only darkness now. No point of reference. It was impossible to tell where the camera was pointing, whether it was still attached to the board, whether Ellie's body was nearby. She'd been wearing her wrist-strap, but it could have come loose. I had no idea if the camera was even still moving, or if it had come to rest somewhere. There were still a few minutes of video.

I heard some glugs and bubbles. Perhaps air escaping from the cave, or the camera. Or Ellie. There seemed to be some movement. I couldn't tell.

Then a soft splash. Like waves against stone. Then dripping. Dripping and waves. We weren't underwater anymore.

Then a cough. Spluttering. Choking. Gasping words: "Oh my god oh my god."

And the footage ended. And I put my head in my hands and tried to resolve the impossible.

Ellie Dawes was alive. Or she had been, almost three weeks ago, when this was filmed. She'd been dragged into an air pocket—some place where the architecture of the cave had freed a section of it from the sea. She'd washed up there, alive, and we had left her.

No light. No food. No drinkable water. How long had she lasted? The battery in her camera was dead, so she would've been unable to film a message. A cry for help. A final request. Was it just chance that this had washed back up, or had she placed it in the water herself? Perhaps taken it with her, when she made the inevitable strike for the surface. Perhaps that was where she'd died—trying to get home.

Or had she found another way? Things had been living in that cave before we found it. For years, if the bearded man were to be believed. They were sea creatures, obviously, and no indication of fresh water or food fit for people, but the possibility was there.

It would have been enough for Jane.

I went to the back room and checked the lockers. We kept some scuba gear in here, chiefly for recreational diving. There wasn't much at Learmonth that you couldn't already see with a snorkel, but sometimes it was about the experience. Jane and I were both certified to eighteen metres. We'd used the tanks a few months ago, when a pod of dolphins had come by. One of them was gone. I grabbed the other, along with wetsuit, fins and mask.

When Sam saw me come out, wearing the wetsuit and tank and carrying the fins in one hand, she started shaking her head.

"Are you kidding? Is this a joke?"

"The other set of dive gear is gone. I think Jane's down there."

She looked out to the ocean. It was already getting dark. "What, right now?"

"Right now."

"Shit."

"I need your help."

She blanched. "You mean, go with you?"

"I need you in the boat. No, listen. I don't know what Jane's doing right now, or what she's thinking, but I know someone needs to be there when she comes back up."

"She might not come back up, Tim. *You* might not. She went *yesterday*—how much air is in that tank?"

Not nearly enough. Unless there was more down there. "Grab some food. And a light. And probably that blanket."

"You've actually lost your mind."

"Please, Sam. I don't want to do this alone."

She bit her lip, her eyes huge, and shook her head again. "This is nuts. This is totally insane."

We dragged the boat out together, and Sam started the motor

while I checked over the gear. The gauges were slightly scratched, but I could read them easily enough, and they seemed to be accurate. I'd filled the tank from the compressor outside the clubhouse. It needed a new filter, and the few test breaths I took were stale. The mask was filthy. I let it trail in the water as we motored out to the cave.

"Why, Jane?" Sam was asking the sky. "What the hell was in your head?"

I told her about the camera. About what I'd seen. Heard. Her face went white and stayed that way.

"How is that even possible?"

"I don't know."

"I wish you hadn't told me."

"I'm sorry."

We were at the hole now. There wasn't much else to be said.

"I don't know how long we'll be. Maybe wait a few hours, then—"

"How about you just go down there, grab her by the hair, and fucking come back up?" said Sam. "How about you make that your plan?"

"Okay."

"I hate this. I hate everything about this. Just come back up."

I sat on the edge of the boat, fitted the mask, and tested the regulator one last time. Then I nodded at Sam, leant back, and dropped into the water.

And now, down. And down and down. The hole stretched wide beneath me. The sun had just set, and there was barely enough light to see by. I unclipped a heavy-duty waterproof torch from my harness and flicked it on. It did nothing to that swallowing darkness, but at least I could see its edge.

I floated above the hole for a moment or two, looking down. Drifting over that dark, imperfect circle. The water distorted it in such a way that it appeared to be moving. Breathing. A throat, a pore, a pipe. Darkness organic. Inhale me whole. I drifted for a few more seconds, then adjusted my buoyancy and descended.

It was a tunnel, I realised. It had always been a tunnel. There was something at the end. Hopefully Jane. Perhaps Ellie. Maybe even that light, after all. I still didn't want to know, but now I needed to find out. I kept going down. My depth gauge showed seven metres, then eight, and then I was truly inside.

Almost immediately, I was seized by the urge to rise. To get out of there. It was something similar to what the divers had described. A powerful and irrational dread. Maybe not so irrational for someone without their experience or training. The gauge showed ten metres. Come back up. Just come back up.

I kept descending, keeping an eye on my air and depth, scanning the walls with my light. I'd lost sight of the surface now, and in the dark it was easy to lose track of myself, where I was, which way I was moving. Several times, I discovered myself kicking, fighting back against the buoyancy compensator, trying to go back up. It was stress, maybe. Or instinct.

I'd expected the chamber to widen out, but it hadn't. I was descending through a column of dark water, entirely uniform so far. The walls were smooth and even and absolutely unlike rock. Had the others noticed this, too? Or had their minds been somewhere else? Perhaps somewhere further down?

I passed eighteen metres quicker than I'd expected to. I wasn't sure how deep I'd need to go to find Jane. Thirty or forty metres is the limit for most non-professional divers. It gets dangerous long before then, but, below forty, the statistics aren't kind. Ellie had made it without a suit or a tank—though probably not without water in her lungs. And she had been riding the current. I didn't even know what I was looking for. I didn't have a clue what I was doing. I didn't want to die down here.

Oh help. Please help. What have I done?

I realised that I could see something, now. A vague shape. I was descending towards something, or something was rising to meet me. I checked my depth gauge. Fifty. I checked again. Five hundred. That wasn't right. I'd broken a world record. One more check. Five thousand. Five hundred thousand. Something was down there.

It was much too cold. The wetsuit wasn't helping anymore. I had enough presence of mind to realise that this—along with the dive gauge—was likely the effect of narcosis. The martini effect.

One martini for every ten metres you dive after twenty. It would have explained the lights.

Little blue specks beneath me. I'd seen them on the shore, and here they were. Returned, perhaps, or had they never left? Twinkling shapes that looked like eyes sometimes. Neon blue and so beautiful. I fumbled with the compensator, started descending faster, until I was among them. They touched my face, my hair. Some tried to crawl behind my mask. They looked like jellyfish, but their bodies were shaped and their tentacles thicker—like a squid's. I thought I heard them singing. Or was that the narcosis again? The depth gauge had popped. Couldn't take the pressure. I was giggling now.

I followed the trail of blue creatures. They led me down, and then they started to hook around and up. A gap in the wall, only visible from below. An open rectangle with four straight sides, all of different lengths. There was light up there, slightly green. I swam. And swam. And wasn't moving. Why not? Too heavy. I shrugged off my tank and compensator, then tugged the regulator out of my mouth. I watched it sink. If Ellie was down there, now she could breathe again.

But that rhombus hallway. It was longer than it looked. I swam it without oxygen, and when I broke the surface, I realised what I'd done. Realised that I might never leave this place.

But my gods, what a place to die.

The walls were metal and stone, a grey-green alloy that seemed to light itself from inside, worked into maze-like friezes that panelled and repeated up towards a ceiling I could not see. Square snakes in right-angled spirals. Inwards and inwards like tracks on a microchip. A geometric geology. Natural like honeycomb is natural. Like orbits are natural. And somehow still perfect. Beautiful and wrong.

I was standing on a smooth floor. That same alloy. That same light. Where I'd come from was a pool of dark water, lapping at the slope. Looking ahead, I could see the room extended several metres before it hit another wall. Between that and me there was nothing. The space was empty, extravagantly so. A grand hallway and a dead end.

I stripped off my mask and flippers and left them together by the waterline. I started checking the walls for a doorway or some other opening. If, by some chance, this wasn't where Jane had come, if there were perhaps other chambers off the main tunnel, then I'd need another way out.

And then, sweeping my torch beam around, I spotted something I'd missed. A flat shape by the base of the wall. Ellie's board. It was scuffed and scratched, but otherwise undamaged. The wrist-strap dangled to one side. As I approached, I realised there was something on top of it—a bundled-up rashie. Ellie had been wearing it in the video. She'd been using it as a pillow.

Imagine that. Lying on a surfboard bed and waiting for the cold and thirst and hunger to set in. Alone in what might have been a dream for all you knew.

"We weren't quick enough," said a voice behind me.

Jane was there, barefoot, still in her wetsuit. She looked pale and cold, a sickliness encouraged by the light. Her hair was stiff with salt.

"Why?" was all I managed.

"You watched it. You heard her. She was alive when she got down here. She was *alive*. She must have thought it was a miracle. And then we left her. Left her down here for weeks."

"So she's dead?" I asked.

She ignored the question, pointing to the end of the hall. "I tried to get through. I got stuck up there and couldn't get further in. So I waited. I knew you'd be coming, eventually."

"I came to get you, okay? Sam's waiting for us up top. I lost my tank, so we'll have to share yours—"

But she was shaking her head. "I'm not going back. It goes further. Much further. But I need your help."

"Jane, we're not doing this. She's gone. How much air's in your tank?"

"Some. Probably enough for one of us. She's not gone, Tim."

"We'll figure something out. What do you mean not gone?"

She stared as if I'd said something mad. "Don't you hear it?" she asked. "You're telling me you…can't…hear *that*?"

"Hear what?"

"Tim…" She was shaking her head again. Tiny movements. "It's Ellie. She's singing. She's scared—god, she's so scared—but she's singing. Calling out. The others heard it. We should have listened to them. We should have realised what it meant."

"Jane, this isn't…I don't hear anything. There's nothing there."

"Do you not get it?" she snapped. "I can *hear* her, Tim. I can fucking *hear* her. Right now. You think you can make me go back? You'd better be ready to drag me." Then her eyes changed. She was shivering, but she didn't seem to feel it. "We owe her, Tim. We owe it to her."

"Jane, just…We'll talk about it. Just let me see your tank, then we'll decide."

She hesitated for a second, then started walking towards the far end of the hall, motioning for me to follow. Our feet slapped quietly against the floor, the sound echoing up into the high reaches of the chamber.

"What is this place?" I asked.

"Why are you asking me that?"

"You've been here longer. I thought you might've—"

"No, I mean *why* are you asking? Do you think the answer's going to help you make sense of this? Do you think it's not going to just open up a million other questions? This place shouldn't be here. We shouldn't be here, in it."

"So why aren't we leaving?"

"Because I can hear her, Tim. I said this. And because I can't not know."

The light from my torch seemed to leave trails on the walls. Faint greenish marks as the glow faded out. I mentioned this to Jane.

"Yeah," she said. "The walls take in light, I think. You remember how dark it was on the video—that's how it was when I got here. After I'd been using my torch for a bit, the place started lighting up."

Which meant Ellie had been in total darkness for those days she spent here. She might not have even realised where she was. And maybe it would've been best if she hadn't.

Jane's gear was piled up in the corner. Her air tank was half-full. Or half-empty. It didn't much matter: between two people, it was half as much as we needed to reach the surface.

"Do you think there's any other way out?" I asked.

"Maybe. This is where I got stuck." She pointed at the wall. Looking up, I could see that it didn't extend all the way to the ceiling, but tapered off a few metres above us. "There's a ledge up there," she said. "And then a drop on the other side. It's pretty easy to climb, but that's obviously not how you're meant to do it. It feels more like a water lock. Like you flood this room and then swim up. I don't know."

"Any idea where the air's coming from?"

"None. I'm just glad it's here."

"We should really—"

"I know, okay. I just need to see her. I know she's dead. I just…If I go back now—if we even make it—I'll still be down here. I'll always be hearing her voice. So we're going to do this."

"What exactly are we doing?"

"Here." She turned to the wall. "I'll show you."

She started to climb, and I followed as best I could. Cubic patterns stuck out from the surface, everywhere and anywhere. It was as good as a ladder, if you didn't slip. I'd left the tank below. It would have been too much extra weight. We'd need to return at some point.

The climb was tough, but Jane had clearly made it before, and, by choosing the same handholds and replicating her movements, I was able to follow without too much difficulty. Still, I was breathing heavily by the time we reached the top.

It was a flat ledge, maybe two metres wide, bare except for some short, square pillars. On the other side of it was a pit. Exactly like the tunnel to the surface, but wider, and more obviously constructed. Perhaps the two shafts ran parallel. Maybe they linked up at some point. Vents or chimneys to the dark beneath.

"Tell me you're joking," was all I could say.

Jane was kneeling by one of the pillars. A bright yellow climbing rope was looped around it to make an anchor.

"On the video—when Ellie speaks, you can hear how big

this place is by the echo," she explained. "I figured that meant a massive cave, so I brought this just in case. Like, if she'd fallen, or…" She stopped. "There's only forty metres of rope." She gestured to the edge. "So we'll have to multi-pitch it. I'll go down and anchor off, then you follow, and we repeat. Same on the way back up."

"Jane, I really don't think this is a good idea."

"I know. And it probably isn't. But I have to see." She shook her head, wincing at a sound I couldn't hear. "Just quickly. Then we'll go. We'll find a way out."

She dropped the end of the rope over the side, and I heard it swish down into the pit. The darkness took it quickly.

"I'll be fine," she said, tying herself in. "Just keep an eye on the rope and listen out for me. I'll call when I'm safe."

She started to move, but I caught her elbow. "If we find her— her body—you know we can't bring it with us?"

Her eyes were on the pit, but she nodded. "I just want to see. It can't hurt to look, can it?"

Maybe it could. "See you soon," I said.

She dropped out of sight, and the place became very quiet. I sat down next to the pillar and watched the rope shift back and forth. Jane couldn't have been too far below me yet. I could have called out to her—just to check—but for some reason I didn't want to make any noise. I also couldn't pretend that she was acting normally anymore. Needing to see Ellie. Hearing her sing. The descent had done something to her. Perhaps to me, too.

I knew there wasn't enough air in that tank to get us out. Not both of us. Maybe I was hoping she'd find another way. Maybe I was hoping she wouldn't come back.

Minutes went by. I had no sense of time in this place. I'd been wearing a watch, but the glass had cracked. I remembered the depth gauge bursting. But that hadn't happened. I'd imagined it. Narcosis. Why was my watch cracked? How deep were we, really? How much had I *not* imagined?

The rope went slack.

"It's okay!" Jane shouted from a long way below. Her voice seemed to echo forever. "Your turn!"

And so I undid the anchor, tied myself in, and started down the wall. Jane had turned her torch on. I could see the spot of light on a ledge below me. I immediately shouted for her to switch it off. It was easier to climb when I couldn't see how far I had to fall. The rope would save me, in theory, but it wasn't a theory I was keen to test.

I got to the ledge after a few more minutes. It wasn't a natural formation—more like a sculpture carved out of the wall. Blocks and right angles. Though, looking at the sides, I could see that they weren't quite straight. Just a few tenths of a degree off. Just enough to frustrate your eyes. Maybe just enough to make you misjudge the edge.

Jane had wrapped the rope around one of the features, and was tugging to test its strength.

"All good," she said. "Ready?"

And we went again. And once more before we reached the bottom.

"Okay," said Jane, as I untied for the final time. "Good. We just have to make sure we come back this way."

"Unless there's another way out."

"Maybe. But let's not take any turns we don't have to."

We switched on our torches. This chamber was like the one above, though slightly smaller, relatively speaking. There was an arch at the end. A doorway, but massive. We passed through slowly, and came to the staircase.

I call it a staircase; it's the closest word I have. A bridge across nothing. A slope. It was pocked with circular divots— platforms a metre wide. The spread was uneven, but there was an unmistakable pattern to it. A staircase for something giant, that walked in a way I could not comprehend.

"Where the hell are we going?" whispered Jane. She was asking herself, I think.

We began making our way down, crawling and crab-walking between the divots. The slope was manageable, but steep. Both of us lost our footing several times, scrabbling our fingers bloody to stop ourselves from sliding. We could not see what lay below.

And then, at last, the floor levelled out, and we were all the way down. And we pressed forward, and we passed through another doorway, and both our torches died at once.

That darkness. Mesmerising. Shaped darkness. Degrees of darkness. So complete I ceased to move. A mirror placed before a mirror, and all the lights turned off. Nothing but that unending lightless depth. Still there when I closed my eyes. Visible always and never. How could I look away?

But the walls take in light, Jane had said. And they had. And now, they gave it back.

Brilliant and bright. Architecture as agony. Angles so keen it cut our eyes to look on them. Sculpture-things so beautiful my body moulded to mimic their design. Make me this way. Unmake me all. Beside me, I heard Jane retch.

We walked in a vast room, but the architecture was such that we walked on its ceiling. Me, she, dangling above an endless chamber of steel and stone. Columns and mazes and things that I saw, but which produced no image in my brain. A place built by colossal minds. A palace or a prison. *Exit*, he had said.

We walked on. When I looked at Jane, I saw other things—things that were not Jane. I do not know what Jane saw.

Sometimes I was below myself, inside the maze, looking up. Other times I was crawling along the walls. I wasn't always me. My body did not always obey. Memories, not mine, of a marble-smooth earth. Planets piled inside planets. A collector's cosmos. Words that would form stars, if only my tongue would lift.

Ellie had passed through here, too. Drowned girl undrowned. Awoken in darkness, caught between walls and water, she had tried to survive. Slept in the damp and cold on her surfboard, twisting at noises she could not be sure she had imagined. Set the camera adrift in hope, or hurled it away in helpless fury. Then, thirsty and sightless, she had climbed, and come to the edge. And blindness or despair had sent her over. But not to end.

We came to a chamber of arches, and above us were the stars. The blue creatures were here, and they danced in space. Tiles of stone spread out—tessellated pentagons. Jane moved forward and knelt, head bowed, murmuring little words I could not understand. I approached and knelt beside her, knee bent to that thin, resplendent thing.

My god, Ellie. My goddess. Ellie in elegy. Ellie eclipsed by all else Ellie. Ellie elect. Ellie elevated. Ellie-gant. Ellie-quent. Ellie-mental. What have they done to you?

Stretched girl. Her body unravelled like pale netting. Cast between arches. Wired into the heart of the earth, still beating. She was not dead, nor would she ever be. Singing, yes, she was singing, but also screaming. And silent, too. That awful silence. The impossible resolved, dissolved and now absolved. Grief is simple. We wept for her, and she watched us and wept too.

How long we knelt does not matter. Time was trapped with us, here. The mazes would keep it lost and circling. Already, in the other arches, more Ellies were forming. Half-Ellies, imperfect Ellies. An Ellie factory. She, the template for a machine that did not know how to make her; a machine designed with no knowledge of her kind, but one which would not stop, because it was not built to stop. A beetle crawls into an engine.

"We have to do something," said Jane. "We have to get her out."

But there was no way. This was a thing built well. To break it, we would have had to understand it, and to understand it, we would have had to break.

"Help me," said Jane. "Tim, help me. Pull her out."

But there was so much of her. Ropes and sheets and swaying ribbons. We could not have gathered it all. Nor was all of it Ellie.

I touched a piece of her—singing, screaming, soft—and felt her move between my fingers. Oceans. The sound of waves. Ellie dreaming. Salt on the wind. A better place, he had said. And I hoped so.

"I'm sorry," I whispered. "We weren't quick enough."

Jane was still tugging at the strands. Ropy like gum. "We can't leave her like this."

But now the water was coming in. Ellie's ocean, pooling at our feet. Dripping from her ruined self, pouring from her dreams. Her salt, her story. It reached our shins, then our waists. Still Jane would not let go.

"You called me," she was saying, over and over. "You called

me, Ellie. Don't send me away."

It was up to our necks now, and we did not float in it. Then I was beneath, salt stinging my eyes and nostrils, and the blue things swirled around me. Peppering and prickling. Sparks beneath my skin.

no way out, said Ellie. *but here you are*
not for me, not for us, not yet
but maybe someday
so close
and still only at the surface
someday
we shall go
all the long way down

Then the water was in my throat, and the last bubbles eked out. Their surfaces swam with dreams, like oil. A face with blonde hair and freckles. A girl alone in the dark and the deep. She reached for me with hands transformed. She lifted me into the stars.

In those days that followed, I could never quite convince myself that Ellie had set us free. After Sam had seen our bodies floating up from the cave. After she had pulled us, one by one, into the boat, and attempted resuscitation, only to discover there was no water in our lungs. After she had taken us to hospital, and the doctors had treated us for mild hypothermia, but pronounced us otherwise healthy.

We microwaved the camera at Sam's place, all three of us. It sparked and cracked and produced some foul smoke, but at least we had seen it done. Jane refused to speak of anything that had happened. Sam asked me instead, but I always seemed to run out of words.

"You should come with me," she said, in her kitchen. "Not like, permanently or anything. Just until you get through it. I don't think you should stay, is what I'm saying."

She was right, but I had nowhere to go. No energy to get there.

"I'll be okay," I said.

Sam frowned, not believing. "I'll give you Silvia's number—she's really good. Just do a few sessions. Promise me."

I did. She seemed satisfied, but not any happier.

"Jane, too. You'll have to make her go."

"I don't think she'll—"

"I don't give a fuck, Tim. Something's wrong with her. With both of you. I don't know if it's a psych you need, or drugs, or whatever, but I'd be a shitty friend if I just let you carry on like this."

"You're a good friend, Sam."

"I know. That's what I just said. Now go talk to her."

Jane was out in the yard, drinking lemonade from a can. She'd been obsessed with sweet things since we'd come back. Nothing savoury. Nothing with salt.

I came up quietly. "Sam's worried about us."

"Yeah. I know."

"Are you going to talk to her?"

"You know I can't."

I squatted down beside her. It was late afternoon, and insects were circling above the grass.

"Has it stopped?" I asked. "Her singing?"

Jane paused, then nodded. "I don't understand. She was calling for me, calling and calling, and then she sent me back. And now I can't hear her—I couldn't bear to hear her. Even the memory of it."

I had wondered about this. That for some, Ellie's song had been a call. For others, a warning. Some divers drawn in, others sent flailing for the surface. Jane had heard it as music at first, but now she was feeling what I'd felt. That dread. That frantic need to turn and flee.

"Did Sam tell you about the cave?" she asked.

"Yeah."

It was gone. Sealed. Sam had said it was a collapse, that we'd just got out in time. But somehow I knew that if someone were to clear away the rubble, they would find nothing beneath. Not that it was no longer there—it had been bored when the earth was new, it would always be there—but, for now, we could not reach it from here.

"I'm going to go down to Melbourne for a bit," said Jane. "See a few friends. Maybe think about university again."

"That sounds like a good idea."

"I'm not sure if I'll be back."

"No argument here. I think we're all a bit done with this."

"Except Darren."

"Lucky fucking Darren."

She smiled at that. "Yeah. Can't hate him for it, though. Not openly, anyway."

"Poor guy."

"Poor us."

We watched the insects, caught in the slanting light.

"Sam wants us to stay for dinner," I said. "She's cooking something."

"Not in the microwave, I hope."

"Ha. Yeah. No." I stood up, shifted. "I was thinking about a walk. Interested?"

She sipped her lemonade. "Nope. On your own there."

"Okay."

I left through the house, spoke briefly to Sam, and started down the street. The sea was visible from here, a thin line against a yellow-pink sky. I continued to the beach.

The surfers had come in. Most were in the car park, packing up, and only a few remained on the sand. Just past the tower, an elderly couple were walking a Labrador. It bounded in and out of the water, shaking its head and ears. Every so often, a wave would catch it in the chest, and it would sprint back to the shore.

I kept going to the water's edge, then kicked off my shoes and let the ripples run over my feet. Somewhere behind me, the sun was setting, and the shade was suddenly cold.

Those she had called, she had sent back. What of those she had tried to send back? The first diver. Several of the others. All driven off by dread. Spat back out. What would it have taken for one to resist? And what would it have proved if they had? If a person had felt that fear, had forged on despite the screaming in their mind, and had made it—all the way down—who would they then be?

But she had sent me back, too.

The couple and the dog had moved on. The last surfers were walking up to their cars. I stripped off my clothes and waded into the sea. It was warm, so much warmer than I'd ever felt it before, and the salt was sharp against my skin.

I found the rip by looking for the darker water, where it was waveless and smooth. It was still only waist-deep, but I lowered myself in and let the current take me. Then I turned onto my back and floated. Don't fight. That's what'll kill you.

Jane had not heard her speak. That was obvious to me. And I didn't bring it up. Didn't mention the drowned woman's words. There are certain things you don't need to hear. Jane could keep her faith a little longer. I owed her that.

Because we hadn't gone all the way down. Not even close. We had thought we weren't quick enough. The truth was that we had been too quick.

A tunnel through the earth to somewhere else. A light at the end, both beautiful and wrong. A way out, for all of us. Exit. Not yet. But someday.

Someday, she would call us home.

The water was warm. Rocked by the waves, encircled by the stars, I ducked my head below the surface, and let my ears fill with her song.

FAREWELL TO ELEPHANT

CAT SPARKS

The little kid's hair was matted with neglect, rough and stiff, like the nest of a black-faced woodswallow. Snot ran down its grime-streaked face—girl or boy, impossible to tell.

Beside the kid sat another, slightly older; skinny-limbed with knobby knees, left arm ending in a stump. A boy, eyes shielded with his one good hand, staring out across the flat expanse of sky, oblivious to the random, shuddering booms resonating from the GoldStar mines. Glancing down, attention caught by the nest-haired kid crawling towards him through the dry, red dust. The boy flicked a look at the nearest boulder where the older kids hid in the shadow of the camo net slung across its top and down one side.

"Pick it up, Olly, else it's gonna start screaming," called out Neve, the oldest girl, always telling the others what to do.

Olly nodded, but he didn't move. Eyes darted up to the sky again, shielded, ears straining to make out a faint mechanical hum.

"Shit, drone's coming—everybody stay down," cried Neve.

"One moment…one moment…" Hazzy shot out from under the camo net, moving pretty fast, despite his limp. He made for the kid with the bird-nest hair, aimed and squeezed the bottle he'd clutched tight against his chest. Red stuff squirted all over the kid's grubby t-shirt.

"Get the hell back under!" ordered Neve.

"I'm coming, just one moment…"

"Shit's sake, Hazzy, drone's in range, it can see you. It can…it can…hurry!"

Hazzy ducked back under the net before anyone could say anything else, a wide grin splitting his grotty face.

"Ketchup—that is total overkill."

"For impact!"

Neve shook her head. "We're pushing our luck. Don't wanna—"

"Shush, it's coming. Zip ya suits up."

The nest-haired kid started bawling. Olly glanced sharply at Neve and the others crouched in the shadowy sanctuary of the net.

"Don't look here, Olly, look back at the kid!"

Neve gave the net a mighty tug. It slid down soundlessly into place as the drone descended. She peered out through the reflective webbing, trying to catch the drone's insignia. Olly hefted the kid on to his lap. Both stared, wide-eyed, as the drone set down a few feet in front of them.

"It's a Doco, an XLG45," whispered Bindy from under the net. Her brother, Bunja, whispered something back.

"Will you two shut it!"

All sounds ceased abruptly, aside from the mechanical hum emanating from the silvery contraption, a bloated, bulbous orb with micro-props and three visible lenses.

Somewhere in the distance a wild dog started barking. The drone emitted a sharp pop, followed by a grinding clunk and whir as a geometric segment broke free of its outer casing, releasing a slender appendage, like the feeler of a giant insect.

More popping sounds in sequence as an array of additional ocular apparatus bloomed from the drone's lumpen surface, recording the kids from multiple angles. The insect-limb reached out to poke and prod, gently exercising calculated caution. A second appendage shot out abruptly from the drone's far side. It bent like an elbow, then plunged down deep into ruddy sand.

"Charge!"

The older kids leapt from their hiding places, each one clutching a rock or a metal bar. They pounced upon the drone and started bashing as Olly hugged the kid hard against his stomach.

"Don't smash the lenses—careful—quick, the antenna, take

them all out of commission."

Neve's team knew what they were doing. In twenty seconds they had the casing peeled like rind, transmissions halted, self-defence apparatus inert and harmless.

"That's a whole ten seconds too long, folks," said Bindy, checking the stopwatch that hung around her neck, a clumsy looking, old-timey object, still working despite its shattered glass and dented sides. "Ten seconds is plenty long enough to report."

"It didn't see nothing," said Bunja. "Nothing but Olly and the kid."

The nest-haired kid wailed harder and louder as an underground explosion sent a shudder trembling through the dirt. Bunja pulled a rusk from the linty depths of his pocket, but the kid kept screaming until he picked it up.

"Whose brat is that, anyway?" asked Bindy.

"Dunno," said Bunja, "but it sure looks the part."

"Better get that hair combed out before you stick it back in Crèche."

Bunja wasn't listening. He jiggled the little kid up and down, talking baby babble in a calming voice as the others stripped the drone down, piece by piece, with an array of tools brought specifically for that purpose.

Bindy took a large screwdriver and started jimmying the company logo.

"In yer dreams," said Neve grimly, snatching the tool from her hands.

"I was just gonna—"

"Nice try," she said, prising off the enamel logo with a deft twist of her wrist. She tossed the shiny thing in the air and caught it, single-handed.

"How many's that make?"

"Dunno," she said, which was a lie. Everyone knew *precisely* how many trophies they'd collected since Mungo Base put itself on drone patrol. Everyone knew how many and what kinds, from Fatboys (surveillance only, great for target practice), through to Skippers, Hurdy-Gurdys, and the much-sought-after Marlboro Men. Most even kept track of the value of the salvaged innards on Station-to-Station's open barter market.

Such a popular sport, drone baiting. Banned by the elders of Mungo Base, especially when there were little kids around, even though they loved the hunt. But nothing attracted doco drones like filthy, 'abandoned' children crawling around like savages in the wilderness, fitting the stereotypes adhered to by big city folks, not to mention the inhabitants of the GoldStar compounds, which were practically cities in themselves, propped up with foreign corporate coin on land leased from a broken Australian government who'd never had the strength to claim it back.

Leased land was all this country was good for anymore according to Sigurd and Jeep and Marguerite, and half the grizzled-up Council talkers who had dug in deep since the olden days, not giving up their posts until they died—which might be never, considering what they'd lived through, what they'd seen, and what they'd had to do. From Jihadi Nukes and the quicksilver spread of toxic Jericho Blush, to the fires that raged and roared like living beasts, and the tsunami that sucked the Gold Coast into the sea.

The lands surrounding Mungo Base were leased for weapons testing and whatever GoldStar was currently mining with explosives. So far Mungo had been lucky; no mushroom clouds or impassable subsidence. Just endless underground explosions and acres and acres of stalled Lantana Raze—a failed 'experimental' ground-clearing weed from a company brandishing a logo of three crossed swords. But lately there'd been Elder talk of moving inland, away from dangerous waste and widening fissures. Nobody wanted to abandon a decade's laboured, clandestine infrastructure, but Jeep reckoned they weren't gonna have much choice.

"Get those little kids back home," said Neve, rubbing her fingers across the shiny logo, a NatGeo, as it turned out. The thing had looked like a Disney in the air, not that anyone had bagged a Disney in more than a year. Times were getting tougher in the lands beyond the Risen Sea. So said ancient, wood-skinned Philomena, who clung to the remains of the decaying interwebs and lived in a grotto resembling a spider's lair, festooned with wires like dune melon roots, some bundled thick, like dreadlocks, others hanging free like dead grass snakes.

You could still glean useful intel off the web if you knew how to hook in. Philomena was how they learned about the West Sumatran quake, Montevideo's killer supercells, the final dregs of the last Greenland ice and a bunch of other stuff they didn't talk about. Philomena reckoned they were safe out here, dug in around the fringe of GoldStar land. Dug in and under, taking over abandoned tunnels and repurposed, forgotten bunkers from the '46 uprising. All ancient history. Nobody cared, just so long as Mungo didn't get too greedy; didn't bleed too much juice off the grid. So long as they kept clear of coastal diesel and desalination plants, and didn't hunt more drones than could be blamed on rogue militia. But Jeep reckoned things were turning for the worse. More explosions only amplified his theory.

That far-off dog started yapping louder, closer now; and then there was more than one of them.

"Move it out, people," snapped Neve. Whatever was spooking those dogs was likely to be trouble. No rifle fire, so they were probably ok, but *probably* didn't count for much in the lands beyond the southern boundary fence. "Take the safe way 'round old Elephant Rock."

As they wrapped the last of the lenses in salvaged polyester, Bindy leapt to her feet and pointed. "Plane!"

All squinted against the sun's harsh glare, trying to see what *kind* of plane, because they knew them all, every make from every country that dared to chance illegal inland flyovers. Not so many in recent months, just GoldStar growlers and sneaky Cessnas, but now and then a big, old Salvation Army Fokker or Red Crescent DC-3 went rattling over on some half-arsed mercy mission, relief for some long-forgotten outpost. Planes that never seemed to fly back out again.

This plane appeared to be made of solid silver; shiny new, without a single bullet hole or dent. Sleek design, kind of round and fat, as if formed from a mix of clouds and light.

"It's aliens!" piped up little Olly, who spent his whole life desperate for outer space, which was not surprising, considering his passion for ancient anime.

As the plane passed overhead it made no sound. Later, some would claim it cast no shadow and glowed with otherworldly light, but nobody was checking the ground for shadows that day.

And then everything started happening at once. A swarm of Blackhawks darkened the skies. The silver plane launched two rockets directly at the Goldstar Corporation mine. That set the kids off shouting and shoving, fighting each other over a battered pair of nocs, as two GoldStar growlers swooped out of the sun, diving too fast for any of the kids to run for cover, so they all just froze there in the open, locked in fright like startled rabbits, not moving, just staring.

The growlers looped and made a second pass. The silver plane, much bigger and slower, rumbled steady on its trajectory. And then, a sickening screech as something like hot shadow sliced the plane in two. One minute it was there, and then it wasn't. Nothing left but silvery disintegrating shards.

Shoulders slumped—that strike proved the plane was just a regular kind, not aliens from the moon or far-off worlds.

"Shit—what just happened?"

"Get undercover," screamed Neve and Bindy. Both had experience of falling blast debris, how torn and spinning, burning metal could fall like rain and cover many miles. Only Olly remained out in the open, oblivious to danger, staring slack-jawed as something dark and fast took out the growlers, metal fragments scattering like seeds.

It took a moment for them to piece it all together. Neither the growlers nor Blackhawks had attacked that silver plane—all craft were firing directly at the mine. Each rocket hit with a mighty whomp, sending towering plumes of debris skyward.

Now the Blackhawks swooped above the mine. One by one, they were swatted from the sky like they were bugs.

Swatted.

Something sliced the dusty air, a blur too indistinct to focus on. Something big and dark and way too fast—Hazzy had never heard of any weapon possessed of such speed and grace. Some kind of blade, perhaps? Only there was no knife, no edge, no metal glinting in the sun. The bulk of the weapon—whatever it was—was nestled deep within the mine, lashing at the sky with frightening precision.

Hazzy limped across to Neve, both gawping at the dirty smoke-streaked sky. Nobody saying what everyone was thinking: there was no chance that aerial display had gone unnoticed. Mungo Base would be under full alert. Battle stations, head counts, bed checks, lockdowns, everyone being accounted for; everyone except Neve's crew, because they had crossed the southern boundary fence, drone-baiting on lands from which they'd been forbidden.

If they went back now, perhaps, if they were quick and stealthy, taking one of the older tracks across the scrub…

"Come on," Neve said sullenly.

"Wait," said Hazzy, still staring at the crisscrossed trails of smoke.

"There's nothing we can do."

"Shhh…" He pressed a finger against his lip. "Listen."

They all stood still, listening, wiping sweaty dust out of their eyes, glad of a chance to catch their breath. Beneath their feet, the ground shuddered, continuous rumbling punctuated by occasional chunks of thudding, falling metal.

"The mines…" Neve sucked in her breath. They shouldn't be hearing anything. The mines had been blown up right before their eyes.

"Shit." Neve chewed her bottom lip. "Come on. We need to get out of here *now*."

"I saw it," said Olly.

"Saw what?"

He wiped his nose on the back of his good hand. "The shadow lightning." He sniffed. "Coming *up*, not *down*."

"Nobody knows what we just saw," Neve's gaze stayed focused on the dissipating smoke columns.

"You know I can get out there and back before—"

"Forget it, Hazzy. It's too dangerous."

"But I'm the fastest. The mining camp's been busted up. There might be food. Or medicine. What if—"

"Something's really wrong out there, Haz," Neve weighed their options. A strange plane, a swarm of 'hawks and two growlers down. A blasted mine continuing to run itself. The mines were mostly automated—everybody knew that—but they'd all seen and heard those rockets strike. It should have been more than enough to stop the machines. The ground would soon be swarming with GoldStar soldiers in any case. This was corporation land. Jeep wouldn't bother coming out to check. That aerial fight would be all the leverage he needed.

The kid with the bird-nest hair began to bawl.

Hazzy limped across to where they'd stashed their stuff beneath the camo net. With a soft thud, he plonked down on the sandy ground, pulled the blades out of his rucksack, one by one, untwining the protective fabric. He unhitched the prosthetics he wore below his knees, wriggled out of his cargo pants, then into the cutoff camo skinsuit that was stuffed into the sack as extra blade protection.

Neve watched all this with a critical eye. "Wait up, Haz—none of this makes sense."

"You need me to do a recce," Hazzy shrugged, attaching the running blades to his padded stumps. He held out both his hands impatiently, until Neve and Bindy stepped out to haul him up. He took a moment to get his bearings, bouncing up and down to test his weight, adjusting the padded straps that held the blades in place.

He wound a faded keffiyeh around his neck as Neve glanced over his shoulder at the thinning coils of dust and smoke.

"Don't say it," he said, face lit up with another wicked grin. "Like you could stop me if I didn't want—"

"Like you're not dumb enough to get yourself killed," she snapped back, but her heart wasn't in it. With his blades on, he *was* faster than the rest of them put together, and then some. He refused to tell anyone what had happened to his legs. All she knew for sure was that he hated living underground, and that he would do pretty much anything to prevent the relocation of the Base. For Hazzy, further out and deeper down was a big step in a very wrong direction.

She placed her hand upon his arm. "You don't have anything to prove."

He shook her off. "Never said I did." His eyes were fixed on a solitary wisp of smoke.

"I'll wait for you at Elephant Rock. Two hours. No more. Got me?"

He nodded enthusiastically, bouncing in kinetic preparation. The others watched in silent awe as he spun around and shot off suddenly in the direction of the mines, a feat involving dodging several rocks, one small child and a twisted heap of broken, metal drone fragments.

Neve stared after him, distracted. She was still staring when Bindy yelled her name: "Neve! Come on, gotta smuggle all the little kids back in before they're missed," which was bullshit, everybody knew. The exploding planes had blown their cover. A month of digging new pit toilets would be the lightest punishment they could hope for.

Neve kicked the untidy pile of drone scrap metal. They'd salvaged all the pieces they could use. Wind would take care of the rest.

They travelled back to Mungo Base in strict formation, lookouts posted, spaced out, armed, with wide gaps between them. They knew they weren't safe out in the scrub, not truly safe anywhere beneath the open sky.

Neve waited till the last of them had cleared Elephant Rock, the place she'd promised to stand vigil and wait, bag slung across her bony shoulder, one eye on the sky for drones and planes. If Haz returned to Elephant with swag, then everything was going to be alright. Particularly if be brought medicine, but anything from the outside world was good.

Hazzy ran beneath the smoke-tinged air, the back of his throat tainted with oily smear. Truth was, he'd been waiting for a break, a chance to show the others what he was made of. A few had questioned his right to food and board at Mungo Base, written him off as one of Sigurd's pets. He should've got passed up the line to a sit-down job repairing boards and circuits like the other maimed and battered travellers who'd fronted at the old base camp at 2:00am in that busted army truck. But Hazzy could not stomach life underground. Hazzy needed sun and air and sky, three things Mungo people took for granted. He was okay so long as he was free. Free so long as he was up and running.

Nobody ever talked about Al Kharaz, just as nobody ever asked about self-destructing pursuit denial munitions placements, or about the human wave attacks—children and old men forced to run through fields ahead of tanks. Nobody talked about how he was the lone survivor of an entire village.

The blades cut into his tender flesh. They hurt. They'd always hurt. No way around it, Sigurd said. Sinewy Sigurd, snow white beard hanging down to his pot-belly navel, always in a filthy mood because none of the blades ever fit as right as they should; as right as they used to, back in *his* day. And he wasn't wrong—those blades dug hard and fierce into Hazzy's stumps. But they were blades made from layered carbon fibre, prefabbed illegally to Sigurd's own design, smuggled in along the very same route that brought the things they couldn't make or steal: solar paneling, medicine, scientists, and news.

Sigurd did the measuring, he did the best he could, because there was no end to the tide of landmine-blasted refo kids in need of replacement limbs. The best he could do for most of them was prosthetics made from scraps. Hazzy's Cheetah blades, on the other hand, were works of art.

Those Cheetahs strapped on well enough, but he lied about the pain. And he always would—he'd keep on lying so long as it got him what he needed: the kind of speed only scored from mighty Cheetahs, blades that made him faster than the wind. Sigurd's work was based on old designs, back from before the Big3 Bombings changed the face of reason, changed the world so it could never be put back right.

Hazzy pushed those thoughts out of his head, his gaze focused on a final, thinning plume. Now and then he changed direction randomly, mimicking a roo, hoping to fool any algorithms he imagined might be tracking him from above. That unmarked silver plane meant something big was going down, something people weren't supposed to know about. Fresh coltan seams as yet untapped? Perhaps it had all been some kind of accident, which meant other planes would soon follow, filled with electronic smarts. GoldStar would be digging in to protect its assets. More soldiers—more bad news for Mungo Base. Meanwhile, the earth still shuddered with relentless blasting, tearing up the mine-scoured Southern stretch of sandy desert. Not just blasts, either, but that other deeper, gut-sickening sound the folks who heard it didn't have a name for. *Tearing, grinding, pushing, choking…* something evil, he was sure of that. New weapons being tested underneath the desert, out here where GoldStar could do whatever they wanted.

He slowed when he came to a patch of ground littered with broken mecha, evidence there had once been mining here. Beyond, rising higher than a dune, the half-buried carcass of a bucket wheel excavator. Such monstrous relics made brilliant camo, but weren't much good for anything else. Everything useful had been scavenged already—drone innards were the thing that brought good barter. No matter how many of the things they caught, there were always more. What remained of the civilised world seemed captivated by the 'savage lands', those places off the grid.

He'd come this far, so he might as well keep running. See if he could get up close. Find a hiding place amidst the scatter of rusted dozers and haul trucks. Neve would not leave Elephant without him. She would wait—she always waited, he could definitely rely on that. But he wouldn't head back to base without scoring something cool as salvage, or without finding out what the hell was going on.

Hazzy tugged his keffiyeh to cover his nose and mouth as he crept up slowly, close as he dared. He came to an abrupt halt when he rounded the side of a mangled, burnt-out chassis. GoldStar soldiers, obvious in their trademark red, lying on the ground as still as stone. Every single one of them was dead.

Death was different to other forms of stillness. He'd learned to recognise death at fifty paces—he had seen so much of it in the time before he made it to Mungo Base.

All traces of the smoke had blown away. Hazzy ducked behind an upturned truck and watched for fifteen excruciating minutes, waiting for whatever was in the mine to show itself. He was mindful of how the day was draining into twilight, how Neve would be pacing up and down by that old elephant's side, how much shit he was going to cop if he failed to get back before the sun went down completely.

Neve. That girl thought she knew everything, but she didn't. None of them did. They were all innocents, raised up soft in Mungo's arms. This time he would be the one to do the talking, and Neve would be the one who did the listening.

Pain intensified as he balanced on his blades, cutting only half as much as his curiosity. A lone Blackhawk sat idle on the sand, emitting random bursts of electronic chatter. When he shifted to a different spot around the far side of a hydraulic shovel, he stumbled upon a burnt-out pile of drones, damaged way past recognition. No point in even picking up the bits. More GoldStar soldiers lay where they had fallen. Up close, he could see the puckered purpling across exposed skin. What kind of weapon left traces like that?

Hazzy's heart banged hard against his ribs. He should be heading back to Elephant, back to Mungo Base, his home. He should do anything except the thing he was going to do: surge over on his precious blades and get a closer look at whatever lay in the mine. Because he could not live without knowing, because he was wearing Cheetah blades and because Jeep and Sigurd and Marguerite and Neve would all be clamouring to learn the truth.

By the time he realized his mistake, the damage had been well and truly done.

Sundown at Elephant Rock, their favourite place of all, despite no kid from Mungo Base having ever seen a living elephant, nor a rhino, a whale, or even a bear. All such creatures had gone the way of dinosaurs long before any of them had even been born. Yet Neve knew all there was to know about elephants: how poachers used to bag them for their tusks, how soldiers used to ride them into battle, how they mourned their dead and never forgot. Not like humans. Humans had forgotten everything.

Over time the Mungo Base kids had made this elephant their own, embellishing its natural bulk with chisels, shaping a trunk, wide ears and sturdy legs. One time they'd even painted it brilliant colours in imitation of something from an old NatGeo mag, but Marguerite had made them scrub the stone clean and said they shouldn't go raising flags so glaringly obvious.

Three hours stretched into four and it was getting late and cold and dark, and still Hazzy was out there somewhere. To make it worse, the ground was still alive with incessant rumbling. The mines had not stopped detonating since those planes came down. No other explanation made any sense. She'd spotted several GoldStar drones patrolling the sand as usual. Hopefully her skin suit was continuing to mask her vitals, but the thing was old and patchy, like every other thing at Mungo Base. It didn't fit properly, and made her feel unsettled. The taser hanging from her belt was old and dodgy, too. Not much use against a well-oiled GoldStar uzi.

She sniffled, getting more cold and angry as the hours passed, angry with herself and Hazzy in roughly equal parts. He wouldn't be coming back with empty hands, which meant he'd keep on looking 'til he scored. He'd keep poking and prodding at whatever lay in that mine. Kids who made it out of refo camps were reckless beyond measure. Risk takers, every single one, which was how they made it this far out, of course. What Sigurd called *Natural Selection*. Only the fittest had the nerve to jump a truck, or trek across open desert, scam passage on a garbage barge, or board a battered dhow across the Timor Sea. Only the tough survived a minefield, made it out towards a better life—a life where you got the chance to fend for yourself.

She should have stopped him. She should have said no. They had it good at Mungo Base, right under GoldStar's eyes and ears and hands. The company had no idea so many were dug in deep like rats and roaches. Sigurd reckoned they weren't worth the cost of flushing out. Probably. Maybe. Mungo Base had endured for thirty years, with its secret labs, pilfered stores, and offshore communication that was theoretically supposed to be impossible. Hijacked connections to cables undersea, hacked and jacked and piggybacked, slashed and reconnected a dozen times as far back as memory would take her.

The sky lay streaked with pink and orange. It was way past time. She should be getting back to Mungo. Sigurd and Marguerite would throw a fit when they learned of Hazzy's stupid, reckless risk, and Neve would be the one to cop the blame. Marguerite knew all about her secret trophy cave and the altar built from scavenged weaponry that used to fly and shoot. *Better on the ground than in the air*…how many times had Neve tried out that line? The elders didn't take kindly to her well thought-out explanations. *You weren't born when it all kicked off. You don't remember the bad years gone to hell.* Maybe not, but she'd seen the pictures, spent hours flipping through yellowed catalogues of things no longer in existence; beautiful things that used to be and would never be again, things the world had forgotten how to make.

Neve hated that she'd never seen the ruin of the coast, never seen the inland sea that Jeep referred to as *That Abomination*. Just pictures, digital and holo, and those guys with the gliders she met last year when GoldStar clipped them—they'd both said it was amazing.

The snapping of a thorn bush branch brought her back into the moment. Chills of early evening seeped inside the elephant's stone skin. It didn't sound like Hazzy's blades. She should be able to hear him jiggling with what always seemed like pent-up rage. She knew all about the pain. How Cheetahs were impossible to keep still.

One hand on the taser. Too late to make a run for it. Damn it, GoldStar—Marguerite was right. Neve was an idiot. She shouldn't be out here alone so close to dark.

"Hazzy?"

Keeping as still as she was able, one shoulder pressed against hard rock, hoping irrationally that whoever was there—if it wasn't Hazzy—might think her carved from stone. Hoping the kindly elephant of olden days might somehow be able to protect her.

"Hazzy?"

Neve swallowed. If not Hazzy, then who, or what? If she never made it back, would anyone come looking?

"Neve?"

"Hazzy!" Relief flooded through her as she stepped forward. "Stop. Don't come any closer."

The glinting, curve of his blades were unmistakable but she couldn't see his face.

"Neve, listen carefully," said Hazzy, calmly, as if he were asking something small and insignificant. "You must leave this place. Go back and warn the stations. Tell Philomena to broadcast warnings through the web."

"What are you talking about?" Her words came out much weaker than intended. "Did you…? The mines…what did you find?"

Hazzy and his Cheetah blades were standing still as stone.

She stepped forward, reaching out.

"Don't move!" he screamed, his voice a peculiar mixture of rasping bark and terror, fracturing the surrounding desert silence. "It knows we're here."

"What do you mean *it*? GoldStar?"

"It." He swallowed hard. "The thing in the mines. Go back. Warn the others. Make everybody understand they have to leave."

"Hazzy, if you don't tell me what's—" she fumbled for her torch, unclipping it from her belt with trembling fingers.

"No—don't look at me!" He raised his arm, tugged the keffiyeh across his face.

She gasped. "Shit—what happened to your…?"

"Go." He used both hands to bind his face up tightly, legs trembling from the strain of keeping balance. "Go. You haven't much time. Make the others understand. Get away while you all still can!" He staggered, momentarily losing concentration and the force of will required to keep himself upright. He tensed, preparing to run once more, something Neve had watched a hundred times with utter admiration, but this time was different. This time she couldn't bear to watch.

"You're sick—let me help you!"

Hazzy looked on past her to the elephant. "You were the biggest animal on land, but I will be the fastest." He turned his face to Neve and shouted "Go!"

Neve whimpered, spun and fled, fuelled by rising, overwhelming horror, hating her fleeing, coward self, but keeping up a steady pace, itchy sweat dribbling down her spine, dodging spinifex and prickly pear, rocks, more rocks, and broken-down machinery. But she stopped when she reached the burnt-out antique school bus, pausing to catch her breath. She *would not* leave him out on the sand to die. Marguerite and Jeep and Sigurd—surely they would know what must be done? She'd bring them out to track him down. They would find a way to put things right.

She ran in time with her own ragged breath, scrubby brush scratching her pumping legs. She was too frightened to look back over her shoulder, terrified of the thing she thought she'd seen.

Hazzy ran faster than the wind, pushing past pain and sickness, fatigue, exhaustion, memories, and the point of no return. He tugged at his skinsuit, exposing his scrawny chest to open air, revealing infected flesh and bleeding heat. He could feel how he was changing. He would not take this sickness back to Mungo Base. The thing in the mines was out of luck this time. He would run faster than the dogs, hurl himself into an impassable ravine.

The dogs were close. He could hear their hungry howls. Running made him feel like he was alive. In this world, the fastest lived the longest. In this landscape, nothing traveled faster and smoother than graphite fibre-reinforced polymer.

The Cheetah blades propelled him onwards, cold air on his skin. Moonlight illuminating his path. He ran for all the ones who didn't make it out of the camps, around the mines, across the Risen Sea. The memory of Elephant, dead but not forgotten. The huge sky, brilliant with stars, opened wide to swallow him up completely.

THE THIRD PARTY DOCTRINE

STEVE PROPOSCH

The orgy was not as expected. In the entrance hall we were greeted by Verdi and a modest, well-dressed couple who spoke softly, ticked off their list promptly, and reassured us of welcome. There was no sign of the messy flirtation or toxic masculinity I had expected at the door.

"Welcome aboard," the couple said unanimously. "Many guests have preceded your arrival."

No questions. No hint of suspicion, a free and easy pass. In retrospect it was my first clue to the impending disaster.

In the main room there was an apparent seaside theme in play. I was certain there had been no mention of this in the group post, and said as much to my trustworthy companion.

From the vantage of a slightly elevated entranceway our vision was assaulted by an abundance of pearly seashells, garish fins and suckered green tentacles. It was a mishmash visually; and aurally, with 'Chorus of the Hebrew Slaves' (of all things) really hitting its leather. In addition to the completely *wrong* soundtrack to accompany our entrance, we were dressed as if for cocktails, in gown and sharp suit. Everyone else in the room wore costumes themed to the decor—sexy mermaid, sexy aqua man, a not-so-sexy in my opinion swamp thing with bulging eyes and long scaly arms, sexy pirate, sexy sailor, etc. This would not stand, I decided. I was rewriting the script of the moment already in my head as we stepped down into the piranha pit.

The room radiated that warm sense of moral relaxation in the presence of some higher purpose that you find at the best parties. Money and effort was the first superficiality to notice, and evidence of long preparation at trying to look your best, spending, pampering, tanning and posing in front of mirrors. It was a good-looking crowd of people laughing and drinking together, but also watching with hooded eyes, jealous yet attracted, conflicted, hungry. A deeper dive would reveal a less-than-diverse, highly spoiled bunch of wealthy white cats of approximate age ranging from twenty-five to forty, in good shape physically but drained mentally and spiritually by their debauchery. They had all been around the block, and most had done more than one circuit. Many had young kids, exes, alimonies, lawyers, payoffs, failed companies, dead friends and dead enemies pushed to some back pocket of their minds. For them, now was sacred. There was no future or past. And tonight was all about quick fixes.

This attitude had permeated every part of their lives. If a pill could literally or metaphorically help to ease the problem of the moment, knowing that the problem would return once the pill's effect wore off made no difference. They took it anyway, and then took two the next time around to extend their period of relief. Addicted to money. Addicted to ego. Addicted to shame. Addicted to sex. Addicted to happiness. They had it all. Their money was their enabler. They could afford a multitude of habits, impulses, scandals, failures, fuck-ups and peccadillo dependencies without ever ending up living on the streets like vagrants. They were highly functioning junkies with property portfolios, personal trainers, and the ability to travel the world on a whim, to one another's parties, little knowing or caring that it was all a performance to take their minds off their own trauma. Their greatest fear was to discover that they were as scared and lonely and miserable as anyone else in this world. Their difference to anyone else in this world was that they could afford to run from that truth day after day, hour after hour. They had become disconnected, weak, complacent, oblivious, and altogether corrupted in mind and soul. As such they were all perfect prey for the Chariot.

In my experience, not all wealthy people are like this. All Chariot people, however, are.

No matter how far you run from fear, loneliness and misery

they catch you up eventually. While the intellectual gap between the reality and fantasy of the privileged life can be treated with good times, pills, therapy and distraction, the spiritual gap continues to grow, ever widening. No one knows that fact better than I. So when someone comes along who promises to bridge that spiritual gap, to fit with your ideology *and* love you and appreciate you always and forever, you are like a dressed lamb, slaughtered, beheaded, gutted, and ready for further processing. Despite their youth every one of the sorry cats gathered there that day was ready to be processed. We were partying in an abattoir.

Perhaps they had simply seen enough of life already to despise it. I didn't blame them for that. The Chariot was the problem. For them it was a saviour, a spiritual organisation that ticked all of the mental and physical boxes for them to feel better about themselves. The Chariot professed to be the bearer of sacred texts that would change the very fabric of society. It claimed to hold undeniable physical proof of the existence of the afterlife, and that it would reveal this proof 'when the stars are right', thus resolving the bulk of human suffering — the fear of death — in one fell swoop: a Revelation on a massive scale. Although it had not yet set an actual date and time for that Revelation to happen, or provided anything more than their Word and a raft of clever marketing events by way of evidence; and although it charged a membership rate that was untenable for ninety-nine percent of the world's population, the Chariot had quickly gained tens of thousands of followers. The cats in this room alone had poured millions into Chariot coffers, and used their power and influence to spread the Word all over the world. They started out by attending lavish and expensive spiritual 'workshops' and ended up devoted to, beloved of, and believing in its leaders, a small, anonymous group who called themselves The Deep Ones.

For everyone outside the organisation it was just another sick cult. Rumours had spread of its practices, that it was anti-feminine, that its leaders had multiple sex partners, that they frequently took those partners by force, that even willing members of the cult were being starved and brainwashed to fit with the ideals of the organisation, that it treated many worshippers as slaves and branded their skin appropriately with the Chariot logo: the canopy of six-pointed stars that had become an image of evil to most, and a symbol of divine grace to these few. None of the rumours were confirmed. Interestingly, and almost uniquely in the strange recorded history of cults, the Chariot had not yet had a single defector.

But there were pigeons among the cats. The Greater Good had infiltrated the Chariot years ago on a mission to discover its secrets. Having now discovered those secrets, we had determined to destroy the organisation utterly. We believed this was for the good of humankind. We believed that bloodshed now would prevent much greater bloodshed in the future. We believed we were attacking an evil force, and we were determined to win. Tonight the pigeons would be armed with AKs.

The cats sat, stood or wandered about, many otherwise armed with drinks or nibbles as they chatted, relaxed, tensed, laughed, frowned, fawned, and were fawned upon. They snubbed, allied, broke up, made up, bemused, benighted, enlightened, beloved, hated, befriended, pissed off, and all the time appraised our progress as we headed towards the bar, acting as though we were sizing up each in turn as possible sexual partners, rather than numbers on a rap sheet. It was just as we'd practiced. There was no sign yet of the writhing, humping masses of naked and semi-clothed flesh one usually tends to associate with such gatherings. Perhaps it was not that kind of orgy after all, I thought. A base note of sexual expectation was in the air, of course, but any such gathering of good-looking people engaged in celebration had that. Almost any gathering of people had that. This was no more or less pronounced than a good straight party when clever, beautiful people who have not seen each other for a while start chatting excitedly about philosophy and big ideas around an open fire, and get a little drunk and start releasing their love of friends and food and drink. I had attended two such parties recently that would have rated ten times hotter on the barely-concealed desire scale than this little shindig, and they were Brethren-only affairs. No girls allowed.

A genteel violin sonata by…Corelli, I guessed, because they

seemed to like their Italians, picked up the ambience as we breasted the post-industrial concrete slab bar. We were quickly offered a pair of old-fashioneds before we could voice an alternative.

"Hennessy?" the bar horse asked by way of telling.

I chose not to be choosy and took it with a smile. My trusty companion was equally charming. I felt my pockets for a carrot in recompense, but came up empty. The attendant waved its hoofs indicating such a gesture was unnecessary in any case. This made me smile a second time, tip my drink and take a sip. The appreciative press of my lips together with a small eyebrow raise would be thanks enough for the nag's effort, I thought.

By surprise my reaction was genuine, raising my eyebrow even higher than planned. That horse could mix a good drink no doubt; bittersweet is a delicate measure.

Despite its initial banalities and disappointments, I knew this was no common circus but a carefully arranged orchestral performance. Every guest had their place in the orchestra, yet all remained ignorant of the instrument they were to play. All, bar one. It was for that audience of one that my companion and I were to be the conductors, sorting out the treble clefs from the quarter notes and making sure the whole thing kept time once the curtains finally opened (the Corelli was getting to me). No one was getting out of this performance alive.

My companion soon dispersed to nod, hob and nob around the room. Wandering alone I was surprised to receive mostly cold, uninterested stares in return for my appraisement of others. Was my slip showing? I had to ask myself. Or had I suddenly become unhandsome and ungainly? The thought flashed on and off again. I chided myself. The first scenario was far more likely, though still entirely *unlikely* in the long run. We had not paid to be here, as all these degenerates had. We were being paid, and our purpose was higher than any of these cats could imagine, beyond whatever his or her fortune may hold. Our payment would be the most precious gift any living being can receive. Not Revelation but Redemption: freedom at last from shame. These jokers had no inkling of what they were up against.

Thankfully the Corelli was switched with surprising alacrity to Notorious B.I.G. at the next opportunity. I relaxed my thoughts, and noticed the whole room loosen up and smile at the change of mood the music affected. On the other side of the room, a certain clam-headed merman bearing a tray of drinks approached my companion. I sought out a similarly dressed creature myself. My sweet bitters were already drained.

"Costume, sir?" the merman inquired, thrusting his sizeable chin towards the back of the room before I'd had moment enough to grab a glass.

I turned slowly in the direction his chin inferred. In my peripheral vision I espied my companion indeed heading that way with her mer-guide in the lead. I could see a curtained archway through which a pair of seahorses in revealing orange skirts were just emerging, laughing at themselves and their silly dress ups on their way back to the bar. Bless them. I turned back to my man and shook a finger—no, not yet—as I picked out a fresh brew. There was no need to rush.

On the opposite side of the room, near the entrance to the conservatory, I spied a squid with a short skirt-like arrangement of tentacles to which I was attracted. Even from afar I knew that this was someone to whom I might be able to speak and break the chill of arrival. I subtly changed tack to move closer to my vision. She noticed but was bordered by a couple who were plainly more plain and shallow of mind than her, and gracefully attempting not to cringe whenever they spoke. I made a quick decision and approached the three of them with confidence and intent. By way of introduction I leaned right in and kissed my target's cheeks in an exceedingly familiar way, as if seeing an old friend.

"Babe, so good to see you again. Aren't you all recovered from trauma and looking fabulous tonight?" I complimented her dress and shoes and made a leading reference to 'Marcus,' who, "always had such fabulous taste."

As the spontaneous use of first names is discouraged at these kinds of parties, where even warm friends use pet names for each other—Pussycat, Pet, Sugar, whatever—the reference was obvious.

Marcus was our mutual friend, and had recently, tragically, dearly departed. It had piquancy, history, and romance, even hope. It was sure to scare the plain Janes away.

My confidence was not misplaced. The sexy squid responded by hanging her head slightly, shrugging sadly but not dismissively, saying: "I don't know what to say. It's just so good to see you again, baby," and reaching out for a big, warm hug. I hugged her back.

The two extraneous wraiths were quickly feeling uncomfortable around such an open and genuine display of emotion. They were gossips to the core, and to them we were a couple of older, more experienced ghosts who could use a little privacy to catch up, perhaps on orgies past or orgies future? It was good cover. It gave us seniority, a dominant hand to play, and they soon parted singing our sycophantic praises. I was confident that word would spread, and that would give us space. Once they were away I joked to my new-old friend about us having just pulled off the Orange stagecoach robbery.

"The perfect crime", she replied, and laughed politely.

I guffawed rather less politely and sprayed a jot of old fashioned at the floor.

"Hopefully not the last brave act of a long and prosperous friendship," I opined while dabbing my lips with my sleeve, as yet blissfully ignorant of how devastating a combo of brains and brawn she would be.

"Fuck that, I'm off to California," she said, and her sailor's mouth looked carved, yet soft and warm, and wore an unexpectedly lopsided grin

I laughed again, afraid I may have stared for too long a moment as I realised just how perfectly impure she was. Her face was a poem, not a pop song. Her eyes were wounded, with heavy lids and the gentle asymmetry of a hedonist. It was a simple enough face to be described as beautiful, but it had gone through a lot of life to get here, and to find 'here' wanting was a major disappointment. Much to its credit, the face had remained simple despite all of that, being realistic at heart, practical and hardworking, it maintained the illusion of being merely beautiful in absence of workable options. Her gently rounded form and short blue hair, and the way she spoke and joked and crossed her eyes at her now departed suitors, was similarly short of perfection but rendered utterly charming by the whole set. She aroused me intensely with nothing more than that look in her eye that seemed to say she was up for anything; any pleasure, any trial, any adventure. I suspected it would all end in tragedy, but vowed then and there to be her witness, to follow her to the end of time itself. Somehow, I just knew.

In the light of my continued numb silence the woman was forced to pick up the conversational slack. "What's with this whole deep-sea theme anyway?' she said, indicating the crowd. "There was nothing about that in the group post...was there?"

Her uncertainty about the fact—including that it mirrored my own—made me smile and wake somewhat from the brief carnal fantasy that had formed, wherein I had abducted and inducted this amazing new being deep into my strange life and she understood and loved everything about me, and I about her. We could speak with complete freedom about anything in the world, anything we could think of, without repercussion, without judgement, without limits on our thinking, our desires, or our designs. There were no secrets left between us. We existed outside of society, free of all intellectual constraint and buoyed by her wealth to enjoy all the comforts that society had to offer. We went to a place where we could be alone and undisturbed for many days. We did things I had never tried before and sunk ourselves wholly into pleasure and each other and forewent all else for all time.

I laughed lightly. "That's exactly what I said when I came in."

She giggled too. "Hmm, I think you would make a nice... goldfish!"

"They're freshwater only, aren't they?"

"A carp, then." She laughed.

When I realised she was projecting the same kind of hunger that I felt but hoped I was able to obscure, I thought for a second to tell her about my little abduction fantasy, but quickly aborted the notion. We made small talk instead to cover our ensuing feelings of both eagerness and timidity. Had she noticed my excitement as I had noticed hers?

We complimented the house and decor like idiots. We looked over the room and subtly pointed out groups of guests we thought looked funny or interesting, and laughed at them together. Slowly we headed toward the garden, where the expansive grounds might allow us to wander and wind as we met.

She told me I was handsome. Her beauty was not perfection, I said, in so many words, but it was all the more beautiful for that, and obvious enough to require no comment.

"Ahh, guess it's a little late for that," she said, and took an ironic swig of booze. "Only that you've been commenting on it for the last twenty minutes."

I agreed, and we laughed again. I took note that since the moment we met we had barely stopped laughing together.

"What possible circumstance has brought such sweet humour amongst all these sour pussies?" I indicated the Doncaster McMansion and all who now occupied her.

She replied plainly that her young, twice-removed cousin had tenderly groomed and seduced her when she was but fourteen years old, and, after much drama and the deep heartache that followed, she'd been left with an obsession to please, and please often. Though the cousin did not actually commit a physical sexual act with her until two years after their 'affair' began, he planted his seeds well. There was timeliness to it, she insisted. He had been very tender and slow about it, allowing her to come to boil. There were fervent images now in her fertile young mind that rolled and rolled, so that by the time their playful union was finally, urgently, tearingly, sweatily, bumpingly, grindingly consummated she was over-ripe and ready to burst. She would have done literally anything he asked of her, she admitted.

Cuz proceeded, in later days, to ask her to pose for photos and 'star' in videos, which he posted online. Initially, this was done without her knowledge, and when she discovered what had been going on via a chance encounter with herself online, she raged and spat and threatened and pleaded and raged and spat again. Against the odds Cuz displayed such shame and regret, such devotion, and such willingness to do anything to make it right between them, that she soon began to lose sight of how sick an act he'd committed. As cream on the cake, he showed proof of the income his work had provided them both.

The promise of a sixty-forty split her way combined with his claim that in truth he was always more excited when he knew others would be watching, sealed their deal. It was simply his kink, she reasoned, not that unusual considering the options, and a profitable kink at that. She was comfortable enough to do it for the camera when it was just the two of them, and had to agree it had been effective enough in promoting a rock solid performance from him. When she thought about it in just the right way, in fact, she supposed that it turned her on quite a lot too, to imagine all kinds of people, all over the world, in all states of arousal, watching them fuck.

They fucked hard. They fucked for real. They fucked for an audience. And so it goes.

It all got out of hand, of course. Money came in every day— bags of money. Sometimes literally, as when a suitcase containing thirty thousand in small bills turned up on his doorstep one morning, accompanied by a neatly handwritten note requesting that a very specific act be performed in their next video. The realisation that the sender knew his home address and could theoretically afford to have them surveilled, kidnapped, or even killed was at least as persuasive towards compliance as the cash.

"It was weird not so much in the act itself," she said, "but in the fact that we did it for that one, anonymous person. It was almost like he was in the room with us."

Again, her feelings were familiar to me. I thought of our own audience of one for tonight's ensuing drama, our Priestess. The years of research and planning of which she had spoken culminated for us all, tonight, in this event. For close to a decade she had been making contact with all the right people, ingratiating herself into their lives, going to all the right places, hanging out, being a friend, hating them all the while, and secretly planning to bring it all down on their heads.

"'When the stars are right'," our Priestess would spit those five words at me like bullets the few times we met. "I say there's no time like the present." Her hate was profound.

The squid woman continued her story. I still did not know her name.

As the money flowed in so did the excess. Parties turned into fuck-festivals. There was blow, pipes, needles and pills. Their contacts grew, a list of the rich and powerful. She began taking on more and more partners. It hardly mattered who they were anymore. Cuz started working more behind the camera than in front of it. Now they were earning more than fifty grand a day, and at times there were more than thirty fricking guys smooched up and gathered around her couch, all desperate to come on her face.

"Why was that not totally appalling to you?" I blurted in wonder, temporarily forgetting my cover.

A moment of profound sadness and uncertainty flashed across her features, before she brushed it away like a pro. "Well, you know how it is," she giggled and fluttered.

"I guess I do," I replied with a laugh, recovering quickly.

The good times couldn't last, she said. Before long first one, then three, then the rest of her extended family discovered their antics, and heard the rumours. Cuz consequently went on the run, and she was captured, recovered, tried, and judged by a jury of her familial peers. There were rivers of tears, a devastating sense of shame, emotional outbursts, a period of total rejection, followed by cautious understanding, and finally an outpouring of genuine love. She was eventually considered largely blameless for it all. She was a victim of circumstance, not the perp. The well-intentioned efforts of her parents and siblings helped her to realise that she did not, *could* not, love her cousin, or ever see him again, and that was all for the best.

Cuz eventually paid his price in being threatened by extreme violence and ostracised so completely that his last known whereabouts were a remote camp in a Siberian forest. Thus ended *his* lesson, she said, but once the dust of his disappearance had settled she could see how the wolf's sudden departure had unfortunately left her alone in the wilderness with a watchful, self-righteous pack who had vowed never to let her stray from their gaze again. And yet there was this ravenous, pornographic appetite to feed.

It was a whirlwind. My head was spinning. Why was she telling me all this?

It was then she heard about the Chariot.

In an effort to ease her soul she had attended a weekend workshop: 'Introduction to Mindful Healing'. She found the course helpful, the staff delightful, and the organisers had been vocal about wanting her to return for the 'Healing with Meditation' follow up. For the first time in a long time she felt wanted for herself, not as a sex object, but as a real person. Her family agreed that such a course of action may be beneficial, and supported her in that course. It all helped her feel better about being herself again.

Before too long she had freed herself from her restrictive family structure and struck out on her own path with their blessings. Soon after that she donated a staggering sum to the Chariot to become a lifetime Patron. Any course of her choice was free after that.

She was her own boss now, she said, with her own small production company, and rarely needed to work more than two days a week, all of which was in administration. When she got in front of the camera these days it was purely for her own pleasure, or for that of someone she wished to please.

"Maybe one day I'll please you," she purred.

"I should be so lucky."

Long story short, here she was, at this place, on this night. There had been many like it previously, she said. "But I've never met someone like you before."

Now she was making me blush.

"Fuck, we should get back inside," she said to her gold Giorgio. 'It's almost time."

"Time for what?"

"The presentation of course," she replied with a smile.

"Oh, right," I acted like I knew what she was talking about.

Back inside I scanned for my companion. There she was, dressed as a tentacle. Nice choice, I thought. The costume was definitely something you could hide a weapon in. And there was another of our Brothers, little Gary, got up as a starfish. He could fit his twin Glocks in there, I realised. Obviously they had accessed the stash already. According to my Skagen we still had twenty minutes. It must have been an opportunistic grab.

To the left of the concrete slab of the bar a small stage was lit, and the room lights dimmed a little. A couple approached the stage, working their way through the crowd. As they reached the lights I saw it was the door bitches, who hadn't been bitches at all. They were heading for the mike stand. They were going to make a speech. I was sure none of this had been mentioned in the group post.

At the periphery of my vision I noticed little Gary nudging towards me. Of course he was on this job. There had been no way of knowing the Priestess's final list, but the main contenders had been fairly obvious choices. Little Gary was military grade and near as fanatical as me, so he was a lock. This is it, I thought, the point of no return. With one hand remaining at my squid girl's waist—suddenly reluctant to give up my prize—I nudged casually towards him.

Oh, God. This was it. Christmas had come twenty minutes early.

For many years I had trained against fear and doubt, but my thoughts were racing now. My squid girl and I barely knew each other, but for a moment in her presence I had felt normal, accepted, calm, understood, even hopeful. This was all so new to me. Could I abandon it now?

Feelings I had never felt before rushed through me when I looked at her. Her depraved, degraded past only made her the more attractive to me. I saw it all with love, and with the knowledge that she could be saved. She knew, deep down, and her spirit longed to be clean. She would soon forget all the rubbish this cult had fed her, these stories of many gods, all unto themselves, these stupid space monsters that were supposed to appear 'when the stars are right'. Such bullshit. Their tricks had never worked on me. It would be easy to erase their shadows from her and start from a fresh perspective. I'd found a dream that I could speak to. How could I risk that now? And why, just as I had prepared to leave this earthly plane, here, amongst the very people I'd planned to slaughter?

Who else among them might be treasures, like her? If there were one did it not follow that there could be many other soulful and passionate and beautiful minds such as hers among the crowd? As I scanned the room frantically thinking in this strange new way, my feelings of love grew stronger, not only for her, but for everyone gathered here…for humanity in general. People were good, I knew. People loved each other, and that was more beautiful than anything else I could think of. I felt tears swelling my head. I was not normally so emotional. What was happening to me? What did it really mean to send them to oblivion before their time? Would those they loved and who loved them in return not mourn them bitterly? Was I not a villain to even consider perpetrating such an atrocity? Why had I never thought this way before? What the fuck had I been doing with my life?

It is difficult to describe the wild emotion I felt at that moment. It was such a mixture of panic, confusion and uncertainty shot through with desperation yet suffused with an all-consuming love for life and most especially for her in the very face of everything I'd worked towards. Apocalypse may come closest, but that is barely a word. It was as if I had been drugged. It was beyond belief that I had not realised the true potential of my actions before, or that I had thought them justified. Did there even exist such a drug, one that could make me feel love? Was MDMA like this? I'd heard of it, but never tried it—liquid ecstasy. It might easily have been mixed in those bittersweet cocktails, I supposed.

The old fashioneds of course. How quaint.

Intoxicated or not, it no longer mattered. Despite half a lifetime of indoctrination into the Greater Good—the hate-speeches, the endless lessons in duplicity, mimicry without involvement, the suppression of empathy and encouragement of self-sacrifice— the notion of suicide had fled my mind, and along with it had gone the desire to destroy the lives of these people I barely knew. I had judged them. I had demonised them. My judgement had been off. Escape was now my priority.

I turned to her. I had to tell her of *my* revelation. She was the cause of it, after all. There was still time. We could escape together.

Her eyes were full of tears. "There is little but pain in the world," she said, sadly stroking my cheek. "And, you and I, we've spent our lives and our fortunes pursuing pleasure to avoid it. But it is still there, don't you see? It won't go away."

My own eyes were overflowing now. I moved closer to her, ready to lay my soul bare. "Without pain, we cannot understand pleasure."

She looked surprised. "But…it's too late."

The bouncer couple had taken their places behind the podium.

"Welcome, everyone," said he.

"To this very special evening," said she.

"When *the stars are right*!" They said in celebratory unison.

Dance music swelled and the crowd clapped and cheered and whooped and danced. They raised glasses and hugged and some kissed. Everyone was smiling. They are all beautiful, I thought. I placed one arm around my woman and pulled her gently into me. I had gained an erection that felt like rock. There was something cold and hard in the small of her back.

"What…? Look we need to—"

"Look! This is it," she clapped and wiped away her tears.

"We need to get out of here," I said.

The boy bouncer left the podium with a great flourish and headed for the rear of the stage, where he stripped off his shirt and flexed his muscles. The crowd whooped some more and the girl bouncer laughed. The boy retrieved a decorated wooden box from an alcove and returned to the front, holding the object reverently between outstretched palms. He presented it with bowed head to the girl bouncer. She opened it with equal reverence, and with slow deliberation, removed its contents.

The blade flashed in the stage light, long and curved and razor sharp, I guessed. She held it up for the audience to see. They oohed and ahhhed. More people were kissing now, and some had taken it further than mere kissing. Some had sunk to the floor, embraced, began freeing themselves of their costumes and clothes. My girl started rubbing at my crotch, softly moaning. I was taken by the moment and reacted in kind.

A strange bell rang out of the speakers; a weird tone I'd never heard before. It vibrated through my whole body, causing my knees to weaken and my balls to tingle. My cock was now free of its confines and safely in her hands.

"The Deep Ones are coming!" the bouncer couple intoned from the stage. I heard a statement in a language I couldn't understand, but which seemed to have a great effect on the crowd. Almost everyone had sunk to the floor now, entangled in sex.

My girl climbed into my arms, wrapping her legs around my back. I was harder than I'd ever been. She was swollen and wet as my fingers slipped inside her. I wanted so badly to taste her. I took us to the floor gently, lay her down and put my head between her legs. Even with her thighs clamped over my ears I could hear and feel another vibrating bell sound out from the stage. My cock twitched and leaked pre-come. I lost myself in ecstasy. My tongue and lips played over her clit while my fingers dived deep inside her. She writhed and squirmed. I heard her moan and cry as she climaxed magnificently in wave after wave. A block of cold heat smashed agonisingly into my shoulder. There was a dull but fierce thump first, before I felt the point of the knife, driving deep into my back, scorching bone.

I screamed and awoke as if from a spell, spiking up from between her legs. Something splashed hotly over my face and neck. I wiped the liquid from my eyes and opened them to horror; her slashed throat, the knife in my back. She had killed herself. She had tried to kill me. Blood was spilling out of her neck, streaming to the floor.

I became aware of screams and cries all around us. Multiple knives flashed in the dance floor lights. Everyone was stabbing, slashing, and killing each other where they lay. A red sea of gore, steam rising, the familiar scent of steel on wet moss. What the fuck? This was not supposed to happen.

The couple on the podium were spilled down over it now, their knives buried deep in each other's necks. My back felt broken. The irony was not lost on me as I realised that my explosive vest had saved my life; had stopped her knife from severing my spine.

I had been the fanatic of the group, a certain choice from the beginning. For this job I would go the extra mile, do the thing that no one else would do, commit the ultimate. I built my vest in private as a safeguard against failure, keeping it secret even from the Priestess. It was light but powerful, undetectable in a cursory body search, a backup if it all started to go wrong. No one would get out of there alive.

With her strength fading, my girl realised I was not yet dead, and lunged sloppily at me again, slashing her knife in the air, aiming for my throat, or stomach. Somehow I avoided her—deep training or simply my amygdala, adrenaline coursing through me. I managed to stand, slipped in blood and my own rage and pain as I rose, and backed away. How could she have done this to us? She had destroyed all hope of our future together. I wanted to hold her and sob but she was desperate to kill me. She began crawling after me.

"Join…us," the words gurgled from her lungs, but she had done too fine a job on herself after all. She collapsed like a broken machine, splashing in blood as she sprawled on the floor.

I stepped on her hand and removed the knife from it, weeping. Our time together had been too short. I looked around—moans, cries, dying screams—most were dead already. Those who were not were finishing the grisly task, on themselves or others. Some were still wrestling. I saw my companion in the midst of the carnage, punch and scamper away from her prone partner, who collapsed in a heap. She was holding a bloody knife by the blade, embedded in her fingers, and looked as soaked and shocked as I felt.

I looked for little Gary, saw him dead in a thick red pool with a merman draped atop. Only the two of us had survived the onslaught. Everyone else in the room was dead or dying, and we had not laid a finger to a trigger. My mind raced for answers.

Was it some kind of double cross? Had the Chariot discovered our plans? Or was the Greater Good not as it seemed? Had we all been set up to fail?

A third bell toned and I staggered beneath its weight. Its reverberation failed to die, instead rising in weird echoes. I covered my ears to stem the pain, but the sound only grew through my red, slick hands.

The immense vibration rose in intensity until it shook the whole place. Near the centre of the room I could see the air ripple. I felt a wave wash over me that chilled my blood. It was not sonic, or kinetic, but rolled through my very *being*. Then, as if the real world was merely being projected onto a cinema screen, a tear began to open in mid-air. Another world appeared behind it, peeled open; another dark dimension.

Incredible. I saw black clouds roiling in a red and purple sky, a strange, impossible citadel with monolithic towers of unknown stone. There were huge, dark gates in the foreground, and as the rent opened further I saw terrible things clamouring at those gates. Sloppy, mossy blobs flinging slime from their tentacled jaws. The tear now stretched across the room from floor to ceiling. The gates cracked open and the surreal creatures began flooding through. Immediately they attacked my one remaining comrade.

Surely as stunned as I was by proceedings, that brave woman nevertheless reached for her weapons. As the terrible claws of the four-legged creatures scrabbled onto the slick wood of the dance floor she fired. She hit the first four, and managed to shoot the head clean off their leader, but the sick, slimy body of the creature moved on regardless to drag her to the ground and spread her guts among the gore. Other creatures sprang towards me, spitting slime.

HALT!

Detonator in hand my dazed attention snapped towards the powerful voice. It had stopped the creatures in their tracks, too. They heaved where they stood as if eager to tear me to pieces, yet came no closer. Even the dimensional rift seemed to obey, sizzling, popping, but growing no larger. An army of creatures still waiting on the other side howled their frustration.

A figure moved out from behind the curtains at the rear of the stage, a short, muscled figure in black pants and turtleneck. Neat, brown hair, a handsome face. He surveyed the scene with a palpable sense of triumph, and burned my soul with his gaze.

He was dragging something behind him. It seemed both heavy, and of little effort for him to carry. It was a body, dead, in red robes.

With a flick of his wrist the body flew across the room, over the heads of the heaving monsters, landing with a dull thump and sprawling to the edge of the dance floor, in front of me.

It was her, our audience of one. Our Priestess. I had never seen her look so defeated, or so peaceful and calm.

He, on the other hand, was powerful and regal. He seemed to glide across the floor towards me.

"You see now?" he said, though his lips did not move. "You see there is no God, but many gods, unto themselves, who are older than time, older than space. Finally, they will take their rightful place in this world."

I fell to my knees, somehow grateful beyond words for this mercy.

"Your pathetic little plan—you think we didn't know? Imbeciles. We knew of it before it began."

He had betrayed us all, and I loved him more for that. I wept and wept. When I looked again he was near me, his mouth black, his awesome eyes reading my every thought and deed. I will obey him, I thought. I will obey.

"So now you can be witness to this, our triumph, before you die."

"I will witness," I sobbed.

He was gathering his cohorts around him now, gathering his powers, ignoring me. He began to chant in that same nonsense language the bouncers had used. The sloppy monsters stood as upright as they were able, and moved around him, equally vocal. The portal rippled and tore. It was not yet stable, I thought. The sacrifice was not complete. He would be the final offering. He was tremendous.

Still on my knees I moved automatically, without thought. I took off my bloodstained jacket, peeled off my soaked shirt.

I started unclipping my vest. I had no conscious idea of what I would do next. Everything I thought I knew was wrong. Our belief was a pathetic fake; the Greater Good was a joke. Only this was real.

I shucked free of my heavy gear. Slowly I stood. Such power as this could not be resisted; it could not be fought. The C-4 packed in my vest might as well have been Play-Doh for all it was worth…

No, I thought, and then there was no more thought. I had only to do.

I whirled as I had practiced, moving by instinct and training. I threw the knife in one smooth motion. It found its target perfectly. The man screamed and staggered, his chanting interrupted by the blade stuck clean through his neck.

The monsters returned to all fours and bounded toward me. I sprinted towards them. Likely they were expecting me to run and were caught unawares. Still their claws tore gashes through me as I ducked and rolled and knocked out their sloppy excuses for legs and they stumbled. It would be time enough. I flipped into a run and went full pelt at the portal. It fought my progress, the rank breath of that other, impossible world blowing back my hair. The slavering monsters on the other side roared and spat their hate in my face. Fuck them, I thought, and threw the vest through the hole. I leapt towards the bar and pressed the detonator.

In mid-air I experienced a moment of stillness. Perhaps time itself slowed down. After all I had seen I did not discount the possibility that it could.

The expected explosion did not come, but heat spewed from the dimensional hole. Then came a sound like boots being pulled from deep mud—a wet sucking. Then I was crashing head first into the shelves behind the bar. Bottles smashed and rained glass on my back. The world shook and began to implode. Concrete crumbled.

Everything was being sucked into the portal as it shrieked and began to close. The wind and noise became deafening as furniture, fixtures and bodies flew across the room. Nothing was spared. Walls cracked. Even the slab of the bar wavered but did not completely break as I cowered behind it. The noise and chaos seemed to last for hours but could only have been seconds.

When, finally, it stopped and I could once again hear my own panicked screams, I looked up. The bar horse was there, cut and trembling behind his own piece of concrete. A survivor, like me.

"I'll have another," I said to him. "Best make it a double."

COME HIS CHILDREN

ALAN BAXTER

octor Canton looked through the glass panel in the door to see a blonde woman of about thirty. She sat on the bed in grubby jeans and t-shirt; barefoot, arms around her knees pulled close to her chest. She stared vacantly, rocking gently on the mattress.

"What's the story?"

Nurse Mason opened a patient folder. "A trucker nearly flattened her, staggering along the highway about eighty kays from here. He tried to talk to her, but got no sense. She was clearly traumatised. He brought her in."

"Any ID?"

"None. Just the clothes she's wearing. No bag, no wallet, no phone."

Doctor Canton nodded. "Any responses at all?"

"Nothing. Catatonic."

"All right. I suppose I should take a look at her."

The nurse glanced at him, brow furrowed.

"Probably upset someone and suffered the consequences," Canton said gruffly.

"Seriously, Doctor?"

"You know how these country people can be."

The nurse drew breath to speak again and Canton knew it would only end in an argument and more bad blood, more insults about him in the staff rooms.

"Come on, let's take a look." He strode into the room, the heat of Nurse Mason's disdain on his back.

"What's your name then?" he asked the woman.

She stared right through him.

"Sunburn," Canton said, as Nurse Mason scribbled notes. "Some light bruising and grazes that could have originated from stumbling along the road." He looked at her arms, frowning, then her legs. "Abrasions at her wrists and ankles? Was she tied up?"

"Tied up?" The situation took on an immediate and disturbing urgency. The nurse paused, pen hovering over her clipboard.

"Merely a best guess," the Doctor said.

Canton gently lifted the woman's arms from around her knees, eased her back onto the pillows. She complied, but gave no signs of awareness.

"We will have to take these clothes off, okay?"

The woman stared at the ceiling. Canton glanced at Nurse Mason, who nodded and put the clipboard down to help. They stripped away her dirty and ragged jeans and t-shirt. Canton stared at several half-moon shaped red marks around her stomach. "These look like bites."

"Animal bites?" Nurse Mason said, but her expression showed she knew better.

"Human. Adult human. Good God."

They stood in silence for a moment. Eventually, Doctor Canton said, "We'd better examine internally." He leaned over, into the woman's field of view. "We are going to need to have a close look at you, okay? I need to do an internal exam, to look for signs of sexual assault. Do you understand? Would you like to tell me anything?"

She stared, empty of all emotion.

The exam showed no signs of violent assault or rape; nothing that Canton could detect. He sighed, stepped back.

"She's dehydrated, but I don't imagine we'll get her to eat or drink. Let's put her on a drip, and into a gown. Once you organise that, call the police."

"Yes, Doctor."

Canton turned to face the nurse. "Eighty kays you say? In which direction?"

"North."

"But there's nothing up there. It's desert for hundreds of kilometres."

"There's a couple of old settlements, abandoned gold mining communities, but the nearest of those is more than forty kilometres from where she was picked up. I checked, and the nearest actual town is Lightning Rock, about a hundred and ten kays west of where the truck driver found her. It's a tin box town in the middle of nowhere, famous for nothing. Cattle farmers, mostly, I guess."

The doctor turned back to the woman, lifted a sheet to cover her. "Could she have come from there?"

"She's ragged enough to have walked a hundred kays, so… maybe?" The nurse used a black, felt-tipped Texta to mark the scant patient details on the board above the bed, then clipped the pen back into its holder. She slipped out to attend to the doctor's requests.

Canton looked down at the patient, disturbed. Without a conversation there was nothing more he could do. She had been through something horrible, that much was certain. The police would come shortly, and maybe they would have more luck identifying her. That might shed some further light. Or it might not. Canton went back to his office to book a psychologist to come by. He doubted one would be available before morning.

The next day, Doctor Canton made the strange woman his first port of call. He needed to see her again, to understand. To help. The police had been the previous afternoon, and had peppered him with questions he couldn't answer. The patient had been as unresponsive to them as she had been all along. The police said they would do all they could to learn the woman's identity and movements, but Canton had heard nothing more since. As he approached the door to her room, he saw she wasn't in the bed, but on the floor, tucked into a corner of the room. The cannula from the drip had been pulled from her arm and lay inert on the white tiles. Her gown had been cast aside. She sat naked, staring emptily. Had the nursing staff not seen any of this? The woman held a pen, the Texta from above her bed. Despite the movement and acquisition of the pen, her vacant gaze remained the same as before.

Frowning, he entered the room, drawing breath to speak, but stopped, dumbfounded. The wall beside the door, and all around one side, was covered in tiny scrawled script. She must have been up through the night, scribbling on the plaster. He moved closer to see the tiny, cramped lettering. His brows cinched together in confusion. He found what seemed to be the beginning of her scrawl near the top of the door, and began to read.

Moonlight pierces the window of this strange cell and seems to light my mind. I need to get the story out, before the shadows close over my thoughts again. That place was real, it had to be real, but it can't possibly have been. Such things should not exist.

Start at the beginning.

I was driving, that much I recall. I was supposed to be heading towards Broken Hill, farm supply catalogues piled on the back seat of my Toyota, but somehow I'd ended up in the wrong direction. I began to suspect a mistake after the empty highway continued for too long. I tried my GPS, but it kept blitzing out. My phone had no signal and as I watched the battery indicator drained like water pouring down a drain. I was momentarily distracted from panic by marks in the road and in the red dust to either side. Blackened indentations—miniature craters—dotted the landscape like strange acne.

Then a town appeared on the horizon.

As I passed the sign saying Lightning Rock, my car coughed and died. It just shut off, as if it had suffered a heart attack and expired. It wouldn't turn over, not even the dashboard lights came on. And it's not a crappy car, only a couple of years old. But thankfully it had waited until habitation to break down, so I climbed out into the dry, brutalising heat and walked into town to find help; a mechanic, a landline, a human face, for comfort. Little did I know the first face I saw, and every one after that, would be no comfort at all.

The town was deserted, not a soul in sight, though it was the middle of the day. The streets were wide with deep stone gutters, single and double storey buildings lined them. A bakery, a country store, a hairdresser, a newsagent. Most had an apartment above. In between the shops were old weatherboard houses painted in pale pastel colours, peeling, with rust-spotted tin roofs. Every sign and awning was sun bleached. It reminded me of a dozen other country towns I'd seen in recent weeks. Except for the lack of people. And then I saw movement in one large window, *Jack's Hardware* in bold yellow letters across the glass.

I smiled, raised a hand to wave as I turned towards the store, then stopped dead. The man behind the window was fish-belly pale, his eyes wider than seemed natural, his cheeks hollow, his frame gaunt, like someone in late-term cancer, eaten almost to the bone. He had one hand pressed to the glass, and his fingers were overly long, unnatural, spider-like.

> *Iä Nyarlathotep cf'ayak'vulgtmm, vugtlagln vulgtmm*
> *stell'bsna tharanak gof'nn*
> *ch'yar ul'nyar shaggornyth*
> *fhtagn li'hee fm'latgh*
> *gof'nn hupadgh Nyarlathotep nog*

What happened? I was writing and...Clouds passed over the moon, I think, and my mind closed to darkness again. What do those things I've written mean? When the night is dark, those words crawl through my mind like worms and I understand them, but in the clarity of the moon, my own mind returns and that language becomes senseless again. Why?

I must get this down.

The drums.

I remember the drums.

I still hear them now.

As I entered town, I heard them. A rhythmic, repetitive phrase that seemed to be saying...something. And when that man in the shop window caught my eye, the drums became louder, suddenly more present, cajoling, entreating me. They drew me somewhere.

I turned, looked around to see where the drummers were. The sound was so insistent, and nearby, pounding out the same beat over and over, four, then nine, four and nine. But no one was near. As I looked away from the man, the sound of the beat faded. When I turned back, he was gone.

In the road ahead I spotted another of those blackened indentations. A small crater, deep and steep sided, the edges ragged, but melted somehow. Something extremely hot had impacted there. Moving over to it, I peered into its depths and saw a ragged, ruddy lump of normal, sandy earth at the bottom. Whatever had landed had been dug free, leaving the ochre soil stark against the dark, molten crater above. What had been removed?

Looking up the street, I saw several more benighted craters, and each had been dug out the same way. A shop front, perhaps a grocery store, had been destroyed. The front of the building was broken and blackened, the interior gutted by fire, and just inside the boundary of its front wall, a crater like the others.

As I turned away from my inspection of this impact, I saw movement in a shadowed alley between the burned-out shop and its neighbour. A woman of indeterminate age, gaunt and sallow like the man had been, eyes stretched disturbingly wide, mouth open as though she gasped for air. I called out to her. "Excuse me. I need help!"

The drums intensified again, four beats then nine, rapid and repeating.

She backed away, long-fingered hands before her face, making high noises like a frightened animal.

I spoke again. "Please, I need a phone, that's all. Can you help me?"

She wore loose shorts and a stained singlet, and as she retreated her shoulder collided with the rough bricks of the wall. She yelped as her skin peeled away from the muscle like wet tissue paper. Pink-tinged ichor, pale and sluggish, rose up through the red meat beneath, and she sobbed, pressed the skin back into place with angular, too-long fingers, then turned and fled.

Close to panic, I wandered the empty streets of Lightning Rock, several times spotting the pale, wrong citizens, but never getting close enough again to converse with anyone. Every door I tried was locked. In an hour I had covered the entire small town twice.

I had been driving far longer than I intended and the sky began darkening towards night. I had no idea what to do, or where to go. I sat in the driver's seat of my Camry, the door open to the hot, musty breeze, and cried. I bawled until my eyes swelled and my heart fell empty. I had never felt so alone.

> Iä Nyarlathotep cf'ayak'vulgtmm, vugtlagln vulgtmm
> stell'bsna tharanak gof'nn
> ch'yar ul'nyar shaggornyth
> fhtagn li'hee fm'latgh
> gof'nn hupadgh Nyarlathotep nog
> gof'nn hupadgh Nyarlathotep nog
> gof'nn hupadgh Nyarlathotep nog

Ah, the moon and clouds play with me.

I must tell this more quickly. Soon the moon will pass overhead and shine through the window no more.

Night sank in. No lights came on in the town. The few streetlights remained dark, and no glow emerged from any window. Was the entire place as devoid of power as my Toyota? Perhaps, I thought, I could sleep in the safety of my car, with the doors locked, and try again to find help the next morning. If no one would let me in, if no door was unlocked, I would take up a rock and smash a window, force entry, and find a telephone. Would a phone even work in this place?

I was thirsty and hungry, with only half a bottle of warm water, and a muesli bar in the glove box. These I consumed for a meagre supper, and settled across the back seat to sleep. It was cramped and overly warm, but it felt at least vaguely secure. Yet still those drums rolled on, four beats then nine, over and over, distant and muffled, but persistent, inveigling.

Sleep would not come, my restlessness caused cramps and discomforts. I sat up to turn around and saw the main street ahead of me full of people. I gasped, my heart stuttered.

The drum refrain increased again, pounding against my

mind. I stumbled from the car and hurried back towards town. But within fifty metres of the crowd I stopped, crying out in horror. In the darkness, from a distance, they had appeared to be a crowd of the thin, pasty inhabitants of this desolate place. But closer, illuminated by the pale half-moon, they were anything but.

Certainly, they had a vaguely human shape, tall and thin. But their skin, slick and rubbery, was as black as tar, darker than the night. And they had no faces, only smooth, featureless expanses of blackness where eyes or nose or mouth should be. Eyeless, yet they all turned as I skidded to a halt, and I knew without a doubt that each one was staring at me.

Above those smooth, non-faces, each had a pair of inward-facing horns. And whipping in the shadows, each had a long, barbed tail that quested like a snake's tongue. And then they unfurled wide, membranous wings. Soundlessly, they launched and swept towards me. Unable to hold back a scream, I turned and ran for my car, thinking only of steel doors I could lock, and toughened glass to keep them out. Would it be enough? It didn't matter. In near silence, the flock descended upon me like a cloud before I'd made it twenty metres. Their long-fingered hands roved over me, digging and driving, causing me to squirm in every direction, trying to avoid that prickling touch. Their tails wrapped around and dug in, spiked and coiled around me. Against my will they manoeuvred me with their appalling, diaphanous touch, back into town. Everywhere I grabbed, trying to prevent their limbs from touching me, they seemed to slip away, but another would immediately take its place. I cried out again when I spotted a shop door wide open and several pale citizens of Lightning Rock waiting in the shadowed depths beyond.

I was guided inside with them, and the citizens parted to reveal an open trapdoor in the floor. I fought harder against the swarming black creatures, but it was to no avail. The floor beneath my feet vanished and I stumbled and fell into the deeper darkness underground. Something struck the side of my head—a stair?—and oblivion swallowed me.

gof'nn hupadgh Nyarlathotep nog
gof'nn hupadgh Nyarlathotep nog
Iä Nyarlathotep cf'ayak'vulgtmm, vugtlagln vulgtmm
fhtagn li'hee fm'latgh
gof'nn hupadgh Nyarlathotep nog

It's in me. It's growing.

I need to write more quickly.

This pen, against this wall, it's not easy. I hope someone can decipher this scrawl.

When I came to I felt tightness at my wrists and ankles. My shoulders burned, the muscles shaking from sustained effort from the moment I awoke and tried to haul myself up to relieve the pressure. But my bonds were too tight. And those drums pounded on, soft and distant, but relentless.

As I gasped for breath and tried to clear my head, I realised I was tied standing, my arms above my head, out to either side, and my legs held similarly wide apart. Where the ropes were secured I couldn't see, but somehow my arms and legs were connected. If I pulled with an arm, my leg on that side would move, but not far. I was stretched to the limit of my flexibility. For several minutes, in a panic, I screamed and shouted for help until my throat was raw and torn. My muscles shrieked with pain.

Weak moonlight flooded down from above as the trapdoor was opened, and my screaming ceased as fear paralysed me silent. Pasty, gangling citizens descended, one, then two more, then a fourth. They looked as scared as I felt, but there was determination in their too-wide eyes. One of them carried a dark wooden box carved with strange symbols that looped and whorled. The one with the box shambled over to stand before me, and another used her stick-like fingers to open the lid.

Inside lay a smooth, spherical rock, no bigger than a tennis ball, cracked open. Inside the rock was something like an egg. Only a few centimetres long, it glowed a soft green, and specks and motes danced and glittered inside. A stench rose from it, cloying and thick, bitter, yet somehow spicy.

The woman who had opened the box took up the glowing

object between the tips of her middle finger and thumb. She made small, suppressed noises, high-pitched and gasping, as she held it up. I knew, beyond a doubt, that this was one of the things that had been dug from those molten, blackened craters. It was beyond question. Why were they showing me this thing? What did they expect from me?

And then the presence of the other two became obvious. Both men, both equally as scared as the woman holding the egg. They moved to either side of me and one took my head in his spider-leg hands and gripped with horrifyingly intense strength. I cried out, tried to resist. The other used long, bone-hard fingers to force his way between my lips and pry at my teeth. I growled through a clenched jaw, refused to give him access, but he dug and clawed, sobbing and weeping as he worked. I felt the skin on his palms tear as I thrashed my head in his grasp. My cheeks greased with his pale ichor.

Suddenly the one holding my head released one hand and struck with shocking force my abdomen, making me gasp in pain. Held by the ropes, I couldn't curl up around the injury and, lightning fast, the woman thrust the bright egg into my mouth. The one who had struck me slapped a hand up under my chin before I could eject the foul thing, and it burst, flooding my mouth with acrid viscosity. It burned, throbbed, and made my head swim. The man gripped my nose, worked two fingers at my throat, and I was helpless, with no choice but to swallow it down. He released my mouth and I sucked in air and used it all to scream and curse them all for animals.

They quickly turned and slunk away. They hurried up the steps pushing against each other, all desperate to be the first out. The last dropped the trapdoor shut again and I was lost once more in darkness. My mouth and throat burned, something roiled and agitated in my gut. I wanted nothing more than to vomit, but could not. I hung against my bonds, defeated, utterly violated.

The drums beat on, four then nine, four then nine. Over and over and over.

Iä Nyarlathotep cf'ayak'vulgtmm, vugtlagln vulgtmm

Under the eye of Nyarlathotep, his will manifests
gof'nn hupadgh Nyarlathotep nog
gof'nn hupadgh Nyarlathotep nog
He returns
The children of Nyarlathotep born in pain in pain in pain in pain
Come his children
Nyarlathotep walks and he dreams
My eyes burn. It's in me, writhing, coiling, ready.
I can't stop it. I have to tell it.

I felt whatever they had forced into me travelling through my flesh, my veins. It seemed to soak through me like blood through a tissue, invading every part of me, seeding me in some arcane and abhorrent way.

No one knew where I was. Not a soul in this whole wide, brown land. I was as lost as a person could be. I have no idea how much time passed, but scratching, scrabbling sounds aroused me. I craned my neck to see behind, to find the source of the noise, and spotted sleek, brown bodies tumbling over each other in a dark corner. How could I see in the pitch darkness of the cellar?

Then I saw a low gap, ceiling height to the subterranean room, but street level above. It was barred with short lengths of iron. The moon had not been bright enough, but the wan light of dawn leaked through. My eyes fell back to the rats, and for a moment I couldn't see what they swarmed over and chewed into. Then the image resolved and my mind rebelled. Stacks of bodies, human bodies, blackened as if burned; leathered and shrunken as if mummified. The rats gnawed at that tough, dead flesh. But more upsetting, every body was burst open at the abdomen, a flower of ragged skin and bone protruding from where something inside had thrust its way free.

Whatever they had fed me squirmed and thrashed.

I struggled anew, desperate to escape my bonds. But they were as tight as ever, thin but far too strong nylon ropes. With the light I saw there were two, tied around each of my ankles, passed through a steel loop close to the floor, then another loop in the roof, and down to be secured at my wrist. If I hauled hard enough with my arms, I simply pulled my legs further apart, and already I was at the full extent of my muscles' ability to stretch. I didn't dare risk falling and hanging suspended. The ropes remained taut. My muscles sang with pain.

And as the dawn progressed I saw more clearly the desecrated remains of those who had gone before me. Were the strange, pale, long-fingered citizens the nannies of whatever foul offspring had emerged? Or were they themselves the offspring? Birthed in violence and grown in darkness, afraid of the sunlight. My mind began to unhinge at the prospect.

At how it might feel to give birth.

The trapdoor opened and a sickly white, angular, lanky creature descended, eyes too wide, fear etched on its face. A woman, but was it really? She came close, crouched. With a grunt of annoyance, she scrabbled in her pockets, then lit a candle against the gloom despite the rising day. I felt its heat on my skin as she lifted my shirt, and ran a hand as cold as ice over my stomach. My flesh pulsed as if in answer. Then, unbelievably, she began to bite at my abdomen. It was hard enough to cause me pain, but not enough to break the skin, her mouth exploratory. My mind began to fray. I felt my sanity at risk. Despite all that had gone before, those questing bites appalled my mind into some kind of permanent submission.

The creature stood, reached up one frozen, bony fingertip, and drew my lower eyelid down, looked intently at my eye. And I saw her neck craning, scrawny and soft. I saw her clavicle arching from the sallow flesh. I remembered the paper-soft skin of the woman in the alley, her pain when it tore. And I slammed my face into this woman's shoulder as she perused me, clamped my teeth over that protruding collar bone, and bit as hard as I could. All I wanted was to cause pain, to fight back despite the hopelessness of it all.

The woman wailed and thrashed, but I refused to relinquish my grip, my jaw a death-vice. Her skin tore, her thick ichorous blood welled into my mouth, but I ignored it all. The candle fell to the floor as she hammered at my head and shoulders with those long, bony hands, but they were as nothing, like being battered with balsa wood. Her bones cracked against my skull. Her pain was strident. She kicked her feet. And I saw from the corner of my eye that the candle still burned.

Refusing to release my grip, I watched as the candle rolled and came to rest against the steel loop in the cement floor. The woman's ichor poured over my chin, dripped to the floor. She wailed and battered, but weakness and pain made her ineffective. Panic and hope made me strong. The small candle flame flickered against the nylon rope. The bone between my teeth began to crunch and crack. The woman screamed and thrashed.

If I ended up biting right through the clavicle, she would escape, albeit maimed. I had to hold on, just a little longer. The distant drums beat louder, four beats then nine, four beats then nine, deafening in their intensity. My brain throbbed with their pulse, my insides roiled.

Sobbing, she spoke haltingly, begging me, I assume, in a stilted language I couldn't understand. I strained downwards with my left arm as the tiny flame melted the rope, and suddenly it gave way. The rope fell slack, my shoulder screeching with pain as the muscles were finally allowed to change position. I cried out in agonised relief, and the woman staggered free, slapped one hand to her torn and ragged wound, then turned and ran up the stairs and away.

> Come his children
> Nyarlathotep walks and he dreams
> Come his children
> Nyarlathotep walks and he dreams
> Come his children
> Nyarlathotep walks and he dreams

It is so hard to concentrate, but it's nearly told.

I knew I had little time. She would surely call for others. Despite the pins and needles, the numb fingers, my left hand was free, and my left leg. Twisting, causing whatever squirmed inside me to writhe and contort, I reached across and pulled at the knots on my right wrist. It freed, and my foot with it.

With nonsensical noises of relief, I ran from the dark basement up into the dawning day. The pale light was pink and yellow on the horizon, stark against the orange sand, the rusted roofs, and worn weatherboards that lined the streets. I stumbled out into the road with no idea where to go, just away. The drumming pounded in my mind and I knew it had been in there all along, ever since I had come near this place. Never outside, growing nearer or drifting further away. Always inside me, echoing.

From every doorway they came, walking stilt-like as if those long thin legs were not an entirely perfect fit. Their arms angled out, fingers writhing and clawing at the air. Refusing to look, I stayed to the centre of the road and staggered on. In pain, starving, desiccated with thirst, sickened by whatever squirmed within me, I stared only at the pale, broken asphalt and tried to run. I managed a stumbling jog.

I kept going.

I expected those fingers to close around my limbs any moment, but none came. I blinked, eyes watering. I realised that the sun had breached the horizon and everything was bathed in early morning gold.

Looking back at the town I saw the last of them hurrying into the shelter of shadows within the homes and shops. The sun had brought me a reprieve. Whatever these things were, they were of the night.

I didn't know which way to go. Nothing but desert lay all around. Low scrub, snakes, merciless sun. None of it mattered. I would gladly die in the middle of nowhere, as long as it wasn't in Lightning Rock.

Whatever lurked inside me leapt and twisted, and I felt my sanity tearing away, shredding at the edges of my mind like weak canvas in a strong gale. I just had to be away from there; away from them. I put one foot before the other again and again and again come his children Nyarlathotep walks and he dreams come his children Nyarlathotep walks and he dreams come his children Nyarlathotep walks and he dreams

Doctor Canton crouched near the bed, staring at where the last of the text trailed away, and the woman's account ended. Every part of it was surely lunatic ravings, hallucinations from exposure, from whatever trauma had truly befallen her. She had been bound, that was certain. He had seen no other signs of violence than the bite marks, but that didn't mean she hadn't been terrorised in who-knew-what ways. Enough to trigger these elaborate, fantastic delusions.

He swallowed hard and stood, wincing as his knees popped. Taking a deep breath, he went back around the bed to where she sat, once more catatonic, in the corner. And he gasped.

In the time he had spent reading, her skin had begun to blacken. Dark spots bloomed across her abdomen, chest, thighs. Dark flowers, with tendrils like questing tentacles; filament thin lines, snaking out in every direction.

Doctor Canton's hands were trembling as he crouched for a closer look. The vein-like growths spreading across her skin seemed to seek each other out, one dark patch striving to meet with another, and the veins intertwining like lovers. And everywhere they met, the woman's flesh pulsed slightly, rose and fell, as if something sentient moved beneath. As the blackening spread, the flesh beneath the skin reduced, drawing tight to the bones, as if consumed.

"Hello, Doctor Canton?" said a voice from the door. "I'm Doctor Alison Carter, the psychologist. Can I come in?"

Canton moved his mouth to reply, but was unable to form words, mesmerised by the rapidly spreading blackness, the swiftly reducing musculature. The woman's remaining flesh undulated in ever bigger motions, her stomach swelled as if inflated with gases that flexed and pulsed.

"Doctor Canton?"

The woman's swollen belly split.

THE DEPICTION

JULIE DITRICH

"**I**f you remove that painting from that wall then I will die!"

This astounding proclamation tumbled from my father's mouth and had an instantaneous effect...I froze...suspended mid action with my hands clasped on either side of the gold frame that bordered the artwork he was referencing.

His utterance hung in the air like a ghostly, prescient shroud, waiting to envelop him. I felt the delicate hairs on my arms raise in goose bumps and heard a movement behind me. I glanced over my shoulder to see my brother, Mark, silhouetted in the doorway, with a strange expression on his face...shared shock, no doubt.

"Oh...so, you finally made it!" I exclaimed in exasperation, breaking the silence, "Only an hour late this time."

"Long work hours, sis. Not that you'd know anything about that."

I gave him a filthy look.

"Come on, Dad..." he said eventually, turning towards my father who was lying on top of the blankets of his motorised single bed, "...that painting's ugly. Actually, I think the more correct word is 'repulsive'."

I rarely agreed with my brother but on this particular occasion we were on the same page.

Mark sat on the lounge chair beside my father's bed at the nursing home. I wondered how it was he always looked so fresh—the epitome of sartorial suaveness—even at the end of a long day's work. He was dressed in a custom-fitted black suit and a crisp white shirt with a sapphire-blue power tie…he looked more like a politician about to front the cameras at a press conference than an IT project manager.

On this occasion, however, Mark was the audience and I was his entertainment. His mouth rested on an angle, betraying his ever-present imperious attitude.

He was a younger version of my father…they were both tall and excessively handsome in a bronzed, corporate kind of way. I was the opposite…a pin-curled red head, white-skinned with rouge lipstick and peridot green eyes like my mother and dressed in a 1950s polka-dot swing dress with ballerina flats, which was my signature look.

I'm pretty sure Mark saw my struggle and revelled in it, as I awkwardly wrestled the painting back onto its hook on the wall opposite my father's bed. The artwork wasn't particularly heavy — just slightly wider than my wingspan — maybe about one metre in width by ninety centimetres in height. I was a lightweight not only on the bathroom scales but also to some degree in life. Or so I was reminded time and time again.

Eventually, with a grunt, I slid the painting back into place and then straightened it. I turned around again with a feeling of unease.

My father, award-winning Sydney architect Luke Darwell, was now a resident in the high-care unit of a high-end nursing home in the Sutherland Shire—Gammell Garden. He was in his early seventies. He was angular and gangly and didn't eat much anymore. The vibrant masculinity and virility that had emanated from him when he was at the peak of his professional life was rapidly waning as he retreated more and more into himself. Right now, he was staring at me and had a frown on his face. His crinkly eyelids drooped over his smudgy grey eyes but his look was unmistakable…he was profoundly unhappy with me.

His shirt was dishevelled, sticking out of his trousers and it had a yellow stain on it…a splat perhaps from the chicken soup he had had for lunch. I made a point of reading the menu in the dining room each time I visited so I could encourage him to eat. He had a blue sock on his left foot and a black sock on his right.

His loafers were flung haphazardly under the bed.

My father's mind was dying well ahead of his body...as though his memories had been locked up in a safe and tossed to the bottom of a dark, deep ocean. Occasionally, one would break free like a bubble of oxygen and ripple to the surface. But this occasion was different.

He had uttered those words with clarity and distinction... with a quiet and resolute lack of ambiguity. He was present in that moment when he had spoken and even though I considered his statement to be completely bizarre and downright ludicrous I thought that maybe, just maybe, he was on his way back to us. Except that it didn't make sense...

...the painting was incongruent with my father's personal or professional aesthetic. There was nothing contemporary about it. The image lacked symmetry, and it was definitely not rendered in muted or natural, earthy tones of the other abstract gallery-bought artworks hanging inside the waterfront Taren Point family home.

My father had been in the facility for about five years. The wall opposite his bed had been naked prior to the painting's coming. The artwork had arrived unexpectedly and mysteriously about twelve months before, and my father had insisted it remain despite my constant objection to it. For some unfathomable reason, he admired it...no doubt his illness talking.

When he was still working and living at home, he abhorred clutter. It was another matter entirely at the nursing home. On his bedside table was a wedding photo of him and mum; a caricature from one of the top-shelf editorial cartoonists in the country; a couple of the beautiful sculptural awards he'd won; a shoe horn; and a prescription list of the various medications he needed for his heart, blood pressure, anxiety, insomnia, and constipation.

He also bought junk incessantly from the local newsagency staff who came by once a day, selling newspapers and magazines, soft toys, and lollies. And the residents bought this stuff because those who were still high-functioning were bored, and those who were low-functioning had lost their ability to exercise good judgement and decline the offer. My father was in the latter category and the cupboard in his room was now full of teddy bears, puzzles he could no longer solve, and tins of chocolate-covered caramels he would never eat. All of these expenses were charged to his monthly account.

I had been lobbying to remove the painting for a long time— my father had refused but now that his illness had progressed, I didn't think he had the mental wherewithal to put forth his argument. I was wrong. He had put it forth most powerfully.

On this particular evening while he had been dozing and I had been waiting for Mark to make his appearance, I had the opportunity to examine the painting a bit more closely.

I was no expert but I estimated it to be an antique…maybe a 100 to 150 years old. It appeared to be painted on a linen canvas mounted on a wooden stretcher and held in place with iron tacks in the margin. It had wedges in the corners to keep the tension. If it was the age I calculated it to be, then the canvas would have been primed with a mixture of chalk and glue made out of gelatinous animal parts. I only knew these things because I had wandered into the many antique shops in the Paddington, Surry Hills and Woollahra area, and eavesdropped as the shop staff explained the features of old paintings to customers who could afford them. Plus, I had a good memory for detail.

The painting was rendered with thick raised dollops of oil paint—the term I believe is "impasto"—and glazed, which gave it a kind of translucent sheen. It reminded me of the early 19th century English artist William Turner, who painted expressive and atmospheric seascapes. But that's where the resemblance ended.

My father's painting was chaotic and frenzied, and that particular ferocious energy threatened to spill outside its containment—an ornate frame, which appeared to be more expensive than the canvas. Indeed, the gilded frame had a scoop profile with black relief details and accents that resembled calligraphic flourishes.

The painting didn't seem to fit in any fine art period I recognised. Instead, I thought it would have been more likely to have adorned the cover of a modern-day pulp horror novel.

Despite my distaste for the painting, nobody could dispute its artisanship. The image was that of a tempest under a full moon. Rising up out of the deep blue hue of violent ocean waves was a god-like creature unlike anything I had ever seen.

The depiction…well…the only way I could describe it was that it was of a hybrid monster with a green, anthropoid leathery body, the expansive wings of a dragon, and the face of an octopus with a proboscis of slimy cephalopod arms and tentacles. Horrible!

I turned my attention back to my father. He seemed to have forgotten the commotion a few minutes before but began addressing me by my mum's name and whispered to me that he suspected his food was being poisoned. I reassured him that it wasn't, which he seemed to accept. I felt a sad kind of helplessness because I knew he'd forget everything I had said in a few more minutes.

After Mark and I said our goodbyes, we walked into the corridor and around the corner.

Then Mark blurted out, "Dad's either just pointed the bone at himself and has truly gone crazy or he's a freaking genius."

"That's insensitive on all fronts, Mark."

"Well, he knows you've been wanting to get rid of that monstrosity since you first saw it and now he's finally put a stop to it. Wily old bugger. Got to give him that."

In this respect, I had to quietly acknowledge my brother's assessment of the situation. Either way, there was nothing I could say or do. If the painting brought my father comfort, then who was I to argue…I certainly didn't want to be held responsible for provoking his new-found superstition or invoking a self-fulfilling prophecy. I sighed and headed off into the night to catch the train home. Mark walked in the opposite direction towards his Audi sports car.

I usually visited my father on Wednesday nights after my shift had ended, as well as on Sunday mornings. I worked as a casual assistant in a trendy Darlinghurst florist shop on Oxford Street and lived close by in a small studio apartment where I wrote bad poetry. I was supposed to have followed in my father's footsteps and studied architecture at the University of Technology, Sydney, or UTS as it is more commonly referred, but had taken a sabbatical…that was ten years ago.

When I was a child I used to wander around the CBD with my father. He taught me to look up. We criss-crossed the streets together and wandered down towards The Rocks, hand in hand. There were the obvious places such as the Sydney Opera House and the Queen Victoria Building that were universally admired. And then there were the buildings that people passed by in a rush and rarely noticed. I loved Macquarie Street the best…our mutual favourite was the British Medical Association Building, which was decorated with grotesques (or gargoyles as they are also known). On the 11th floor balconies are a series of medieval knights, holding shields to ward off evil from entering through the façade. To this day, I can't pass by without looking up at them and feeling nostalgic.

These excursions ended when my mother died of breast cancer. I was ten and Mark was eighteen and had started a computer course at university. After that my father lost himself in his work and I had to make do with answering architecture questions during television quiz shows in the afternoons after school. When I got them right, which was most of the time, I would jump up and down on the couch like a female version of Tom Cruise. But nobody was ever home to witness my victory.

Gammell Gardens was about a 15-minute walk from Cronulla Station, so it was easy for me to hop on a train at Central then get off at Cronulla and walk there. I had no need for a car and couldn't afford one anyway.

The nursing home was originally an old office building that had been converted and modernised with tall blade walls, quartz tiles and glass into an L-shaped plan, which opened up into a gorgeous garden at the back with ocean views.

It was 10:00am and I had bought some fresh croissants so my father and I could have breakfast together and sip our daily cappuccino, courtesy of Heidi the dread-locked onsite barista.

My father had developed a taste for coffee when previously he had found it repugnant. Heidi would wheel her giant-size, double decker, stainless-steel coffee cart through the nursing home and stop by to visit each resident. Perched securely on the top of her trolley was an expensive coffee machine and in the closed-in compartment below she would keep the milk, sugar and biscuits. If she was busy, then she would just sprinkle powdered chocolate onto the frothy milk. If she wasn't busy, she would create complex froth sculptures of suns and moons and other fixtures of the cosmos, which delighted her elderly customers. Right now, I craved one with or without its artistic head.

I pushed open the door into the foyer.

One of the residents, wearing pineapple earrings and a tropical flowered shift, promptly wedged her walking frame to block the backward swing of the door.

"Not today, Joyce," I said gently, then manoeuvred her away ever so slightly until the door swung shut. Surprisingly, the skin on her elbow was soft and smooth.

She didn't say anything but smiled in a quiet acceptance...I had thwarted her escape. She would need to be buzzed out or be in possession of the security code to make it to the outside. She turned around and headed off towards the common room—her walking frame tapping on the floor with every step.

Many of the elderly residents in the high-care wing tried to break out. They were able-bodied or on canes, walkers or wheelchairs but visitors had been alerted not to let them leave. To my knowledge there had been only one successful escape from Gammell Gardens—one that had reached legendary status. An elderly woman had made her way to Bundeena on the Cronulla Ferry before being discovered. She was standing in the water in a white nightie at Jibbon Beach, staring longingly out to the ocean with her arms upraised as if she was about to be baptised. She had been brought back safely, of course, but there had been an investigation and the security protocols had been revised and more CCTV cameras installed in and around the facility.

The day my brother and I booked our father into Gammell Gardens I felt as though I was dropping a beloved dog at the pound because he couldn't comprehend what was happening. I was distraught but Mark appeared calm and logical, which was a comfort. I also recognised that neither my brother nor I could provide my father with the medical care he needed. By the time I had contemplated moving in to look after him it was far too late. My father could no longer drive and was forever getting lost. He also posed a safety-risk to himself and others.

On another occasion, he fainted when I came to visit. When I checked his fridge and found it empty, I realised he had forgotten to eat for days.

My father adapted to Gammell Gardens better than I anticipated and, even though I still felt my stomach twist every time I went to visit him, I knew he was in good hands.

As it was, on this particular morning, I waved to Anne the receptionist on the front desk who had given me a smile when she saw me avert the escape. It meant she didn't have to get up. She was a platinum blonde, dimpled woman in her mid-forties and from the western suburbs who had worked in Gammell Gardens since it opened ten years before. She knew everything and everyone there.

"Morning, Anne," I said, "Brought you something."

I dropped off a packet, containing a scone and a container of whipped cream and strawberry jam onto the desk.

"Ooooo…my favourite. Thanks, luv," she responded with enthusiasm.

We chatted happily for a few moments and then my mood changed as my eyes settled on the shrine…a burning votive candle alongside the photo of the latest resident who had passed away overnight. Although I didn't recognise the face of the grey-curled, long-faced woman on this occasion, I did feel a profound sadness.

"That's Mrs Davidson. Poor thing. Heart failure," said Anne.

There were always two things that gave away the inevitable deaths that happened in the facility…the front desk tribute and an empty bed dressed in fresh sheets. Seeing the shrine each visit gave me a terrible sense of foreboding.

"Well, I'd better be off. See you later," I said.

"Bye, Celeste, and thanks again for brekky."

I walked down the corridor into the high-care wing. I was met with the usual wall of smell—a thick mix of cleaning products, flatulence and incontinence. In the background was a sound of quiet moaning, punctuated with the sound of buzzers. You could guess the personality of the person pressing it. Some were hesitant and tremulous. Others were unrelenting. For the most part, the call-outs were valid insofar as the resident may have dropped something or needed help to walk to the toilet but other times it was nuisance attention-seeking behaviour

Right now, one of them was sending an obvious message. Relentlessly stabbing…bzzz bzzz bzzz…and then there was one long insistent bzzzzzzzzzzzzzzzz so there was no ambiguity that the perpetrator wanted action.

I continued walking down the corridor, popping my head into the common room to see if my father was there. A few residents were sitting in tub chairs or wheel chairs, watching the sports on a large TV. Some were reading in the library section in the corner. Others were absorbed in craft activities…crocheting, assembling model aeroplanes, folding paper flowers. A volunteer beauty therapist sat in the corner painting the fingernails of one of the women. It was a lovely homely place.

I approached my father's room. The buzzing had stopped but I was surprised to see one of the nurses, emerging from his room with a worried look upon her face.

"Hi, Cassie," I said with a smile, "Nice to see you."

"Celeste…" she murmured. Then she ever so subtly blocked my way.

"What's wrong?" I asked.

"I have to warn you…your dad's taken a bit of a turn."

"He was fine a few days ago."

"He's been buzzing all morning."

"That was HIM?" I exclaimed. "What happened? Is something wrong?"

"You need to prepare yourself. I've never seen him so agitated before."

She moved out of the way.

My heartbeat sped up as I walked into his room. The first thing I noticed was him, sitting on top of the bed, hugging his knees and rocking.

The second thing I noticed was that the painting was gone.

I instantly knew what the problem was.

"**W**here's the painting that was hanging in my father's room?" I was in the Executive Manager of Residential Care, Robyn Sheargold's office, who happened to be catching up on work that weekend. My hands had curled up into tight fists, and I hid them behind my back.

"You might want to sit down," she said, indicating a chair behind her desk. I reluctantly followed her suggestion.

I hadn't met her before but felt as though I knew her because I had watched the Gammell Gardens promo website video many times. She had been the white-suited, brown-bobbed, well put-together talking head on the online tour that espoused the virtues of the "luxury independent living units, residential and palliative care, and home support" within the aged care facility.

"We actually don't know anything about it," she replied simply.

"Well, when did you notice it was gone? Do you think it was stolen? Have you searched the place?" I pummelled her with questions.

"As I mentioned, we have no knowledge about the disappearance of this painting."

"Do you think somebody could have shoved it out of the window and made off with it? Maybe they thought it was worth something."

"It's impossible. The windows are bolted for obvious reasons. We checked anyway and neither the locking mechanisms nor the glass had been tampered with. The only way out would have been through the door."

"Well, it's fairly obvious that the painting's a kind of—for want of a better word—security blanket for my father. It calms and stabilises him. You must've found that out after you put it there."

"Gammell Gardens had nothing to do with placing that painting in his room. It's just not our style. As you can see…" she said, indicating some beautiful framed prints of rainforest vegetation on the wall of her office, "We tend to purchase professional photographic art…you've seen them in the foyer. Nothing too vibrant or colourful."

Indeed, I had. Benign close ups of plants, tranquil waterfalls, rustic farmhouses in lush green valleys, and jetties on beaches at high tide—all carefully chosen to blend in with the pastel colour palette of the walls.

"We'll make some enquiries for you," she continued, "When did the painting disappear?"

"Well…it was here last Wednesday night when I visited and, according to Cassie, my dad didn't start having his melt-down until this morning so I'm assuming something happened to it in the last twenty-four hours. I'll have to let my brother know, too. He won't be happy."

"Well, when you speak to him…" she said, shuffling through a tray of papers on her desk, "…can you give him this?" she said, handing me a sealed, window-faced envelope.

"What is it?"

"I don't wish to be insensitive, especially under these circumstances but it's an invoice. We've emailed your brother several times. As yet, he hasn't responded."

"He's really busy. And he's going on a cruise tomorrow so he's probably under the pump."

I opened the envelope.

"We only have the best interests of our residents and we wouldn't want your father to go without in your brother's absence?"

"In what way?"

"Well your father's tab is overdrawn."

I looked at the invoice.

There was nothing awry. The only minor issue was that my father's petty cash account was overdrawn, and his latest top-up had been declined.

"Here's some cash," I said handing over sixty dollars from

JULIE DITRICH

my wallet. "It's not much but it should cover any immediate expenses."

Robyn accepted the cash and hand-wrote a receipt.

"There's another problem. Please ask your brother to contact me ASAP. I've left several phone messages for him already."

"Maybe I can help?"

"It's not my place to share this information with you. You aren't authorised and we need to follow procedure."

"I'm his daughter, for God's sake!"

"I'm sure you understand. Please ask your brother to call me first thing tomorrow before he leaves, so we can clear things up."

"Yeah, sure.

"The more important matter is that we start searching for the painting. I'll ask security to review the footage outside your father's room during the last twenty-four hours."

"Thank you. I really appreciate that."

I got up, walked out of the office and headed down the corridor to the recreation room. Out of habit I checked the menu which was pinned up on the notice board. If he was not eating a croissant, today my father could have chosen a hot breakfast of scrambled eggs, sausages, fried tomato, sautéed spinach and rösti.

My phone rang. It was my brother. He told me he had just received a call from Robyn Sheargold. He was as shocked as I was. He told me he had visited our father the evening before and that the painting was still there, which meant there had been a fifteen to twenty hour window in which the theft had occurred. That was a lot of security footage to go through.

"I know we haven't always seen eye-to-eye but I do appreciate you looking into this," said my brother, "and I'm sorry that I won't be able to be much help while we're away. Just keep me posted. You can still reach me by email."

We hung up. It was good to know we were united about something, although I couldn't shake a weird feeling.

I circled the room, thinking that perhaps some of the residents might have witnessed the theft but realised it was kind of pointless because they would either have no recall or would have

112

confabulated a scenario to keep me talking in order to offset their loneliness.

But then I started thinking…Anne knew everything and everyone. Maybe she knew something about this too.

I found her taking the last bite of her scone and wiping some cream from her face. She saw my frantic look and waved me over. She didn't speak until she had swallowed the last mouthful.

"I've just heard, Celeste. I'll help where I can."

I paused for a few moments and then said, "Anne, I feel terrible asking this er…but when you were on shift last night did you see my brother?"

"Yes. He came over and had a chat. He's quite a charmer that one."

"And…and was he carrying anything?"

She shook her head. "No. He came in empty handed and left empty handed."

I felt a sense of relief. And guilt that I had suspected my brother. But I couldn't shake my paranoia.

"Anne," I hesitated, "Do you have any idea where the painting came from? I'm just thinking that maybe my dad pilfered it in the first place and the rightful owner is stealing it back?"

"That would have been very difficult..."

"Why?"

"Because its previous owner is dead."

"Oh. Who was it?"

"A retired nun called Margaret Mary. She had this gorgeous, silver, waist-long hair. She was in palliative care. Her convent closed and she needed medical support after her illness was diagnosed. The other sisters used to visit her until one day they just stopped coming."

"Why did they stop?"

"Well. There's two parts to the story…ordinarily you can take the nun out of the church but not the church out of the nun, if you know what I'm getting at."

I wrinkled my forehead, not grasping her meaning. She glanced at me slyly and then continued.

"Margaret Mary turned her room into a little chapel. She had rosary beads and pictures of her Lord and Saviour all over her bedside table, and crucifixes and religious paintings all over her walls. But then her illness took a strange voyage through her brain...even though she was married to Christ she must have gotten a divorce."

"What do you mean?"

"Well, when the painting went up her icons came down. She used to be dour at times but then she was suddenly...I think the old fashioned word to describe her would be...'merry' like one of those merry gentlemen in the Christmas carol or the merry men in Robin Hood. The other nuns didn't understand what was happening and stayed away. She also developed a strong attachment to your father."

"In what way?"

"Well, there was one incident, which I'm sure your brother has already shared with you..."

"Remind me."

Anne leaned in closer and lowered her tone. "I don't want to be disrespectful but we walked into Margaret Mary's room one day to catch her, as one would say, in flagrante delicto with your dad."

My mouth dropped open.

"Oh, she appeared surprised, "You really didn't know."

"Well, my brother didn't tell me."

I was furious and embarrassed and also mightily disturbed.

My father had always been a bit of a prude but his GP had warned us this could happen...sometimes people with this disease can lose their inhibitions and act impulsively.

"I can't begrudge Dad a little bit of happiness...God only knows I could do with some myself." I muttered. It had been a long time. The year I entered, then dropped out of university. I had no idea if my sexual body still worked or whether it had withered and died.

"So how does this relate to the painting?" I continued.

"The painting's been here for as long as I can remember. Margaret Mary owned it. I don't know its provenance before that. I think it came from another gentleman who bequeathed it to her but I can't really say."

"How did the painting make its way to my dad?"

"She willed it to him."

"What happened to her?"

"She went to Jesus. But I hesitate to say that maybe he didn't want her anymore."

"Why not?"

"She died naked in her bed with her sheets twisted like snakes around her thighs, a smile on her face and a look of ecstasy in her eyes. She was staring at that purple monster in the painting."

I was speechless. And puzzled.

"I don't want to be rude, but are you colour blind?

"No."

"Well the monster in Dad's painting is green..."

"Well, the one I saw in Margaret Mary's room was grey and purple. Come to think of it...and I might be going daft... but the creature on your father's painting looked somewhat the same but the sea looked more turbulent. The painting style was different...it looked like it belonged to another art period. More like a William Blake."

"Which leads me to believe there might be more than one painting," I said.

"You might be right," she answered.

When I left, I was completely confused.

My mind is a bit hazy and I'm still not quite sure what occurred and in precisely what order because everything happened so quickly. But I do know when I got to his place at Botany it was too late to save my brother.

Nobody else was home. His wife and two children had been sent to stay in a swish, five-star hotel near Circular Quay, prior to the family's departure the following day for a three-week cruise on a new liner—the *Starry Wisdom*—which was taking her maiden voyage to the South Pacific. Very convenient.

As I rounded the corner of his brick, heritage-listed, bungalow and into the backyard, I spotted his silhouette. He was standing with his back to me, dressed in a t-shirt and jeans, in front of a campfire stacked with burning logs and surrounded by a ring of rocks. It was typical of him...no council approval, no checking with the neighbour or complying with regulations. At least it was winter.

I saw him heave something into the heart of the fire, and then watched him place his hands with seeming self-satisfaction on his hips. Then I heard a crackle and a roar and was assaulted by a blast of heat. Being my father's daughter, I looked up.

The flames reared up from the pyre to about 300 feet. I didn't know of any domestic accelerant that could cause a fire to burn so hot or so high or so quick. It burned golden yellow in the centre. The outer edges were burnished orange as the flames reached up to the night sky. Its aura was the colour of copper.

And Mark was ablaze.

He was screaming.

It was not a deliberate act of self-immolation. It was as if the fire had been granted life and deliberately sought him out, enfolding around him like dragon's wings.

It was brutal.

I didn't run to him. The heat waved me back.

Instead, invisible fingers pried open my mind and unleashed a torrent of ugly memories that I had never acknowledged before... of every childhood and adult transgression, of every suspected lie and manipulative act my brother had ever perpetrated towards me that left me feeling confused and worthless.

And then I felt my usual warm heart, harden into cold, unyielding glass...

I. Knew. Why. He. Had. Lit. The. Fire.

And it was because of this reason I didn't grab the garden hose to douse the flames.

I ignored him as he lay charred and dying, smelling the revolting stench of his hair igniting and shrivelling into dust, and watching the skin on his front turning leathery white as the epidermis burned away, revealing the dermis underneath. All that remained of his clothes was a seared patchwork of cotton and denim, stuck to his torso and limbs. I witnessed the piteous plea for mercy in his grey eyes…my father's grey eyes.

All this happened within ten to fifteen seconds and then he was quiet…his pain had ended when his nerves had been destroyed. Sheer torment and then none. He was gone.

Instead, I only had eyes for the painting, my father's hideous painting, which was burning like a sacrificial object. Flames licking at the frame. Heating the oils. I knew what my brother had done, and I didn't hesitate to undo it. It was not too late.

I ran to the fire's edge and inserted my hands into the middle and seized the frame. I recoiled at the sheer heat and screamed. I felt my skin sizzle and sear but I grasped the frame anyway and tugged.

I screamed at the effort and the agony. Someone must have heard me because I saw lights suddenly switch on in the windows of the houses on either side of us. A looming 300-foot fiery beast of flame stood out, too.

Somehow, I managed to dislodge the painting from the kindling that was stacked up in a tepee like bones on a killing field.

Then I wrenched the thing out of the flames with such force, fuelled by adrenaline, that I stumbled and fell backwards onto the lawn beside my brother's charred body. The painting fell on top of me—its image pressing down on my chest. My hands did not uncurl from the frame but gripped it like a raptor's talons. The pain was inconceivable. I heard the whine of a siren in the distance and I saw airborne cinders dance around my head like black butterflies. And then I passed out.

I was told later that as the paramedic leaned over me, I whispered in a gravely croaky voice, "Please…please…return this painting to my father."

There wasn't much money left in the will. The only other beneficiary was dead, so when the police had finished questioning me at my hospital bed and were satisfied with my account from "bonfire night" as I came to call it—which is pretty sick, I know—and when probate came through, the entire estate passed to me.

The painting never made its way back to Gammell Gardens because it had been impounded as evidence at the crime scene…I had sacrificed my poor hands for nothing. My father passed away within seven days of its disappearance. Anne reported that he had deteriorated rapidly. Her words were kinder than mine but I read between the lines and extrapolated that he had turned into a gibbering mess, rapidly lost his ability to hold a spoon or fork or to write with a pen or grip the toilet paper. He lost control of his body functions and then somehow, despite all the security precautions, had slipped out to the beach on a nightmarish, rainy night. He was found washed up on the sand the next morning. The autopsy said he had died of organ failure rather than drowning but I couldn't dismiss the coincidence that both he and Margaret Mary, whom I found out later had been the other escapee, had been drawn to the Pacific and wanted to end their days close to the ocean.

I couldn't understand how he could have declined so quickly. In theory, this stage of the disease should have taken another two or so years but it claimed him directly after the painting's disappearance. My brother had set out to test my father's delusion in the hope he would hasten my father's death. He had succeeded.

I didn't have a chance to say goodbye, which just about killed me. Whatever the fire had done to my flesh, the anguish I felt was so much more palpable. My father's body had been found at the same time as I lay in the burns unit in hospital recovering with crepe bandages the size of boxing gloves on my hands.

Unlike Sister Margaret Mary, there was no smile on his face. Only a grimace, and spindly, twisted and contorted limbs like branches of a thorn bush. I didn't get to see his shrine at the front desk of Gammell Gardens.

On close examination of the bank statements I understood why my father's expense account had been depleted and why his residential fees hadn't been paid. It was because his bank account was empty.

I noted a cheque being written here and an internet transfer happening there, as well as a bank withdrawal popping up intermittently since the time my father had been interred into the nursing home. Some transactions were small—petrol or grocery money—and some were up to $20,000…the timing of each larger debit lined up with a family holiday or major renovations to the Botany bungalow my brother's family resided in. The house my father let them live in…for free while I paid exorbitant rent for my Darlinghurst studio.

My brother had been given power of attorney but somewhere along the line had obviously felt entitled to help himself to my father's retirement fund. Half a million dollars in five years! That's what it came down to.

I found out later he had been the one to extract the painting and smuggle it out in the bottom compartment of Heidi's coffee cart when she wasn't looking. Later that night he had liberated it when she'd parked it in the catering wing and when the staff were serving dinner.

I suppose I could have sold the Botany house out from under my sister-in-law and the kids but that wasn't my style. They were blameless—shocked, confused and in mourning at the circumstances—unaware that Mark had been unemployed for several years. They didn't know he would sit in Hyde Park all day in his business suit, reading newspapers and playing the stock market on his computer or that he was drawing his "salary" so to speak from my father's bank account. I decided to spare them the full story. His wife was in complete denial anyway.

Had Mark been patient, he would've inherited his place. As it turned out, the deed to bungalow, as well as our Taren Point family home, passed to me. I was the last one standing.

After the money was released, I paid for my father's cremation and scattered his ashes underneath the palm trees at Taren Point. The wind swept up the grey dust and swirled it into the river and out towards the ocean.

I asked the tenants to leave when their lease expired. The rent had paid for my father's stay at the nursing home but it was no longer needed. I vacated my studio apartment at Darlinghurst. I had lived a simple life. There wasn't much to pack and by the time I took care of all the family affairs and I moved in I was mentally, physically and emotionally exhausted.

I decided to go back to university as a mature-aged student and finish what I had started. Somebody had to keep the family legacy going. I wondered whether it was bad taste to spend some inheritance on myself and experienced heart palpitations every time I thought about it. I couldn't save my father but I didn't want to profit from his death.

I did buy something…

Bedsheets. A queen-size set of Egyptian cotton sheets with a 1000 thread count…the kind you find in a luxury hotel that I had never been able to afford in the past. And I felt good.

After the police investigation, the painting was returned to me. It lay on the kitchen table in a cardboard sleeve for a week until I felt ready to look at it again.

Venetia, the Italian homecare nurse who came by every day to change the dressings and bandages on my hands, volunteered to help.

"Oooo. A masterpiece." Her eyes widened. "Where do you want me to hang it?"

"Dare I say it…on the wall in the master bedroom."

She carried the package upstairs, placed it on my bed, then slit the sticky tape on the sides of the cardboard container with a pair of scissors from her medical kit while I watched. She slid the painting out, tenderly unwrapped the bubble wrap and popped some bubbles for good measure, which made me laugh. Then she unwrapped the multiple plastic and cardboard layers and removed the cardboard corners precisely, as if she was participating in a sacred ritual. As if the painting was an ancient artefact.

"Here?" she asked, pointing to a lone picture hook on the wall opposite my bed.

"Yes. Thank you."

She hung the painting and then stepped back to my side. She contemplated it for a few moments, tilting her head this way and then that way before being compelled to spit out her assessment for the scorched piece.

"Dio santo! It's ugly!" she said finally.

We laughed again.

"Well, don't blame me if it gives you nightmares."

"No," I answered. "It's going to the restorers soon."

I escorted Venetia to the front door and watched her walk away.

That night I put plastic bags over my bandages, had a shower, then clumsily poured myself a glass of white wine. I set it down precariously alongside the bottle on my bedside table. I jumped into my new sheets, naked. I lit some vanilla scented candles and then read for a bit then sipped the wine again until the first glass was empty and then the second glass too. In between I kept glancing at the painting, aware of its imposing presence.

The gold frame was singed badly. Parts of the painting were scorched outright…and in other parts the paint was bubbling, blistering and brittle. I kept thinking the painting should have been reduced to ash due to the ferocity of the fire, but in truth, the damage to it had been minimal…as if it had been protected in some way. My brother was dead but the painting endured. It was a mystery.

I blew out the candles, switched off my lamp and settled in, luxuriating in the soft sheets. I soon transitioned to that gone state but still feeling the lingering heat in my scarred, hooked hands.

I felt as though I was dreaming…a waking dream where my eyelids were at half-mast. In my dream, I felt something cool encircling my bandaged hands. I felt the bandages unravelling. Then I felt a faint yet sublime stroking and massaging of my palms and something ejaculating onto them that felt like a cool, soothing gel.

I moaned ever so slightly.

When that sensation stopped, I opened my eyes. I switched on the bedside lamp. The eco light-bulb took a moment to emit a glow. I looked down at my hands; now somehow sans bandages.

The puckered, stretched flesh had vanished. They were flushed a blush pink…virgin skin. I watched my destiny lines… love, fate, life lines, imprinting before my eyes.

I couldn't make sense of it.

Then I heard a scratching sound.

I looked up. As my hands peeled so did the painting. I became engrossed in it. Watching a fragment wrinkle up like a burnished autumn leaf and then just drop onto the floor where moments later it disintegrated into dust.

And then I felt the effects of the wine on my brain, which was misty but also SO VERY light and dewy if one could use that expression. As I lay on my bed, feeling the luxury sheets on my skin, the sea breeze wafted through the window and the sheer curtains fluttered.

Through the dim light I turned my attention to the relief pattern on the frame and silently absorbed the miracle of it all.

I saw the dark, florid shapes begin to wriggle…writhing under the gold overlay that covered them like a thin blanket. Gyrating languid designs and patterns generated into phalluses and mouths and phalluses in mouths and succulent openings and mounds in an orgiastic frenzy. And I felt my breath and heartbeat quicken as I watched this spectacular relentless showcase and I felt my body wet and alive.

I felt an energy probing and entering me. And I felt my body arch and release, buck and release.

And then I finally understood…

I knew now that Margaret Mary had lived out her hidden desires through the painting. And I knew now that my father innately comprehended the power that lay underneath the brush strokes had somehow halted the escalation of his condition. For I heard a faint chanting as I saw the paint flake off. The artwork was shedding its skin like a snake until it regenerated.

The same God-like creature still presiding over its angry ocean. But the depiction was different. This time he was naked, a marble Michelangelo sculpture with arms akimbo, gazing majestically down at its viewer. I felt the Great Old One's eyes boring into my core.

I sat back and saw lapping tongues and juices. Occasionally the minute figures would look toward me as if they were beckoning to me to partake. And I did not resist. I was now part of the frenzied beat and the rock and the thrust and my poor pink hands with my soft pink fingers moved downwards and started probing, overtaken with bliss and pleasure as the cacophony of chanting entered and swirled through my ears and into my mind and I finally understood that where I had previously been denied I had now been blessed. My sacrifice had been rewarded.

The rush. The sensual rush of it all. I knew I had succumbed. I knew I had been taken. I had been transformed and I didn't mind a bit. For the painting was part of me now and I would protect it at all costs and, because I had proved myself, I would reap all the rewards it chose to bestow on me.

THE KEY TO ETERNITY

STEVEN PAULSEN

The ganger climbed down to join me in the hold of the run-down collier. "You can piss off out of here, Ryan," he said with a jerk of his head.

The light was dim and the air was thick with coal dust so I couldn't make out his expression. "What's up?"

"You gotta go meet your mate, Sardine, at The Hero of Waterloo."

"Now?" I put down my shovel. I was lumping coal on the afternoon shift at the McIlwraith McEacharn wharf on Darling Harbour, and we were expected to finish the load by midnight. "But the shift's not over."

He tapped the side of his nose with his forefinger. "If the boss asks who's missin', I'll tell him Burke and Wills."

I frowned. "Reckon that'll fly?"

The ganger hawked and spat. "He won't know, he's a drongo. Now get out of here."

I laughed, grabbed my coat, and took off.

My light-heartedness quickly faded, overtaken by curiosity. It was the cold autumn of 1925 and the air had a chill to it, so I shoved my hands into my coat pockets as I walked and thought about it. Why would Sardine bribe the ganger to let me off? And why would he want me to meet him at the Waterloo? I never drank there. He knew my locals were the Lord Nelson and the Dumbarton, near my tenement on Kent Street.

When I entered the old sandstone hotel ten minutes later, it smelled of stale beer, tobacco smoke, and a mellow coal fire. I looked around but couldn't see Sardine. It was the quiet time of the afternoon, just before the rush for the six o'clock swill. There were a dozen or so blokes knocking back schooners of Resch's and yabbering at the bar. A smaller group of men in faded bib-and-brace overalls and peaked caps stood around the glowing fireplace haggling with the SP bookie.

The barmaid caught my eye and waved me over. She looked me up and down, noting my dirty wharfie clobber. "You Bull Ryan?" she asked.

I nodded, noticing for the first time a bloke standing alone at the end of the bar. Unlike the other drinkers, who were mostly waterside workers, he was dressed in a charcoal-grey flannel suit and waistcoat, white shirt and navy-blue tie, and a black fedora hat. He had copper written all over him.

The barmaid pulled a beer and pushed it across the bar to me. "Your mate's waiting for you downstairs."

Making my way across the old wooden floorboards to the cellar stairs, I could feel the copper's gaze on me. It made the hairs stand up on the back of my neck.

I found Sardine in one of the sandstone-block cellars, sitting at a rickety table with another man. The stranger had grey hair—prematurely so for a bloke I reckoned was in his late thirties—and a short, pointed blond beard. He was dressed in a grubby, white polo neck skivvy and a navy-blue pea coat. His eyes were haunted, sunken in his pallid face.

"What are you doing down here?" I asked Sardine. "What's with all the cloak-and-dagger?"

"This is Gustaf Johansen," he replied, inclining his head at the other man. "He's in hiding here because he's in trouble. He came to me for help because he's from the same village as me in Østlandet."

"Another sardine," I said. Neither man even smiled at my little joke. "You know…Norwegians: Sardines!" Nothing.

Johansen flinched when I dragged out the spare chair to sit down, his gaze darting nervously around the cellar.

I put my beer on the table, rolled a fag, and lit it.

Sardine pointed at Johansen. "He's the bloke who was towed into port the other day by that Morrison Company freighter."

I raised my eyebrows. The story was all over the waterfront. "You were aboard that disabled island trader?" I asked him. "The one that was shot to pieces?"

"The *Alert*," Johansen agreed. "Out of Dunedin."

"The only survivor," Sardine said. "He needs to get back to New Zealand on the quiet. I came to you because I figured you could use your connections with the Waterside Worker's Federation to help him. And, as an educated bloke, there's half a chance you might believe his story and get to the bottom of this."

Johansen scrutinised me. "Why are you lumping coal if you're an educated man?"

"A few reasons," I said with a shrug. "Well, maybe they're all one and the same. I used to be an accounts clerk in a large firm, but it was a stilted, artificial environment and I was bored to death. Down here on the docks, the work is physical and the people are real. I intend to travel, but before that I want to help the waterside workers fight for their rights. These poor bastards are exploited to the point of poverty."

"That's very noble of you," Johansen said, a note of sarcasm in his tone.

I thumped my fist on the table. "The people here in Millers Point do it tough, mate. I know, I grew up down the road. My old man slaved his guts out on these docks. He was killed in an accident when I was a kid and we were left without a brass razoo. I put myself through school, selling papers, working as a cocky for an SP Bookie, night shift here on the docks."

Johansen pursed his lips, somewhat chastened.

I took deep breath and a swig of my beer. "So, why the secrecy? Why are you in hiding? And why do you want to get back to New Zealand on the quiet?"

"I am being pursued by a fanatical cult," he said. "They're trying to kill me."

"That plain-clothes copper up in the bar anything to do with this?" I asked.

Johansen nodded. "A sergeant from the Detective Branch. Perkins. He's keeping an eye out for me."

"I wouldn't trust the bloody coppers," I said, shaking my

head. "They're anybody's for a quid."

Johansen half smiled. "I went to the police out of desperation. They weren't interested. Perkins was the only one who believed me. He followed me out of the police station and said he couldn't do anything officially but would help me in his spare time."

I shrugged. "Why is this cult after you?"

He lit a cigarette and the match flame wavered in his trembling fingers. "I was second mate on a two-masted schooner called the *Emma*. We sailed out of Auckland bound for Peru but were thrown off course mid-Pacific by an unexpected storm. We chanced upon the *Alert*, only to have the crew fire upon us with a battery of brass cannon when we hailed her."

Johansen paused and cocked his head to listen, his eyes once again darting around the cellar. He took a gulp of beer and went on. "When we began to take on water and sink, the *Alert* pulled alongside and the crew boarded us. They were crazed cut-throats—mostly Kanakas—who fought to the death like berserkers. It was a bloodbath. In the end we prevailed, but only eight of us from the *Emma* survived."

I rubbed my chin and frowned. "How come you're the only one who made it here to Sydney Cove? What happened?"

Johansen shook his head, wiped a tear from his eye, and looked away. "I don't want to speak of it. You wouldn't believe me if I did."

"I might," I said. "There are more things in heaven and earth, as the saying goes. If you want my help you're going to have to spit it out, tell me what's going on."

He bit his lip and lowered his gaze. "I took something from that dreaded ship."

I nodded. "Word on the docks is that you brought back a rare stone idol. I thought the eggheads at the Museum were examining it."

"They are. However, I took something else from the *Alert* too. And even though I haven't told anyone about it, the cult somehow knows I have it."

I narrowed my eyes. "What is it? Is it valuable?"

"It's extremely valuable to them. It's a key. But not an ordinary key. It's a key from another realm, brought here to open the way into our world."

"Another realm?" I stared at him with a tight smile. "That's a bloody esoteric concept. What the hell does that even mean?"

Johansen shifted in his seat. "It's from a place they call R'lyeh. And hell on earth it might well be if the key is used. I believe it opens a doorway to R'lyeh in another time and place; a portal that will let their monstrous deity into our world to wreak havoc."

I let out a long, slow whistle. What had Sardine gotten me into? "Do you believe all this?" I asked him. "Are you two pulling my leg?"

Sardine reached out and laid his hand on my arm. "Johansen believes it. The copper upstairs believes it. Let him tell his story before you dismiss it."

I smiled. "It sounds like bulldust to me."

"It's *true*," Johansen said, his Adam's apple bobbing. A sheen of sweat broke out on his cheeks and forehead. "I took the key from the skipper of the *Alert* as he lay dying. He told me in broken English what it was. He cursed me and said his people would track me down to recover it and kill me for what I have learned. My only hope now is to return to Dunedin, collect my wife, and head back home to Norway. Perhaps there I'll be far enough away from the cult to be safe."

I chuckled. "We're in Millers Point, mate. Not on some primitive Pacific island."

Johansen looked at me with contempt. "This is not some cargo cult or aboriginal myth. These people are organised and implacable. I have seen the blasphemous deity they worship, felt its fetid breath on my face." He shivered. "They call it *Cthulhu*."

This time I laughed. "Cthulhu is myth. I've heard the stories. You're not the first sailor to spin this piece of cock and bull. Either you're having me on or you're crazy."

He lurched to his feet, tipping his chair over backwards. "This is true!" he yelled, his eyes wild. "Cult members ransacked the rooming house where I was staying and they have attacked me on the street twice here in Sydney already. I barely escaped both times."

"Calm down," said Sardine. "Tell him what happened on the island." He turned to me. "Listen to him with an open mind, Bull."

Johansen picked up his chair, sat down and took a deep breath. "After the melee at sea, we came upon an uncharted island. It was mud-covered and wet, steaming under the Pacific sun as though it had just risen from the ocean depths."

I raised my eyebrows in a theatrical gesture. "Really?"

Sardine shook his head at me, his expression pinched.

"What's more," Johansen continued, "it was built up with a Cyclopean city of spires and monoliths and confused geometry that seemed to stretch forever before us."

"'Cyclopean city'?" I said. "What's that mean?"

"It was bigger than Sydney, bigger than New York, but it appeared abandoned and empty. Water poured from its black ramparts and queerly angled towers, green slime oozed thickly down its buildings and walls."

I guffawed. "Pull the other one, it plays 'Jingle Bells'."

"Let him continue," Sardine said, annoyed.

Johansen ignored my jibe and went on. "We made landfall and climbed to the island's peak where we discovered a giant citadel with an immense, carven stone door. Our mistake was to open it, for within its black interior it housed a hideous monster."

"You should write tall stories for the pulp magazines," I said. But I shivered because he was deadly serious and I was starting to feel uneasy. Living and working on the docks I had heard all sorts of stories from sailors, and, as they say, where there's smoke there's often fire. Despite the weirdness of Johansen's tale, I was beginning to believe him.

"You can joke," he said in a low voice, standing up to lean over me. "But only myself and one other crewman survived the encounter. It drove him insane and he died."

I pulled at my collar, my imagination racing. "What sort of monster?"

"I told you," he said, his voice trembling. "Cthulhu. A bloated and lumbering green thing, sticky with ooze and slime. It squeezed its rubbery mass through the enormous opening and slopped into the sunlight. At full height it was as tall as the Empire State Building. It had membranous wings on its back, and tentacles around its kraken-like face that writhed and whipped when it spied us."

I glanced at Sardine and swallowed. He shifted in his chair and licked his lips.

"What was that noise?" Johansen exclaimed, his eyes wide. He ran to the stairs and peered up them. Then he came back to us at the table. "Did you hear that? I heard a noise."

Sardine screwed up his nose. "What's that rotten fish stink?"

A rank odour suddenly filled the room and I almost gagged.

Four huge creatures, croaking and baying, burst into the cellar from a rear passage. Three walked on two legs like men, the other on four like a wild animal. Behind them came a couple of long-haired Kanakas wearing loose sail-cloth shirts and pants, armed with hook-bladed cane knives.

"*Herregud!*" Sardine shrieked.

I jumped to my feet, my heart racing. What manner of beast were these things? They were as big as mountain gorillas, except instead of fur they had wet-looking, greyish-green skin, faces like frogs or fish with bulging eyes, and large, webbed, clawed hands and feet.

My mind reeled. I'd had a difficult enough time coming to terms with Johansen's story, and now I was facing these impossibly bizarre creatures. If he had told me about them I would have laughed, but I wasn't laughing now because these things looked like they meant business.

Sardine seized his chair and held it in front of him in the manner of a lion tamer.

To my surprise, Johansen grabbed hold of me in a bear hug. What the hell was he doing? I had to defend myself against these monsters. I'm a big bruiser, but it took all my strength to wrench myself loose. I turned to face the ungodly intruders.

Johansen leaped for the stairs, but the creatures were upon him before he reached them. Sardine smashed the chair into matchwood over the back of one of the freakish things.

The creature turned and swatted him aside.

I dived into the fracas, raining punches to little effect. One of the beasts clouted me on the back of the head. It felt like the time I was floored by a three-bushel bag of wheat. I fell to my knees. Everything went black, and I saw stars.

I heard my name being called and clambered groggily to my feet. Only seconds must have passed, but I was alone in the cellar.

"Bull!" Sardine yelled from one of the back rooms. "They've taken Johansen down here."

I found him disappearing through a trapdoor in the rear cellar.

I followed him down the rusted, iron ladder and emerged in a damp, lightless tunnel. In the enclosed space the rank, fishy stench was overpowering. I could hear Sardine and the others ahead of me in the dark. I stumbled after them, feeling my way along the rough-hewn masonry walls. There were stories that a secret tunnel ran from the hotel cellar to the harbour, supposedly used in Colonial days for smuggling, or to shanghai drunken sailors. I always assumed they were fanciful tales. But when I came forth into daylight and found myself in a disused part of the Walsh Bay wharves, I knew the stories to be true.

I looked around. The Kanakas had made off along the quay, dragging the unconscious Johansen between them. Sardine was standing half-crouched on the dock, facing the four croaking monstrosities. He lashed out, throwing a punch at one and a kick at another.

I rushed to his aid. But before I could reach him one of the creatures raked its claws across his throat and ripped out his gullet. Sardine's eyes went wide. Blood spurted in a ruby-red arc and splashed across my face and chest. I tasted metal. Sardine made a gurgling sound and crumpled to the weathered timber wharf.

"No!" I cried, my vision blurring as tears welled.

I had no time to mourn my friend. The beasts turned to confront me. It was futile, I knew. I was surely facing the same fate as Sardine. But I wasn't going to go down without a fight.

Everything seemed to slow down. I wiped my eyes with the back of my hand, braced myself and took up a defensive stance, fists clenched.

They circled deliberately around me, croaking in harsh, guttural voices.

My breath came hard and fast, my neck and shoulders tense. I squinted at one of them and lunged in fury. I hit it square in its fish-eyed face. The blow made a sickening, squelching *thud* and it felt like I had punched a side of freshly butchered mutton.

The creature barked and shook its head. Sensing movement out of the corner of my eye, I ducked instinctively and felt what probably would have been a killing blow swish through my hair.

I dived to the wharf and rolled aside.

Suddenly there came the sound of a whistle and shouts close by.

One of the creatures gave a short, sharp bark. As one, like a school of mullet, they turned away and slipped off the edge of the wharf into the harbour.

I jumped to my feet and peered into the scummy water. Except for some ripples and a faint, fishy odour, there was no sign they had ever been here. The docks were momentarily quiet, save for the sound of ships bumping against a far wharf in the gentle swell. I stood there dazed. The Norwegian named Johansen had been spirited away. My friend was dead. And I had barely escaped the same fate at the hands of those ungodly monsters.

The whistle started sounding again as three uniformed police officers burst onto the dock and ran towards me. One of them fumbled for his service pistol. "Hands in the air," he yelled.

Two of the coppers grabbed me, pulled my arms back and cuffed me. One of them delivered a gut-punch and I doubled over, struggling for air.

The third copper with the gun briefly examined Sardine's body and turned to me. "You wharf scum," he snarled. "You've killed him. It'll be the noose for you."

I shook my head, still finding it difficult to breathe. "He was my friend," I said, gasping.

"Well who did this?" asked one of the coppers holding me.

"Fish-eyed monsters," I said numbly, realising how ridiculous, how crazy it sounded even as I spoke the words.

Another man came running. I recognised him as the detective from the pub. He flashed his warrant card. "I'll take over from here, constables," he said. "Take the body to the morgue and leave this man to me." He took hold of my arm and said, "I'm Detective Sergeant Perkins. You're in a spot of bother, Ryan."

"You know me?" I asked in surprise.

"Only by reputation. You're one of those union rabble-rousers. Johansen and your dead mate told me you were coming to meet them. What happened here?"

I explained everything to him. His steely expression didn't change once. Not even when I told him the part about the creatures that attacked us.

"Weirdly enough, I believe you," Perkins said. "Your story might sound fantastic, and the circumstantial evidence points to you as the killer, but I've seen things you wouldn't believe." He turned me around and unlocked the handcuffs. "The people who took Johansen belong to a group called the Cult of Cthulhu. And those creatures you described are called Deep Ones. They usually live at the bottom of the oceans, although they come to shore when they want, or when commanded by one of their deities."

I swallowed hard. "I didn't believe him at first. I thought Johansen was a lunatic."

"I don't blame you," he said. "My superiors think it's all rubbish. Who would believe it if they hadn't seen it with their own eyes?"

I rubbed my wrists to get the circulation moving.

"What did Johansen want from you?" Perkins asked.

"To use my union contacts to sneak him back to New Zealand."

The detective looked at me quizzically. "He didn't give you anything?"

I shook my head. "Nothing. Not even a smoke."

"Tell you anything that might help me?"

"I don't know what else I can say, except that the key he mentioned is supposed to be important. That's what the cult were after."

"He had it on him?" he asked, his eyes sparkling.

"I think so." I choked back a sob. "My god, I can't believe Sardine's dead."

"There's naught I can do to bring your friend back," Perkins said. "I'll try to find his murderers and Johansen, but you mustn't tell anyone what happened here. Aside from people thinking you're crazy, I don't want word of this to reach the wrong ears and jeopardise my chances. And don't leave town because I might need your help. Got it?"

I nodded solemnly. "Yes, I understand."

Perkins took hold of my shoulder and gave it a gentle squeeze. "Good man." He produced a white handkerchief and handed it to me. "Here, clean yourself up. I'll be seeing you."

I found myself standing alone on the dock. A ship's horn sounded nearby. Seagulls squawked overhead. I walked to the wharf's edge, knelt down and wet the handkerchief. Oil and scum bubbles pock-marked the surface of the water. I washed my face. When I was done, I stared at the hanky stained with Sardine's blood for a moment before I tossed it over the side. In the distance came the thump of a coal lumper loading fuel aboard a ship. A cold breeze sprang up. I stood and shoved my hands into my coat pockets. And froze.

There was an object in my pocket. I pulled it out. It was an oily, grey-green stone figurine about three inches tall. A carving of a grotesque, anthropoid creature, in that it had arms and legs, however that was where any resemblance to a human ended. It had an octopus-like head, with evil eyes set deep in a face wreathed in tentacles. Instead of hands and feet it had claws, and it had large bat-like wings protruding from the back of its scaly body. It looked like the monstrous creature called Cthulhu that Johansen had described.

Everything around me suddenly seemed to spin. I retched into the water and thought I was going to pass out. It was only when I shoved the figurine back into my coat pocket that the feeling slowly passed. What in God's name was it? How did it get into my pocket? The only thing I could think was that Johansen had slipped it there when he grabbed me in the cellar of The Hero of Waterloo.

walked up Kent Street towards Chinatown. It was well after 6:00pm so the pubs were shut, but I needed a drink. There was a café there I knew, a sly grog shop that served dark rum in a porcelain teapot with a teacup. It was somewhere I could sit and think, away from the hubbub of the wharves.

The sun had set and it was starting to get dark. The breeze coming off the docks carried the familiar odours of diesel oil and lanolin. I buttoned my coat and felt the weird figurine against my hip. Was this piece of carved stone the key that Johansen had mentioned? It looked nothing like a key. How could it unlock a doorway?

I heard a noise behind me. Someone shouted, followed by the sound of running feet. I turned. The two long-haired Kanakas who had dragged Johansen away on the Walsh Bay wharf were coming up fast behind me.

There were only a few people on the street and not a copper in sight.

I took off at a run, my chest pounding. I clattered across the tarred-woodblock surface of Kent Street, and ducked down Gas Lane. Too late, I realised my mistake. The lane led to Jenkins Street where one end was dead and the other terminated at the gas works demolition site. The rat-proof fence blocked my way across.

Breathing hard, I yelled out for help. A dog barked, but no one replied.

I faced my pursuers. Both sides of the lane were lined with weatherboard houses and rusted corrugated-iron fences, sandwiched between a couple of commercial sandstone buildings. None showed any lights or signs of life. I thought about banging on doors, but the Kanakas were only yards away. Two against one. They were big, but so was I, and by the looks of them they tended more towards fat than muscle.

They charged at me like bulls. I sidestepped the first one who barrelled past me, unable to break his stride. I brought up my elbow and hit the other in the throat. He gagged and fell back, choking.

The first one circled me cautiously, a knife now glinting in his hand in the pale moonlight. I glanced about for something to use as a weapon and ripped a paling off a ramshackle gate. The timber was brittle and half rotten, but it was better than nothing.

He swiped the knife at my face. I parried and whacked him across the arm with the paling. The wood cracked loudly, splintered and broke, leaving me holding a short stake. He lunged. The steel of his knife bit into my left shoulder. I grunted in pain and drove the paling stake into his eye. He screamed and clutched at his face.

I dropped the stake and dashed full pelt back the way I had come, turning along Kent Street towards Millers Point. I glanced behind. The two Kanakas emerged from the lane at a run. I ducked down High Street—away from the Agar Steps and Observatory Hill where I'd be a sitting duck—and let myself into an unassuming house I frequented regularly. From the outside it was unlit and quiet. Inside, Mrs Kennedy sat in her floral wallpapered front parlour and sold take-away bottles of beer on the sly.

"Hello, Bull," she said.

I shushed her and peered out through a gap in the heavy drapes. My attackers ran past, turning their heads from side to side, one of them holding a hand to his gory face.

"What's up, love?" Mrs Kennedy asked. "Larrikins after you?"

"Something like that." I touched my shoulder and winced. My fingers came away sticky with blood.

"Have you been stabbed?" she asked in alarm. "Here, let me help you."

"No, I haven't got time." I forced a smile. "It's not too bad."

"Be careful," she said. "I don't want to lose a good customer."

I peered cautiously out the door. The lane was empty. I thanked Mrs Kennedy and ventured out. Instead of heading for home I went after the Kanakas. If I could follow them they might lead me to Johansen and to Sardine's killers.

I found them in High Lane, searching yards and porches house-to-house. From there they went back to High Street, before giving up and heading north along Hickson Road. I stayed well back, keeping to the shadows, and followed them until they reached Duke's Wharf on the Millers Point headland. There they let themselves into a small, isolated warehouse built on pylons over the water, abandoned by the Goodman Company some years ago.

When they'd gone inside, I crept along the wharf to the warehouse entrance. The worn and weathered sliding doors were slightly skew-whiff, hanging crooked on their rusted cast-iron rollers, and I peered through the gap. The interior was lit by burning candles. In their flickering light, thirty or more people were milling about. A few broken tea chests lay scattered in one corner. Heavy timber beams criss-crossed the roof and supported the walls. In the middle of the mob, Johansen was tied—naked, bruised and bloody—to a wooden frame.

Out of the night, someone loomed up soundlessly beside me. I gasped, my heart racing, but relaxed when I recognised Detective Sergeant Perkins.

"Thank God you're here," I whispered. "The cultists have Johansen prisoner in there."

Perkins smiled. It was an ugly, brutal smile. He thrust the muzzle of his pistol hard under my jaw. "It's good of you to join us tonight, Bull," he said. "It turns out that Johansen didn't have the key, but with a bit of persuasion he told us who did."

My nostrils flared and I bared my teeth. "You bastard! You've been in league with them all along."

He patted me down and dug his hand into my coat pocket, grinning with satisfaction when he pulled out the stone figurine. Then he spoke a string of sounds that I should not have been able to understand nor easily recall but those syllables etched themselves completely into my mind—as if they were words I'd always known and could never forget. "*Ph'nglui mglw'nafh Cthulhu R'lyeh wgah'nagl fhtagn*," he said. The figurine responded to these utterances by glowing with a sickly green light.

He pushed the barrel of his gun harder into my neck and hailed the people inside.

Glancing up at the sky, he said, "You brought us the key just in the nick of time, Bull. The stars are right tonight. And now that you're here we've got two sacrifices for great Cthulhu."

The weathered sliding doors of the warehouse screeched as they were dragged open. Perkins twisted my arm behind my back, sending a sharp pain through my shoulder where I had been stabbed, and marched me inside.

The two Kanakas I had followed here rushed forward and grabbed me either side by my arms. One of them sneered at me, his injured eye weeping blood and mucus. I struggled to break free, but he produced a knife and held it to my throat.

Perkins raised the grotesque figurine—the so-called key—above his head, its eerie, inner green glow visible to all. The people began to dance and cavort around us. The Kanakas shoved me over to where Johansen was being held and tossed me to the floor beside him.

The detective began to chant in a loud clear voice, the same words he spoke when he pulled the key from my pocket, and the cultists joined in. It was again a toneless and sinister incantation that should not have made sense to me, but somehow, impossibly, it did.... I stared at them in terrified horror as they pranced around us; blacks, whites, Chinese and Islanders of all ages and all walks of life. Some wore suits, others rags, but all were caught up in their zeal.

A trapdoor in the floor of the warehouse near where I was crouching burst open with a loud *thud*. Half a dozen fish-eyed Deep Ones clambered in, dripping wet from the harbour water below. Their rank smell was nauseating, but nobody seemed to care. The creatures joined in with the throng, swaying, croaking and grunting in time with the chanting cultists.

Their voices got louder as they whipped themselves into a fervour. The figurine in Perkins' hand glowed brighter and brighter, until it illuminated the room with its bilious, green light. Above us a mist began to form, filling the ceiling space of the warehouse, rolling and billowing in great foggy clouds, cloaking something dark and shadowy beyond it.

I went rigid and began to tremble. It was like a surreal nightmare and I struggled to comprehend what was happening.

I sensed movement close by and twisted around. Another two Kanakas wielding long, hook-bladed, cane knives stepped around the trapdoor opening towards us. They cut Johansen's bindings. The Norwegian fell to his knees and looked up, seeing me for the first time. He began to weep. They dragged us both to our feet, thrust us together and held the cane knives to our throats. I shuddered, knowing this was the end. Whatever these people were up to, we would never see the sunrise.

A howling wind smelling of rot and decay swept into the warehouse in a great gust. It parted and disbursed the swirling fog to reveal an immense Stygian vista in the air above and around us. The walls and roof of the warehouse were disappearing, replaced by an enormous city of black stone. It appeared to stretch interminably in a jumble of towers, bastions, queerly angled ramparts and structures.

I stared at it in wide-eyed awe. Surely it was a hallucination because it was impossible. The warehouse couldn't have just vanished. A city this size couldn't just materialize out of thin air. And yet, there it was, steaming, mud covered and wet, exactly like Johansen had described. The place he called R'lyeh.

Perkins seemed crazed, his eyes ablaze with rapture. His body shaking. The light from the figurine he still held aloft was now so bright it forced me to avert my eyes. The cultists and Deep Ones bobbed up and down as if in a trance, still chanting ecstatically.

The vista that had materialised out of the air continued to grow and envelop us. Soon the entire warehouse had disappeared, except for the warped and cracked floorboards where we stood. Before us stretched a wide path, paved with dark masonry, winding up between colossal stones and gigantic buildings all carved with weird runes and depictions of monstrous creatures.

I found some spittle in my mouth and swallowed.

The sour, poisonous-smelling wind that blew out from the vista into what remained of the warehouse grew in intensity until its wailing and shrieking drowned out the cultists' chanting. Above it all came the rumble of mighty stones grinding as the gate of the massive black citadel that crowned the city slid open to reveal an orifice blacker than coal tar. An ear-splitting guttural roar issued from within the darkness, and a hideous monstrosity lurched into the sunlight.

I went rigid, unable to move, every sense screaming. It was the creature that Johansen had told me about, the model for the stone key. The thing they called Cthulhu. But neither Johansen's words nor the carved figure had captured its corrupt essence. When it looked down on us, the tentacles around its face thrashing, a wave of malignant arrogance swept over me. It radiated tremendous power and hunger.

I smelled urine. I had pissed myself.

In their euphoria, the Kanakas had lowered their cane knives and relaxed their grip on me. The other pair had released Johansen and were writhing in ecstasy. Perkins was now holding the key straight out in front of him, pointing it towards the monstrosity lumbering out of the impossible landscape towards us.

I took a deep breath, the poisonous air burning my throat and lungs, and shook the fog from my brain. Whatever was happening—impossible as it seemed—was real and I had to stop it.

Wrenching free of my captors, I launched myself at Perkins. I caught him unawares and snatched the key from his grasp. It burned in my hand like a lump of red-hot coal. The skin on my palm and fingers blistered and peeled away with a whiff of charred meat. Perkins looked stunned. The cultists stopped dancing and stood blinking, confused. Someone whimpered. There was an angry cry. But most stood frozen in shock and disbelief. The monstrosity lumbering towards us *roared* in rage—a terrible and deafening sound.

What was I going to do with the key? There was nowhere to run. Should I drop it through the trapdoor into the sea? Try to break it, smash it?

My hand burned in unbearable agony.

"Throw it into the portal!" Johansen screamed, suddenly coming to his senses. "It will close the doorway."

I gritted my teeth and flung the key through the portal. Out of our earthly realm into the mind-bending vista that stretched before us.

The portal shimmered and time seemed to stop. The rank wind ceased blowing. For a split second everything was still and silent. I seized the opportunity and shoved Johansen into the open trapdoor, hoping he wasn't too badly hurt and wouldn't drown. He dropped into the harbour below and I dived through after him.

There was a mighty *whoosh* behind us.

Cold water closed in over me, soothing my burning hand, muting the terrible discordant sounds above. I felt disconnected from the tumult, free of the miasma that had held us in thrall. I surfaced and looked up.

The floorboards of the warehouse were tearing up one by one, flying into the air. The vista overhead was shrinking, closing. The tremendous wind howled and shrieked once more, except this time it blew back into the vista instead of out, sucking everything before it into its gaping maw. The cultists and the Deep Ones flew through the air like leaves in a cyclone, turning and somersaulting, arms and legs flapping. Their screams added to the deafening bedlam of the wind and Cthulhu's furious roars.

Johansen surfaced beside me, coughing and spluttering.

With a final mighty *boom* the portal disappeared.

Everyone and everything in the warehouse, including the building itself, was gone. Johansen and I were alone, bobbing in the dark water among the jagged ends of the wooden pylons. Silence descended, or so it seemed. After a while, when our ears began to recover from the assault, the familiar sounds of the harbour returned. Water lapped against the decapitated pylons. In the distance the blast of a horn signalled midnight, the finish of the coal lumper's shift.

In the cold light of dawn two days later, Johansen and I stood on the dock, smoking. Just a nondescript sailor in a knitted cap, and an unremarkable waterside worker. No one gave us a second glance, let alone noticed my bandaged hand. Sail cloth flapped and snapped in the cold wind. Johansen gave me a curt nod of thanks and held out his hand.

I shook it with my left hand, rather than my injured right one. "Good luck," I said.

"What will you do?" he asked. "*They* will be after you too now."

I gave him a grim smile of resignation. "There's talk they're going to build a railway from Oodnadatta to Alice Springs in Central Australia. I reckon I'll head up there. That's about as far away from the sea as I can get. I'll change my name, pick up some labouring work when my burns have healed."

He hoisted a duffel bag onto his shoulder, turned and strode up the gangplank of the *James Craig*, a tired, old, three-masted barque bound for Dunedin on New Zealand's South Island.

That was the last I ever heard of him.

As for me, I'm living in railway work camps most of the time. It's all good, except I don't sleep very well. I'm haunted by dreams and nightmares of R'lyeh and Cthulhu. It sounds crazy, but *he* calls to me in my sleep.

I go into Oodnadatta with the work crew and hit the pub sometimes, and I've never had any reason for concern. Although last time we were there, there was an odd looking fellow drinking alone at the bar. An American from a place called Innsmouth, by all accounts. I couldn't help thinking he looked vaguely fishy, especially around the eyes. But it was probably my imagination, a by-product of my weird dreams.

THEY ARE IMPATIENT

MAURICE XANTHOS

GREECE, JULY 1976

After midnight, at some ridiculous hour between then and two in the morning, the old bus juddered to a stop and its driver switched on the interior lights.

There was groaning from the passengers; curses splashed the air in French, Greek, German and assorted dialects of English. The lights flickered on, then dimmed; the gloomy interior was sliced by a glowing flashlight beam. A squat, moustachioed man in a grey uniform entered the bus and stood beside the driver.

"Border," he said in a thick accent. "Pass-e-ports please."

The driver spoke something in Greek; the word 'passport' was repeated several times.

"What he is telling us," explained Vangellis, who sat across from me, "is that we must hand over our passports to the border official for processing. This should take fifteen to twenty minutes."

Vangellis took Bryce and me on as travelling companions for our journey from Athens to Paris. He especially took a liking to me after I had mentioned that I had Greek blood on my mother's side. He said that he came from the same village as she did, and that he remembered her family well, but I suspected otherwise.

While the border official spoke to the bus driver, Vangellis leaned across and handed me an envelope.

"Take this," he whispered. "Until we pass the border, okay?"

Bryce nudged me. "Nice going, *Philo*," he said not too quietly. "You're going to be sprung for narcotics smuggling."

My hand held the envelope in full view of the guard, and Vangellis pushed it toward me, into the shadows.

"It is five hundred dollars in *drachmae*," he said hurriedly. "Please hold it for me. We are not allowed to take so much money out of the country. They will not search you because you're not a national."

I thought about it for a moment, then I pocketed it and nodded an assurance to Vangellis. He smiled, and fell back into his seat.

The border official, an unlit cigarette dangling from his lower lip, commenced collecting the passports, grunting and mumbling a cursory *"thenk-you"* as he went along. After he stepped out of the bus, the passengers heaved a collective sigh and filled in the time with lighting cigarettes, napping or making small talk.

"Thank you for helping me," said Vangellis. "It is hard to have a holiday abroad when you're not allowed to take any money with you."

"Think nothing of it," I said, again suspecting other exotic motives. "After all, we're nearly related."

"Yes," he said, laughing, slapping my shoulder. *"Philo."*

"Koumparo," Bryce said, somewhat facetiously.

Vangellis laughed harder, probably at Bryce's weak attempt at the Greek pronunciation. Soon, the border official returned and read out several Greek names. Vangellis' was included in the list.

"It's all right," he assured us. "They will ask me a few questions; how much money I am taking out; how long I will be away. Nothing to worry about."

The border official then called out my name, then Bryce's. Vangellis' smile caved in and his eyes bulged in confusion. I looked at Bryce, who shrugged his surprise.

I stood by my seat, and the official ambled down. All faces turned to stare.

He started speaking to me, but despite my Greek background I couldn't understand anything he said. I shrugged an apology.

"It's all right," said Vangellis, "I'll help you."

He spoke to the official, who kept pointing to Bryce and me. They seemed to be arguing, but Greeks always seem to be arguing.

Finally, Vangellis turned to me.

"They want you to renew your visa," he said. "You have exceeded your stay in Greece."

I smiled, relieved. Bryce said, "I thought you were sprung."

"Shut up," I mumbled. We were ushered off the bus and walked toward the border office. Vangellis followed us. I suppose he had an interest that we returned unscathed; more likely that we returned with his kitty.

In the office, a large man in an oversized, unpressed suit greeted us.

"*Kyrio* Stefanos Johnson?" he asked.

"Steve," I said, and nodded.

"And Mr *Proyce* Williams?" Bryce nodded.

He adjusted his tie, and looked down at our passports.

"You cannot continue your trip through Yugoslavia."

"What?" I said. "What did you say?"

"Yes," interrupted Vangellis, "what is the matter?" He broke into a babbling Greek, his voice growing louder.

"*Skasse, vre,*" answered the big man. He turned to us. "I am speaking to Mr Williams."

"What's the problem?" I asked, trying to gain some composure. Bryce stood silently, but I could see that he was waiting to hear an explanation before he had something to say, civilised or otherwise.

"Your passport," said the man to Bryce, "says that you are from New Zealand."

"Yes, that's right," Bryce answered, confused. "I'm originally from New Zealand, but I live in Australia. What's that mean?"

The man looked apologetic, waving our passports. "You will return to Athens—er, should you pay your visa dues—or wherever you wish to go on the next available bus. But you cannot go into Yugoslavia. Australia is okay. Mr. Johnson is free to continue."

"But our bags…I mean," I started, confused. "I can't go on to Paris if Bryce can't continue."

"We're not even stopping in the bloody country," started Bryce, getting angry now, "we're just passing through on our way to Paris."

"Makes no difference," interrupted the official. "It has nothing to do with me. It is…international relations between your country and Yugoslavia." That was news to us. "Your luggage has been taken off the bus; it is leaving now."

"What!" exclaimed Vangellis. He leaped into a barrage of Greek, and a hostile argument ensued. Bryce and I couldn't dare match the outrage shown by our Greek friend, and turned to watch the bus pull out of its bay and drive off into the night. Our bags were left in a dusty pile along the side of the road.

Without thinking, we left Vangellis and the official to their argument, and wandered down to our luggage. We found that Vangellis's bags were not amongst ours.

"*Sto Diavolo!*" growled Vangellis, as he joined us a few minutes later. "You don't pay those bastards." He turned repeatedly, gesturing with open hands back toward the offices. When he tired of this, he sat wearily beside us and exhaled deeply. I handed his envelope back to him.

"Well, my friends," he said eventually, "I have lost my luggage trying to help you. What will you do about it?"

Bryce was about to say something, but checked himself and started laughing. It took him a few minutes to stop, by which time he had both Vangellis and me joining him. "*Philo*," he said, "when's the next bus out of this hole?"

Vangellis shrugged, still chuckling. "I suppose we will find out tomorrow. In the meantime, we should look for a place to sleep."

We could see the flickering lights of a nearby village from the depot, and decided to try our luck. At least Bryce and I would experience some of the country's hospitality first hand. The roads in this area were not lit, and we had to rely on the moonlight to find the off-road trail that led to the source of the lights.

The moon was still high as we lugged our bags into the smattering of milky-painted, high-walled residences that comprised the village. The streets were cobbled and narrow—too narrow to allow donkey carts, let alone vehicles.

Vangellis had resumed complaining, his voice rising to wake the townsfolk. The *Taverna*, when we eventually found one, was closed; its owner wasn't interested in feeding us, nor finding us a bed. Any plea or threat was greeted with a curse, a tired shrug and a twist of the wrist. "This *chorio* is very old," he grumbled. "These people are…*archaios*…very, very old. That man could barely talk sensibly."

"He was very tired," I interrupted. "It must be nearly four in the morning."

"Pah," said Vangellis. "We are still partying at this hour. No— his gestures, his speech was *agnoiya*…er…simple."

"Look," said Bryce, interrupting, trying to quiet him down, "there's a light down the hill. Let's try that."

We stumbled in the darkness, down a graffitied pathway, until we reached a decrepit shopfront. A dingy light gleamed through an open doorway, while grimy windows were covered with a spider-webbed drape coated with years of dust. Someone was moving about inside, howling what appeared to be an old dirge.

Vangellis crossed himself.

"*Theo mou*," he whispered. He suddenly seemed to lose control, as he was breaking more and more into Greek. "That is an old Macedonian song. Old. It is terrible…we go."

"*Se barrakalo*," came a voice from the doorway. We stopped, although Vangellis was pulling hard on us.

In the filthy light of the doorway, a gritty silhouette swayed against the open portal, an arm held out in beckoning pose. "*Se barrakalo*," repeated the voice, gravelly. "*Ella messa.*"

"*Stanio…*" started Vangellis.

The shadowy figure stepped into the weak light. It was a woman, almost haggish. Her face was ropey, the lines meshing almost parallel diagonally across. She wore a heavy, black outfit, more a cowled cloak than a dress. In the heat of the Greek weather, it should have struck her down with exhaustion.

"Sorry, but…" I said, speaking over Vangellis, trying to cut off whatever curse he was about to fling.

"You speak English," she said suddenly, cutting us both off

with her fine neutral accent. "Please, come in, come into my shop. I offer you some coffee and *mezethes,* and you just look around."

Bryce shrugged. "I've given up on sleeping," he mumbled. "A snack'll compensate and keep me going."

"In there?" I asked.

"So, we'll eat and run. You never know what you'll find anyway. Some ancient rune—a fossil from the great wars of Marathon—the original writings of Homer..."

"Shut up," I said.

"No, no; come away," pleaded Vangellis.

"Prosohi," the woman said to him, drawing out the word. *"Ftani pya!"*

I recognised her warning to Vangellis, simple in its meaning, yet he shivered into silence.

"Welcome in," she said to us. "Bring your little Greek friend."

"Please," started Vangellis. "There is much trouble here."

The old woman commenced chanting, as if passing the time to await our decision. Her words and tune seemed to weave into our minds, making it difficult to concentrate. Bryce and I were compelled to turn toward her and listen. I was aware of Vangellis stumbling over his words, stuttering, repeating himself until he kept spitting out the same word repeatedly: "Please..."

Her song became louder, her voice more shrill. Gone was her neutral accent, she now invoked a strange tongue: not Greek, not Macedonian. It seemed to be an alien message, foreign to my ears that have listened to myriad dialects and languages in my travels. I couldn't see her eyes in the black shadows that shrouded her face, but could feel something stabbing at me: a look caressing my flesh, brushing cold against the sultry evening breeze. There were grey, faceless, spidery puppets in my mind, dancing or fighting or wrestling...I couldn't tell, but the images were frantic and shifting their shapes. She suddenly stopped. Bryce and I jumped, startled. Vangellis stood silently, soaking in weaving trails of perspiration.

"Please," she said quietly. "Come inside and browse."

Without knowing why, I moved forward, stepping into the shop. Bryce followed me, and Vangellis was not far behind. As

I passed the doorway, my body broke through a heavy spider's web that covered the threshold. It was as if no one had entered the shop for years; or had left it.

"*Bravo,*" she said. "I have a little gift for you."

The old woman was surrounded by a light that radiated off her, yet threw darkness around the shop. Gradually the light dimmed, bringing the shop to a sickly, amber glow. The interior smelled of rancid seaweed and I considered leaving. She approached us and handed me three small packages; each wrapped in fine, dusty parchment. Cautiously, I unwrapped one. The wrapping crumbled in my fingers.

"It's…" I stuttered, looking around to Bryce. "It's my passport."

There had been no explanations about the passports: mine, Bryce's and Vangellis'. The woman wandered off into a dark corner, laughing like a rude violin, only to return moments later bearing a tray with coffee and a food platter. We were too confused to accept anything, so she placed the tray onto a dust-caked bench.

I realised that Bryce had suddenly become aware of the shop's interior. It took me a while to focus myself, and it was evident that Vangellis was standing behind us, as if in some mild shock. Steeped in his heritage of myths and superstition, despite its strict religious concepts, Vangellis must have been battling with an inner conflict between some perceived or instilled magic and truth.

"God," said Bryce. From the darkness I heard an audible intake of breath.

"Look around; study," came the old woman's voice. "I'm certain you will find something to interest you; or your friends back home."

The shop, in all its murkiness, was a plethora of ancient relics, curios and books. Through the weaving dust-caked webs that spanned the ceiling, piles of rolled scrolls were layered amongst rows of clayed jars. Jewel-specked trays and chalices were displayed on an old trestle, while in a far corner hung a row of mummified beasts: monstrosities that resembled fish with taloned paws, semi-humanoid dogs with faces in snarling pose; withered lizards that once stalked rocky plains on hairy limbs. Musical instruments, bastardised from traditional or acceptable forms, were piled against strangely woven rugs: bagpipes that had retained the fur of their origin, chimes that were created from ancient skeletal bones, a strange violin—long necked and obscenely carved.

There was a feeling of oppression; dust drifted as we disturbed the displays in our uneasy curiosity, clingy material brushed against our tired bodies, and the acrid smell of burning incense or herbs, mingling with the sea-stench, watered our eyes.

"There is nothing that pleases you?" asked the woman, whose voice floated distinctly around the shop. "I am certain that I can select the perfect gifts for each of you."

I found myself back at the entrance, where Bryce had just returned to, and Vangellis had not strayed from.

"Refresh yourselves," she said, suddenly appearing from behind us. She offered us the coffees that were thick and black in small-carved bony cups. I found the brew very sweet, and once sipped, I gulped the remainder quickly. Bryce also drank his within seconds, but Vangellis, still eerily silent, remained unmoved.

Beads of sweat formed on my brow, a new heat, separate from the Greek climate flushed through my body like a purging draught. I immediately suspected the coffee, but the old woman spoke, dragging my mind from any personal thoughts.

"You," she said to Bryce, "admire art, and shall have this expressive landscape." Bryce numbly accepted the painting. It was a flattened piece of timber on which was painted lumps of coloured clay, oils, grasses and who knew what, forming a desolate plain on which loomed spidery trees that resembled searching hands. "There is a history behind this painting, which, when studied, you will find compelling."

She handed me a tubed instrument: musical pipes. As she reached out I saw that her arm and hand was covered in tattoos. Blood red, black and green, the images appeared to be moving. One image resembled some octopod, although the arms were centred around the head, whilst its body comprised of reptilian flesh. "You are more of an artiste," she said, startling me. "This will enable you to realise that the ancient ones were far more poetic in their sciences and arts than most academics would ever imagine."

I studied the pipes—it was finer than the bamboo used in those traditional recitals I had seen in some halls around Europe. There was a fine script along its surface, that appeared to be a mixture of Turkish, ancient Greek and another language I did not recognise.

"Your little Greek friend," she almost spat, but then controlled herself, "is very materialistic. He loves the riches that go without hard work." She placed a large, green pearl into his hands, and he seemed to clutch at it hungrily.

"I know that you each like these gifts, and I have much pleasure in telling you that you pay me nothing for them."

As she resumed speaking, I was again aware of the heat, which was radiating from within me. I had to stop myself from stumbling.

"But remember," she said, "nothing is free. There is always a price to pay. These gifts, you may be interested to know, were created by the same…artist. He was very skilled in the arts, so much so that to him it was a science. His works, you will find, shall have meaning beyond artistic appreciation; they will touch your lives.

"The creator of these works lived many, many years ago," continued the old woman. "His works have been eagerly sought throughout the centuries, by the greedy and the unholy. His crafts have been found by the stumbling and the cunning. But these are yours, and only you will reap their benefits, so long as you remain true to their intent." She smiled, her face now showing in the light of the shop. Her ropy features seemed to writhe in the moving shadows, and the wiry hairs that ran down her face curled as the first rays of sunlight reflected through the open doorway. She had no irises in her eyes, they were only white orbs.

We slept a full day before deciding to think about the events we had experienced.

Bryce, Vangellis and I had awoken beneath a large leafy tree. In the distance lay the village on the rocky hill, and below us ran the highway that crossed from Greece into Yugoslavia.

Our luggage was intact, and for a while we speculated about how we had reacquired our passports. Our lengthy talk only made us more aware that we didn't wish to discuss the weird events of the night; and how we came to wake up in a field a few kilometres from the village.

"What do these mean?" asked Bryce. He grasped his painting, staring at it, studying it. "It wasn't a pawn shop, for God's sake."

"Throw it away," spat Vangellis. "There is evil there, I tried to tell you but she…" he made a gesture across his lips as if to pull a zipper. "*Pana yio, mou,*" he continued, "my soul is on fire from that *maggia,* she is worse than the devil."

"Calm down," I said, "we're here, away from the shop and the crone. Maybe a little surreal, but it certainly is an experience that makes for an interesting travelogue."

"Are you mad?" shouted Vangellis. "Why did I trust you, to help you from the border officers? Think! Look at what she has given you: horrible works—they look evil, blasphemous. Throw them away."

Strangely, Bryce said: "She told us not to get rid of them."

"No, she didn't," I said.

"Maybe not those words," he answered, "but the meaning was the same. And you shouldn't complain," Bryce continued, to Vangellis. "You seemed to have got a good deal."

Vangellis stared wide-eyed at Bryce, then slowly looked down to his hand. He still clutched the green pearl like a clamp. With effort, he opened his fist, revealing a deep pockmark in his palm.

"I wonder," he said. "It possesses a spirit. The pearl, it smells of death." He stood and threw the pearl down the hill toward the highway.

"I am free," he howled. "She cannot touch me. I must find a monastery, a church. I must be cleansed." His words seemed bizarre.

Bryce and I stared at each other. We had both recognised Vangellis as an eccentric rogue from our first meeting, but this was becoming an irrational aspect of his character that frightened us.

Suddenly, through his shouting, Vangellis grabbed his chest and fell to the ground. He rolled a distance down the slope, coming to a sliding stop against some jutting rocks. We could hear him groaning, gasping for breath.

"*Voithia!*" he shouted. "He-he-help me."

We sprinted down the slope to Vangellis, almost sliding into him.

"Breath… breath," he whispered. "I…I cannot."

"Shit," shouted Bryce, "do something!"

Vangellis started writhing, his face turning blue. Suddenly, as if my imagination had taken over my senses, I saw sucker indentations squeezed around his throat. I clutched at his neck; it felt like a thick ropey wire.

"Look for it," I yelled. "Go get the pearl."

Without hesitation, Bryce ran down the hill. I could hear his rising curses as he flung soil and rocks wildly in a mad search.

I continued to struggle with Vangellis, his screams becoming gurgles. Foam and spittle frothed from his thickening lips, and his tongue was swelling.

"Hurry," I screamed. "He's going…"

"I can't…" Bryce shouted. Then, amid the pounding of Vangellis's jerks, I heard: "Wait. I got it."

Bryce was only twenty metres from me. He turned and threw the jewel towards us and I lunged for it. I caught it, pushing the pearl into Vangellis' hand. Like a miracle, his face flushed, and his breath came gushing back, and he exhaled a hysterical scream that went on; and on.

"Keep it," Bryce said, his voice rising. "Don't ever throw it away."

Vangellis stared back at us in pathetic horror. "What can I do?" he pleaded. "That witch hated me from the start."

We were confounded; this was beyond our understanding. Until something could be explained, we had to hold onto our gifts.

People ignored us, not comprehending our terror. We were returning to Athens. From there we would decide our next move; we wanted to be as far away from this place as possible.

Vangellis was verging again on hysteria; he was a wreck. He looked as if he had crawled a hundred kilometres through the rugged, rocky terrain of the Greek plains on his stomach.

We had an hour before our bus, so Bryce and I took Vangellis to a restroom to wash up.

"Do not leave me, *Philo*," he pleaded, clutching my arm.

"It's all right," I assured him. "Have a wash; I should have a shirt that'll fit you."

He stared back at me, wanting more, I felt: protection— possibly substitution. He dazedly placed the pearl in his pocket, and then turned on the tap. I left him, returning to Bryce who paced nervously along the roadside.

"Shouldn't you be with him?" asked Bryce.

"He should be right," I answered. "Anyway, I couldn't stand to be with him all the time. He's like a walking time bomb at the moment: *'Help me…rid me of this…do not leave me'*. I needed some space."

"I just hope he doesn't start babbling on the bus," said Bryce. "He'll probably get us thrown off at another village or in the middle of nowhere…"

"Spare me," I complained. "He needs our support. God knows what happened to him, whether that pearl is possessed, or it's his hysterical imagination. I'd rather just play it safe."

Bryce stared out along the highway. "As for me, I'm playing it safe: I'm keeping my little work of art."

We turned, hearing a disturbance among the waiting crowd. People were rushing back toward the depot, milling around the toilets. Instinctively, Bryce and I rushed back, pushing people from our way. There was only one possibility, and we could hear it.

Vangellis was shrieking in terror. His cries were unintelligible to me, and he kept repeating one word continuously.

"Vangellis," I shouted. "We're here."

Through the crowd, I saw Vangellis thrashing his arms. People were stepping back, trying to avoid his waving fists. They were creating a ringed wall through which he couldn't pass.

"Vangellis," I repeated, waving frantically.

"Steve," he shouted back. "It is gone. It is gone."

Suddenly the crowd was flung back like a crashing wave. Screams filled the air as bodies were hurled into buildings and vehicles. For a split second Vangellis stood alone, standing like a totem amid a pile of rejected wood carvings: his expression was one of pure terror, carved into wide-eyed, open-mouthed torture.

Then it happened with supernatural speed. Vangellis skimmed across the sprawled bodies, their cries rising in fear of the incomprehensible vision. He clutched at the air, his feet kicking impotently. Then he hit the hard tarmac of the road, his body dragging heavily, his voice hysterical. I could see a bloody path follow him as he scraped along the highway. His arms bounced as he tried to stop himself, and I saw a limb suddenly twist and bend at an unnatural angle.

I ran after him, Bryce following me. People stepped aside, moving away from the road. I couldn't make any progress, Vangellis kept skimming along the road, howling, travelling at an incredible speed. I could feel my lungs burning, the heat of the day slowing me down.

Bryce tripped, and I heard his thud as he slid onto the gravel. My momentum was suddenly halted as I bounced off thin air: I seemed to have run into an invisible barrier and I couldn't move any further.

"Bryce," I called. "Help me. Something's happening."

Bryce staggered up to me, then stopped. Before us, Vangellis lay still in the middle of the road. A thick cloud was converging around him, darkness was pouring through a rip in the air. Vangellis started writhing. He clutched his chest, moaning once more, and this time we could see the reason for his agony. From the darkness enveloping him, a series of thick tentacles lashed his body, a wiry, whip-like member whirling around his throat. I tried to move forward, but was kept back by the invisible barrier, and held back by Bryce's desperate arms.

"No, don't," he pleaded; "there's nothing we can do. My God, this can't be happening."

Vangellis was lifted into the air, his features bloated and sickly blue, as if his blood was being drained from his body. I could see his flesh caving into his bones, the fat being chewed out of him. His mouth was stretched to beyond possible limits, and his eyes… his eyes were enormous and white; his tongue looked as thick as my wrist and dangled well below his extended chin.

Like a matchstick puppet, his limbs jerked in a surreal dance. He was continually collapsing; his head lolled, spinning and rolling, threatening to snap from his neck. His arms flayed uncontrollably while his legs buckled under the horrible spasms inflicted by whatever had control of his body.

I attempted to grab him but I was unable to get close, the invisible barrier pushing me back. Bryce ran alongside me; he also tried to approach the gyrating Vangellis, but was prevented from getting within arm's reach of our friend.

The crowd behind us rumbled in amazement, the many voices and dialects created a cacophony. I implored them for help, but in my panic, I could only see waves of bodies surging forward, then receding backward. I was astounded at the surreal movement of the crowd's reaction; it was almost as if they were performing a folk dance in response to Vangellis's thrashings.

Suddenly I heard a wail, then a number of cries from the crowd. Then I heard the screech of car tyres. I spun my head and saw a sports car sliding along the road. People leaped aside as the car picked up speed despite the black smoke that rose from the rear tyres.

I made another lunge towards Vangellis, but was hurled backwards into the crowd behind me. The vehicle veered as it bounced and spun like it had hit an oil patch, its forward movement, though, aimed it toward Vangellis.

With a sickening thud, the car ploughed into Vangellis, the impact hurling him high into the air. I saw him bounce back onto the road, then roll continuously till he stopped along the gravel verge. The car kept spinning, then flipped into the air, landing onto its roof atop Vangellis with a loud metallic crunch.

Seconds later we were engulfed by the crowd as they converged upon the horrible accident. Bryce and I stood there, stunned, disbelieving; we were immediately jostled aside by officials and police from the nearby border offices.

The crowd was in an uproar, screaming, yelling, waving, creating chaos. I pushed Bryce off the roadside, away from the scene. We don't know what the people saw as the result of the accident, and we didn't wish to add any confusion or suspicion by forwarding our eyewitness accounts, so we walked back toward the bus depot. As we returned, we passed a swarthy youth ambling toward the accident. He was playing with the green pearl.

SYDNEY, AUSTRALIA, MAY 1985

I had decided to take a late walk around the Opera House, following a series of business seminars held at the InterContinental. My mind was full of facts, and I had a need to unwind with the splashing sounds along the Harbour, the smell of sea, and possibly a glass of wine from a bistro. At the same time, I was trying to hush the tinnitus whistling in my head by focusing on the information sessions I had attended.

The evening crowd was sedate; I took my time, watching the lights of moving traffic across the Harbour Bridge, and the distant flashing glow of Luna Park.

Finally relaxed, I strolled back toward the hotel, hoping for a good night's sleep in preparation for the following day's back to back sessions. Passing the Circular Quay terminal I suddenly stopped in my tracks.

"Bryce," I said, catching sight of an artist who was working on an unusual cityscape. I don't know how I actually recognised him; we had lost track of each other back in 1978, when he crashed out of university and shot through to parts unknown.

He had changed considerably: his hair was long and greasy, his eyes seemed to be smudged with a deep charcoal. He had a haunted look, and he appeared in need of a good meal and a hot bath. It seemed incredible that my old friend who had so much scholastic potential could have willingly chosen a desolate lifestyle.

"Bryce?" I repeated, not truly believing—not wanting to believe that I addressed my old friend.

The man continued to poke the canvas, one moment scraping a flat blade across a narrow cord of oily paint, the next fanning the sides with a fine brush.

"Steven," he said, not turning, studying his strokes. "Get me away from here. Buy me a beer."

I stood, stunned for a moment. Bryce rose, leaving his gear at his feet, took me by the arm and led me away towards the Cross.

"Your work…" I said.

"Forget it," he answered. "Not worth shit."

We veered from the main street and crossed into a dark, cobbled lane. I couldn't read the street name, but it wasn't far from the bustling city traffic. Our footsteps echoed in the darkness, sounds bouncing around us in a jumbled tattoo. From darkened doorways, I could hear subdued murmurs, shuffling movements.

"The painting," Bryce said, pushing me into one of the doorways that sprinkled the alley.

"What?" I yelped, startled by his aggressive thrust.

"My place," he said. "My shout. A drink and a story. A bloody, god-damned story."

He wasn't making sense. I allowed myself to be hustled into a gloomy corridor, shadows blurred a sickly hue as a fly-specked light globe swung overhead. We reached another doorway, a weathered, dampened entrance; Bryce kicked it. The door buckled slightly then pushed inwards. A light glowed from within, casting a pale spotlight effect on Bryce's gaunt and greasy features. He nodded me to enter, his paint-stained hand guiding me forward.

I entered, watching Bryce as he hesitated at the doorway. He stood still, looking ahead, his gaze suddenly transforming into a glare of hatred, of fear. There was an avalanche of emotion pouring from his fixed gaze, and I could see it exhaust him as he slumped to the floor.

I stood there staring, not moving, studying his shuddering efforts to rise.

"The painting," he gasped, pointing ahead. "That bastard…"

I turned and saw it. Memories flooded back, and I almost reeled as if struck by the visions of 1976. I had not forgotten the events.

Bryce's painting hung against the far wall. It dominated the room; faded wallpaper peeled at its edges, and a slimy substance glistened a multi-globbed trail to the floor. It compelled me to stare at it now, drawing me towards it, exuding a hateful message.

"Do you remember the painting, its vision?" asked Bryce quietly.

"Yes," I replied. "I don't recall feeling this badly about it, though."

I heard Bryce laugh, there was no humour in it. "It's changed since…since I first took possession."

"Changed?" I tried turning to Bryce, but I couldn't look away.

"There are some characters…creatures—call them anything you like—moving about." Bryce laughed again, a touch of hysteria in his pitch. "They come out at night. They come out at night."

"I can't see anything," I said. I could feel something though—there was some force splashing coldly against me.

"Look; look closely," he pleaded. "You'll see them."

"I don't think I want to."

This has been going on for years," he whispered, fighting back a deep sob. *"I'm not mad. You must be able to see them; concentrate."*

"But I can't," I answered. My eyes suddenly stung as if they had been washed with ammonia; salty tears welled and I had to wipe hard to ease the pain.

"There," accused Bryce; "you see? You saw them. Why are you lying to me—tell me about it?"

I swung around. "I saw nothing, Bryce, I don't know anything. Get rid of the bloody thing."

"What? What did you say? You know what happened in

Greece; you were there. I can't throw it away—it's mine, it belongs to me. I belong to it. I don't know how to use it—but you must; look at you. You were given the pipes, and you're here; you're normal—you must know something."

"The pipes," I said, cutting off his rambling, "are still mine. But I haven't become obsessed by it. I bring them with me, but they create this noise in my head."

"Obsession?" queried Bryce. "I was never obsessed with that. It drew me in. It demanded my attention. Its strokes, its colours, it commanded my mind." Bryce shook his head, trying to pluck a phrase that eluded him. "It wanted me, my skill to recreate it. But I can't—you saw my shit down on the quay. But it commands me to continue to paint and paint, and paint...until I make its companion."

Bryce looked at the painting, his eyes again focusing sharply at the thing. "They're there," he whispered. "They're beckoning. I must paint."

Bryce stumbled into an adjoining room, returning moments later with a grubby paint board and a handful of brushes and paint tubes. He wiped at the board with his sleeve, smearing whatever work he had commenced into a swirl of dirt and grease.

"I must paint," he recited, "I must capture it, find its secret."

I stared at Bryce in disbelief as he spread a tube of paint across the board and commenced to work it. His eyes were focused at the painting on the wall, as if he were looking beyond it. Instinctively I stared at the wall and once more my eyes were riveted to the artwork. I couldn't see anything beyond what was painted there, strange and surreal as it was, but I could feel its attraction—more a drawing force—that demanded something of me.

For a moment, the painting blurred—perhaps it was the strain of the dim lighting, my stinging eyes, but I blinked, trying to focus, and the flat vision of the landscape with its clutching trees...beckoning trees...jolted me.

"What are you trying to paint?" I asked, attempting a casual tone. "The painting may be of a strange vision, but it appears to be a straightforward style."

"You don't really understand, do you?" Bryce spat. "You

don't see them. They move; they want to come out. Look at them straining, pushing to be free."

"Paint me what you see, then," I almost shouted, frightened and frustrated. "What can I do?"

I can't paint them," he said angrily. "I've been trying for years. They're there, but it's not a matter of painting a creature; I must paint its essence—somehow that's its key."

"I don't understand," I said

"Shit," he screamed. He picked up his board and threw it at the painting. "Get out, Steve. Leave me." A drooling jelly seeped from the painting, tracing a trail down the wall. It seemed to harden or dry, leaving a sucker pattern on the surface, giving it a resemblance to a coiling tentacle.

"I asked if I could do something," I started.

"No, you can't help at all. You don't even know what I'm talking about. Something is happening here, like what happened in Greece. It's not imagination, it's not madness; it's a force—and it's driving me to its purposes."

"But doesn't painting it—copying it—feed its needs?"

Bryce stared at me, like he stared at the painting, a hard intense glare. There was anger, pain, and fear in it. "I don't know," he said. "I think it can be used both ways. If it's a key, you can lock something in as well as letting it out." There was a sad smile on his face as he thought for a moment. "At present, there's a crack in the door, and they want me to open it. 'Use the key' they're saying; 'let us out into your world'. They won't leave me alone, so I must try. I was hoping you had an answer so I could avoid all of this."

"Wouldn't burning it destroy it?" I asked.

Bryce shook his head. "You're pathetic. You're not listening to me. You think I'm mad…raving."

"No."

"Please," he said quietly, "it would be best if you left. Forget that you saw me; forget all of this—my obsession, my ravings. Perhaps one day, that pipe of yours will start haunting you."

Bryce opened the door. "Sorry, but maybe we'll have that beer another day."

MELBOURNE, AUSTRALIA. FEBRUARY 1991

The dreams had been persisting for several months. They weren't really dreams; it was more a noise than anything visual. Wailing during the night, sibilant sounds like sucking air—annoying enough to waken me during my sleeping hours.

One pitch soon became two, then gradually developed to become many. Persistent, prodding, jumbled, insistent. My sleeping hours were now broken nightly; once wakened, I would lie restlessly for hours until morning when I would drag myself up for the office.

Sleeping tablets had only been temporarily effective. My wife, Julia, was concerned, as our sex life was now being strained as well as my growing lethargy toward work issues.

"Maybe you should have a week off," she suggested. "You've been under a lot of stress, particularly with the collapse of that company that owed you all that money."

"I don't think it's work related," I said. "Sleeplessness is a sign of stress, but in my case, it's the mind ticking over, you know?"

"It's not your work?" Julia asked.

"No, it's not work at all. It's…noises, like I've told you. It's as if there's a crowd standing at the end of our bed chanting at me."

"What do you mean?" she asked.

"It's hard to explain," I said. "They don't seem to be my thoughts nagging at me. I'm awake and I can hear these sounds in my head; they seem to come from ahead of me, like they're not in my mind."

"But I don't hear anything," said Julia. "It must be stress related. You should do some physical activity; maybe that's the answer: go for a morning walk, or run."

I shrugged, and then nodded. "I'll give it a try."

Early morning runs were a refreshing solution for a while. I was able to cope with the mental fatigue of the office, and our intimacy was back on track. The sounds, however, continued, and for a time I was able to push them aside.

But they continued, and became ever more insistent. The

urgency that persisted in the early days was now developing into anger, a demand that I listen and pay heed, although this was more a feeling than an understanding. Eventually I was back to the same situation as before; recurring exhaustion leaving me susceptible to poor judgment and arguments.

I found myself dozing off as my normal waking hour approached, and Julia was finding it difficult to stir me to prepare for work. I finally agreed to take a week off from work so that I could see a specialist who may be able to find the cause of my problem. The time off allowed me to sleep in so that I was able to cope with the appointments that Julia had arranged for me. On the third day, though, Julia roused me awake during late morning.

"Steven," she said. "There's a parcel here for you. It's special delivery."

I struggled up to see what the parcel was.

"Does it have a return address on it?" I mumbled, forcing my clouded head to clear.

"I didn't notice," Julia said, inspecting the package. "It should have something on it."

The package was large and flat. My name was written in large black Texta, but there was no return address printed on the parcel. Julia carefully unwrapped it, then exhaled a confused "What?"

"What is it?" I asked.

Julia's eyebrows knitted together in confusion. "Who would have sent you this? They must have a very disturbed sense of humour, or poor taste in art."

My heart suddenly jerked. "Art…" I grabbed the unwrapped package from Julia, pulling it rudely from her grip.

"Steven…" she protested, but she stopped for I must have looked as bad as I felt when I cast my eyes over the painting—Bryce's painting. I tore the wrapping, and raised the painting with a feeling of dread and confusion.

"What is it, Steven?" asked Julia. "Who sent it?"

"Bryce…" I muttered. "How could you?"

"Bryce?" said Julia. "Isn't he the friend you went overseas with years ago?"

I was silent; I couldn't think or speak coherently. Images flashed through my mind—violent images. Vangellis on the hill, at the bus terminal; Bryce in his dingy room; the old witch beckoning us—they seemed to waver across the painted timber that I held in my hands.

"Steven?"

I roused myself and looked at Julia.

"This was Bryce's," I said. "It was impossible for him to give it away."

"What do you mean?" she asked. "Why would he want to give that to someone? I would have burned it. It's horrible."

"It isn't a question of admiring a work of art," I answered, "or passing it on to someone to appreciate. He had to keep it. Had to, or else."

Reluctantly, I told her the story about the painting. I told Julia everything; she had to know, otherwise she would have thought me crazy. Perhaps she did, once she heard about the weird events that I had experienced.

"So, what are you going to do?" Julia asked. "Are you assuming that Bryce is now dead?"

"I suppose he must be," I said. "But who would have sent me his painting?"

"This is ridiculous," she said. "It has to be coincidence. Are you going to be haunted by this painting? What about your pipes—the one you keep locked away. That hasn't been affecting you, has it?"

A thought crossed my mind. It started as a niggle, but suddenly it screamed at me.

"My dreams. Surely," I said, shakily.

"What?" asked Julia.

"The ringing noises, prodding and abuse. They keep me awake at night."

Julia looked nervous. "Maybe you should take a tablet."

"I'm not mad," I protested. "It's consistent with what happened to Bryce. That has to be the answer."

"But now you've got the painting. What chance have you got if you think that way?" argued Julia. "Surely you should think logically about it. Don't dig your own grave, confront it."

"If you saw what I've seen…Vangellis and Bryce…" I said, shaking my head, "you wouldn't dare give this thing a sideways glance."

Julia scooped up the wrapper, crumpling it. Suddenly she noticed something within it and stopped. "Look," she said, "there's some writing paper in this."

"Let me see," I blurted.

"No," she answered. "Take it easy, Steven."

Julia unfolded the writing paper and read it silently. I saw a quizzical look in her eyes before she looked up at me.

"What does it say?" I asked.

"'Steve—I've found the solution. Now you must find your answer to celebrate your victory. – Bryce'."

"What?" I said, startled. *"Your victory?* What's he talking about? This is madness."

"Maybe more so than you realise," said Julia. "Bryce's note; it's written on notepaper from a place called the Elder Holy Sun Sanitarium."

"This is ugly; horrible," continued Julia, studying the painting. She was holding the painted board at arm's length, examining it, eyeing the detailed strokes and objects smeared and splashed across its surface. "I can understand why someone would be haunted by this."

"It isn't just the painting," I said. "There is something beyond what you see. Bryce looked at it and imagined moving objects. I looked at it and saw only what you see, but I could feel some presence. I can't really explain more than that, because I couldn't see what Bryce saw."

Julia touched my hand and squeezed it. "Perhaps there's nothing left in the painting. Bryce says that he's found the solution. Maybe whatever was in it is now dead, from whatever he's done."

"He was trying to paint a key, whatever that means. Or the opposite to this, so that he would lock its influence away."

"Well, maybe he's done that."

I looked at Julia and responded to her touch by hugging her.

"I've got to find out, for sure," I said. "I've got to speak to

Bryce, find his answer. Then, perhaps, we can get rid of this painting, and the pipes."

"You're not taking this painting with you?" Julia asked.

"I think I must."

Julia took the painting up again. She didn't appear to be nervous about handling it. I dreaded even to look at it longer than a passing glance.

"You know," she said, "the style of this painting reminds me of something."

I suddenly experienced a panic attack. "Don't look at it," I almost yelled. Julia's eyes bulged and her mouth opened wide. She dropped the painting and stepped back, gasping, breaking into sobs. I grabbed her and held her close.

"Shit," she cried, "it's still alive—he hasn't thwarted it. The bastard."

"What—what happened?" I asked, not thinking whether she was up to it or not.

"It reached out at me. Scaly hands, I think. It all happened so fast, I thought they were going to grab me."

"But how?"

Julia trembled in my arms, then took a deep breath. "The painting reminded me of those holographs that you see these days."

"Holographs?" I asked. "What do you mean?"

"I don't really know if that's what they're called. Those magic prints, 3-D art, whatever. I've seen them in art and gift shops: they're like a mass of little spots or patterned lines, but if you look at them a certain way, focusing at a certain point, a three-dimensional object appears."

"But they're only a recent creation; computer designed, aren't they?" I asked.

"It doesn't seem so to me," said Julia. "I adjusted my focus on the painting, and suddenly a clawed tentacle lunged at me. It moved; it seemed to spring at me so quickly."

"That does it," I snapped, picking up the painting angrily. For an instant, the painting spun before Julia and she cringed as if ducking from a swipe. "This is coming with me. Bryce will have to explain himself, crazy or not."

I wondered whether it would be safe to take the two together. Perhaps the combination would be a recipe for something far more horrendous than the power of one. I thought that I would try; it was the only practical thing for me to do.

Julia and I went up to our room to pack quickly.

"Are you okay?" asked Julia, staring at me with a wide-eyed concern.

"Yes," I said, nodding slowly. "As soon as I've taken care of the painting and the pipes I'm heading straight for the airport. If I can't get an immediate stand-by flight, I'll pay whatever it takes to get on anything. The sooner I can get rid of these damned artefacts…it still won't be soon enough."

"Do you know how crazy it sounds?" said Julia.

Things had happened fast, and I knew that there was something more to it. The whole episode had been building up since 1976. The seeds had been planted on the Greek-Yugoslavian border. Three young men had been presented with strange gifts. Two naive students had allowed the artefacts to take root and wrap around their souls, their minds. Now it was tightening into a stranglehold. A third man was soured by fear, anger and superstition eons old, and had been no doubt been presented with a gift that sucked the soul from his body. Now it was time to pull this curse out by the roots, before it commenced its poisonous work upon me. It was inconceivable at this time to envisage what horrors may evolve.

Julia brought me back to the present. "What's keeping you?" she asked. I looked at her, and was suddenly confused by the surrounding darkness. It took me a few moments to realise that I was back inside the house, within the unlit recess that housed the artefacts. I had been standing there for almost an hour, the suitcase in my hands. Some subconscious battle was raging within me, and I needed Julia to help me.

"Please," I whispered forcibly, "help me down to the car."

Julia took me by my arm and led me outside. I absently unzipped the case and clutched at the pipes. I remembered the strange horny feel of the tubes, and browsed across the old strange etchings that I could barely decipher. A phrase of Turkish here, a few Greek characters, other scratches and hieroglyphs: meaningless arrangements, confusing patterns, swimming and wavering before my eyes.

I was attracted by some repetitive symbols. I stared, focusing and unfocusing, as they merged and divided, like a amoeba splitting, regenerating, splitting again.

Then it happened. My face felt momentarily scorched, the sensation of a fiery splash, a savage face slap.

The music leaped out at me from the pipes, a rhythmic pattern was formed, and floated from the pipes like an eerie series of wind gusts. There was a story there, a horrible story. Although I could not identify the words, I visualised the saga that spewed forth. The pipes writhed in my hands, as if flexing. My mind was flooded with visions: torture and death, sacrificial rape and murder, sacrilege and madness. Searing pain spasmed across my face repeatedly.

Suddenly the visions disappeared and I saw Julia standing before me, a moment before her hand blurred from her waist and smacked hard into my cheek. An uppercut tore the pipes from my hands. She then rushed me, hugging me tightly, as she burst into deep sobs of relief.

As I fought for self-control, I responded to her hugging, and stared defiantly at the pipes on the lawn.

SYDNEY, AUSTRALIA. FEBRUARY 1991

In the blinding glare of the late afternoon sun, Julia and I alighted from the taxi and climbed the steps of the sanitarium. The Elder Holy Sun Sanitarium was a dilapidated building that must have dated back to the turn of the century. Julia had decided to come with me; we relied solely on the taxi driver's knowledge of the area and the route, and I felt disoriented in this isolated location.

Its facade consisted of cracking Bluestone, and the timber verandah that extended across the breadth of its entrance was warped in places. Bars lined the windows along the lower floor, while the upper storey shutters were opened, revealing fingers poking through the mesh wire that was bolted into the stonework. Before leaving home, I tried calling the sanitarium, but could only get a voice message telling me of a connection problem. We couldn't wait; we had to come here.

Climbing the steps, I almost tripped on the weathered timber. I rubbed my eyes, blaming my tiredness on the prickling dread that tingled through me.

We passed through the entrance, suddenly stopping, feeling the dread scratching deeper at us. The reception area was deep in gloom; a strong, bitter odour permeated the air. The smell was cloying, acidic; it reminded me of animal wastes and raw meat left out in the sun for too long.

It was strange that a receptionist sat at the front desk, sitting calmly, ignoring the foul vomit stench. I approached warily, trying to suppress my nausea. As I spoke, I gasped, and had to swallow a few times to force back rising bile. I had to speak through clenched teeth.

"You have a patient here," I started, then stopped. The receptionist looked past me, ignoring my presence. Her eyes blinked slowly, and there was a lifeless expression in her pale, dull, dry eyes. I looked at her, studying her features.

Her skin was dry; there was barely any moisture on her face.

In this heat, she should have been shiny from perspiration, but there was no gleam in her flesh. Fine, dry lines ran down her face, a hint of powder floated from her as if her skin was flaking away.

"Pardon me," I said nervously.

It took a while before her head turned slowly toward me. I thought that I could hear her neck muscles creak from the exertion. Her smile angled up with effort, her lips appeared to tear into little bleeding cuts.

"May I help you?" she asked, her voice was dry and hollow. As she spoke, dust-skin flew from her mouth. She spoke slowly, and I could see more of the flakiness floating within her mouth, lying on her tongue. She was also unaware of blood around her lips coagulating, drying into small crimson mounds, forming a horrible moustache on which her flaking flesh settled.

"I—I'm here to see one of your residents," I said, trying to ignore her condition. My mind was racing to conclusions about Bryce and his painting, and what he may have unleashed. My gaze darted around, searching for staff, but the place appeared empty. Then I remembered the fingers that clawed through the bolted mesh along the upper building windows.

"Yes?" the receptionist said, attracting my attention back to her. Her voice startled me.

"Williams. Bryce Williams," I mumbled.

I stared at the receptionist who seemed to be in a world of her own. She raised her arm toward a closed door. "Please go through and wait; the doctor will come and speak to you about Mr Williams."

Julia and I stared at each other, but we moved toward the door and opened it. The room had a heavily draped window, and it was dark. I searched for a light switch. Finding the switch, I flicked it, but was rewarded only with gloom and shadow. There were paintings on the walls, the oily paint smelling noxious. Before us was a long wooden table, surrounded by aged, leather chairs.

"Please come in," a voice said abruptly, "and close the door."

Without thinking, Julia turned and closed the door. We felt impelled to enter further into the room. A cloaked figure stepped from the dark shadows and into the gloom.

At first, I was confused at the theatrical nature of the figure and the oppressive atmosphere. I grabbed Julia's hand and drew her close to me.

"It's very good that you've come to see me," said the figure, "and I see you've brought your gifts with you. As I expected."

Without further preamble, the figure took off his hood and smiled at us. At first I didn't recognise him, but I saw that it was Bryce. He no longer looked as I had known him during our college days, or even when we crossed paths in Sydney. He was gaunt, almost skeletal in his features, and his face had been tattooed in dark black, green and red drawings.

I felt speechless, and Julia grabbed my arm tightly. My eyes were fixated on Bryce, so horrid and hypnotic were his features. His hair was tufted and ragged, as if he had pulled at his scalp, leaving raw flesh mingled with blood soaked hair. His eyes were almost black, but brightly glittered, and beneath his facial tattoos, I could see the scars of the needles that had etched the art work.

His teeth were stumpy and yellowed, as if he had been grinding them for years.

"Bryce, what the hell…" I had found my voice, and all I could think of were clichés. "What's the meaning of this? What's happened to you?"

"My old friend," he said, ignoring Julia's presence. "For fifteen years, the Old Ones have been patient with us. They presented us with gifts, knowing that they would provide us the keys to open their doorway into our lives. They knew that once open, it would be another step closer to reclaiming their domain."

"What are you talking about?" I asked.

"All around the world, over the centuries, they have been distributing gifts, gradually opening doorways," he continued, ignoring my question. "We are at the final portal, and they are now growing impatient. I discovered the key to the painting, and it is now duplicated here on the walls."

He gestured behind him, and through the gloom I could see the paint pulsating, drooling down the walls. I had initially thought that the walls were covered in framed art, but now I recognised that Bryce must have painted the length and breadth of the room in the style of the painting that had been given to him. He no longer needed that framed work; he now had this horror at his disposal. Julia edged closer to me. She had been silent and still, but now I could feel her shaking.

"Who are the Old Ones?" I demanded. "What doorways are you talking about?"

Bryce looked astounded. "Don't you understand, *Philo*? You've had your pipes for all these years, and you've gained no understanding? It's pointless for me to explain something so unearthly to a mind that will only comprehend simple grunts. All you need to know is that the Old Ones have tossed the dog a stick, and the dog will instinctively retrieve it. Now it's time to play your tune, the music that will guide them to this room, through the forest that I have painted."

"You're joking," I replied. "I don't know any 'tunes', and I don't want to guide anything through that wall of paint."

"I'm not joking. The joke will be on mankind. Play."

"I've had the pipes for many years. Not once have I been tempted to play them. I don't know of any music I'm supposed to play," I argued.

"You know them. You've been listening to them throughout these years. The music is embedded in your mind; it's a part of you. Just place the pipes to your lips and blow. The Old Ones will hear you, and leave the halls of R'lyeh to find their way here; their reclaimed kingdom!"

I turned to Julia. "I don't know what's going on here. Go to reception and tell them that Bryce is in here and that he's totally irrational."

Julia squeezed my arm. "Come with me", she pleaded.

Bryce just smiled as we whispered to each other.

"I'll try to keep him calm. I'll show him the pipes, while you get help." I opened the bag containing the pan pipes, and pulled them out, showing them to Bryce.

"Yes," he said. "Just play them. The music will flow from you."

I placed the pipes to my lips, staring into Bryce's cold black eyes. His eyes were fixated on the instrument, his lips drawing into a broad grin. He nodded, encouraging me to start playing.

"Julia," I said. "Go now." She released my arm, and I heard her shuffling towards the door. I commenced blowing into the pipes.

Suddenly, the whistling sounds I'd been hearing throughout the years burst into my mind. It formed into a frantic jangle of piercing fanfare, a horrible, ugly sensation. My hands involuntarily passed the pipes across my lips and followed the strident symphonic rhythm.

I saw Bryce throw back his head and laugh. He raised his arms and threw his hands around like a demented maestro, following the alien strains of music. Behind Bryce, the wall painting seemed to come alive. The barren, spindly trees had an eerie movement, like hands reaching out and closing into fists.

I could see moving, drifting shadows follow a path around the four walls surrounding me.

I turned and saw a gathering of dark, monstrous shapes, while I continued to play the pipes. In a small, dark place of my mind, I wanted to stop blowing, and throw the pipes onto the floor, and smash them with my feet, but I was now impelled to continue with the cacophony of noise, knowing that I was approaching a crescendo in this abominable rhapsody.

Mingled with the music, I could hear Bryce laugh, his voice reaching a shrieking pitch. My gaze, having revolved around the walls, fell across him again. He was now tugging at his cloak, tearing it from his skeletal frame. Soon he stood naked before me, now rubbing his hands across his torso. His body was covered in tattoos, the colours of the wall painting. He was almost camouflaged against the surrounding alien panorama.

Bryce started to chant along to the music, the words alien to my ears, guttural and hollow. Yet, I grasped his utterances, although I still had no comprehension of its intent: *"Now is the time to awaken, Great Old One. Time to feast and command us."*

I heard another noise amongst the shrieking sounds, and my eyes turned toward the doorway behind me. I then noticed Julia, who was still in the room and screaming at me. Her hand appeared adhered to the door, the paint had drooled over it and was crawling up her arm. She was tugging, but her arm was affixed. In fact, the paint had formed into a taloned claw, and was pulling her into the timbered door.

My heart suddenly punched hard against my chest, and with an almighty effort I thrust the pipes away from my mouth. I grabbed Julia and pulled her away from the door.

There was a tremendous "Noooo!!" from behind me, and I turned. Bryce stared at me with pure hatred, his mouth baring his stumpy teeth. "Play on!!" he cried. "Play on."

"No!" I screamed back at him. "Go to Hell!"

Again, he threw his head back and laughed hysterically. "We will all be in a far better place than Hell, once you resume your playing."

"Enough!" I yelled back. "Enough."

"They are waiting. They need to pass through the forest," he pleaded. "You must continue. It is inevitable."

I threw the pipes onto the floor and stomped on them. The bones shattered into jagged shards.

"What have you done, man," cried Bryce. Suddenly around us, the paintwork started boiling on the walls. Dark shapes were rushing discordantly to the fore, and appeared to be pounding against the walls. We could hear thunderous roars as they attempted to come through from their alien dimension.

"You are the final link," cried Bryce above the clamour. "It has taken centuries to arrive at this point. It was ordained that you provide the bridge from R'lyeh to this place."

Bryce clutched at his chest and gasped. His body heaved, and I saw his flesh crawling into a lump. From his tattoos, a figure rose, a head protruded as if to pull itself away from Bryce's flesh. It was a horrendous shape, a cone-like head with cold black eyes, and at its mouth wriggled a mass of tentacles.

Bryce screamed as the beast-shape kept rising from his body. Its shoulders soon appeared, then large claws were raised onto his stomach as if to haul itself free. The tentacles fluttered and vibrated, creating a shattering sound, like discordant violin strings.

Julia gasped. "Steven, we've got to get away."

"How," I said. We were trapped in the room. It looked as if this creature was determined to come through. It had heard enough of the music to find its way into our dimension. Through Bryce's completed task, something had lain in wait within him, ready to lead the way for these unspeakable creatures, pounding their way through the wall barrier.

Bryce continued to scream as the beast lurched its way through his body. I looked down and saw the pipe shards, and desperately picked up the lower jagged portion.

As I picked it up, I could hear the foreign music return, only weaker. Not knowing why, I placed the pipes to my lips and blew. The beast suddenly stopped its motions and stared at me. Its tentacles pulsated and started to harmonise with the music. I continued blowing, and could feel my mind drifting. A dark vision formed and I could see a city of monstrous towers overlooking desolate jagged mountains, bordered by a black lake. The towers looked ancient and covered in slimy lichen. Beasts appeared to be patrolling the ramparts, looking toward a glowing orb. It wasn't a sun or a moon, but appeared to be a tunnel, a gateway.

I knew this was R'lyeh, the place that Bryce spoke of, and that knowledge and understanding was being imparted into my mind.

"In his house at R'lyeh, dead Cthulhu waits dreaming," my mind recited.

"Stop it, stop it," I suddenly heard. It was Julia. In an instant, she grabbed the pipes away from my mouth. In her pulling, its edge caught my lips and scratched them. Julia then grasped the pipes from me, and lunged toward Bryce, who was writhing with the beast embedded upon his chest.

With an effort she broke the pipes in half, and then thrust the jagged edge into the beast. It screamed out, snapping its claws at her. She kept stabbing the pipes into the beast. A fountain of blood spewed into her face, and the beast flailed and screamed. I realised that it wasn't the beast screaming, it was Bryce.

He collapsed onto the floor, shaking uncontrollably in his pool of blood. The beast that had been extracting itself from his body started shrinking, sinking back into his torso. Instinctively, I shook myself from my daze, and reached back for my bag. I took out the painting, and placed it in Bryce's hands.

The painting was back in his possession, and now once more it could no longer be passed on. As Bryce's convulsions eased into death, I knew that the painting could be destroyed. With the pipes shattered beyond use, embedded in the beast that sourced the gift, and the painting destroyed, the gateway passing between R'lyeh and Earth would be delayed, hopefully for a few more centuries. I don't know.

The wall painting had bubbled into a hard cake of blackness. The gateway appeared dead.

After scarring the painting with the pipe's shards, I tried the door and it opened without effort. Julia and I walked from the room into the reception area. The reception desk was no longer there. The entrance was now nothing but a dust caked, collapsing structure, empty of any life and furniture.

Julia and I looked at each other: Julia, soaked in Bryce's blood, me, with cut lip and sweat stained clothing. We would create interesting speculation about our appearance once we attempted to make our long way home.

SYDNEY, AUSTRALIA. AUGUST 2012

After midnight, at some ridiculous time between then and two in the morning, I heard a scratching at the door.

"Who could that be at this hour?" asked Julia. We were used to late nights, and were both sorting through a lot of things we'd been collecting over the years. As one grows older, the need for sleep comes at strange hours, so we occupy ourselves with personal stocktakes. Still, no one expects visitors at so late an hour.

I opened the door, and a couple in the entrance jumped slightly in surprise at my appearance.

"Come in, please come in," I said, delighted that we had company. "We have some guests," I said to Julia.

The couple stared at me, looking confused. They were a young couple; they looked like a homeless pair. He was a young man, probably no more than twenty-four years, and wearing hand-me-downs from a Salvation Army bin; she looked older than him, but I imagined that was the wear-and-tear of street life.

"Um, we didn't think anyone lived here," he piped up, "seeing this neighbourhood looked abandoned."

I chuckled, which seemed to make them uneasy. "Well, the neighbourhood has gone downhill since we moved in some twenty years ago." Julia made agreeing sounds. "We keep an open house though. We've never had any trouble here during that time."

I looked closely at them. "But the fact that you found us, gives us some comfort in the nature of mankind." It was Julia's turn to chuckle.

I invited them in, and they hesitantly entered. "We have some food here. We always have food available in case of unexpected visitors."

Julia gestured toward a table against the wall, which had coffee as well as platters of rissoles, sea food, pastries and condiments.

"We were just sorting through our collection," Julia said. "Would you like to have a look at them?"

The pair hesitated, but I took the girl's arm and led her to the display table. Her friend followed her, and she stepped back into his comfort zone.

"We found much of this after we moved into this place," I said. "In studying the objects, my wife and I have been able to collect a lot of matching sets. Some others, we were able create and duplicate a number of damaged artefacts."

Julia stepped forward. "Here look at this. My husband carved it from memory." She picked up an object and placed in in the young man's hands.

He stared at it, confused at first, then his eyes focused on the intricate carvings. He held the pan pipes, made from the bones of Bryce Williams, which I had hollowed out. The inscriptions represented the music that the young man would learn to play, as well as provide the invocations to attract the attentions of the Old Ones back to this place.

The young man brought the pipes closer to his eyes, looking fascinated.

I handed the girl a flat, shiny plate. "Here is a mirror that originates from ancient Turkey. The inscription on the back dates it before Christ. It's yours."

She looked at it, studying her reflection. She let out a brief gasp, and looked over her shoulder, staring at the wall quizzically. I turned and looked at Julia who smiled at me. I smiled gently at her ropey face, her age lines meshing parallel and diagonally across it.

DEAD LANGUAGE

STEVE KILBEY

1917

It was 1917 when she came to town
She came in on a train from Sydney
She talked like an Italian but her hair was like a
    Swede
She was dressed in white like a Madonna
Her skin was dark against the morning
Her eyes were different colours one blue one hazel
The sunset brought the smell of crushed orange
    blossom
The music about her was triumphant if you could
    indeed but hear it
She moved through the air like a cheetah
She carried a small carpet bag
She wore Roman-style sandals
A white hat on her yellow hair
The people in amazement whispering
For she was a medium and intrigue walked beside
    her
Yes she was a friend to the spirits having flown
The constant dialogue between the living and the
    dead
Yes with a foot in each world
The sighing of the souls
The chatter and the tiny shrieks

The long cold silences when you think you've lost 'em
When the frequency fades and there is only the
	sound of the rain
There was a storm
God there was always a storm
Day starts bright but at three o'clock the sky is
	darkening
A red sun therefore on a black sky
The sound of the trains in the distance or the moaning
	of some spook
Who can tell?
A forlorn bird cries out and we see it briefly white
	and rising
We have lost many here to the maw of the war
Which eats young men in some desolate place
Their souls go crying hastening down to Hades
The brave boys from Wollongong in the sweet
	smelling field of death
Their confused wraiths wandering this earth forever
	disconsolate
So far from the homes they knew and the girls they
	loved
So far from Crown Street pubs and bobbing boats in
	the harbour
The Illawarra lads maybe unknown and trampled
She spoke to them all
On this dark afternoon arriving in town
The green pines moving in the wind with a shudder
The beaches were empty
The picnic tables deserted
A coal ship on the horizon
The waters troubled and foaming
A mournful feeling a shiver a loss
A day from a dream
A night from a song maybe an elegy
She has come for a seance
She is here to speak for the beloved now dead

She is a sorceress she is a medium
In the hotel she takes a bath and is in reverie
All the voices the boys from the war
How can it be she's beautiful and ugly at once?
She's young and old as well
She's defying description lying dreaming in a bath
It was hard to get a fix on her as the changes rippled
    across her
The priest bang bang bang on the door
He's sunburnt and dressed in black
He's the servant of Christ and he burns with a zeal
He's missionary to grimy mechanics in factories
In the drizzle on a little footbridge he touches his
    Bible
In the lamplight and sea mist doing the Lord's
    bidding
Now he's banging on the door
It's Father Jim Ryan and we don't want Egyptians,
    healers or mediums here
As though from a great distance she hears his
    thumping and his voice
From a million miles away behind a door a man is
    bellowing
She stands up and flings open the door in her
    dressing gown
The priest must turn away from such a sight as this
And he looks away muttering an entreaty to some
    saint
Some saint who died an excruciating death who he
    thinks intercedes for him
And his hot blood is a little soothed, yet he still looks
    away
Why have you come here?
A lot of us have had enough
What devil's work is this?
Have you received Jesus the Christ?
She beckons him come to my room

No I cannot accompany you into this room Madam
She hovers on the threshold holding the door open
She smiles like Delilah
Her head on one side like Jezebel
Her hands like Bathsheba
Her eyes like the Magdalene
Her mouth was Eve
Into the room without thinking Father Jim in you go
Into the void of temptation
Like a big black crow inside a hurricane blown off course
We hear the rain beating on the hotel's tin roof
We feel evening condensing around the cemeteries
We hear the horses in the street snorting
We listen as the smoke escapes from a chimney
The yelping of a faraway dog underneath the sound
    of the rain
The waves on the shore
The concrete cracked and penetrated by weeds
Yes go into the room of the medium and take up a
    chair
She sits on the single bed brushing her medium hair
In the flickered light of the candles she exists
A haggard lioness a queen and a crone
The priest and the medium who sit in the room
Wollongong 1917 and everything is dark and fading
For the boys in Flanders it's a cold old morning and
    they are already dead
J. Smith from Thirroul
W. Brown of Unanderra
J. Brown of Unanderra
P. Wright of Corrimal
T. Woods of Figtree
H. Brooks of Mount Saint Thomas
They are one with the mud and barbed wire and blood
They are blown away and screaming through November
In the Australian night where the rain falls like a
    plague

And everything is damp and mouldering and
    dripping
And tuberculosis plies her job in the graveyards
In a house where in five years D H Lawrence will
    write *Kangaroo*
In a hospital where some twins are being pulled out
    of the warmth
In a field of blackberries on Kembla Grange
In a house by the beach where dinner is untouched
And a school for musicians who all went to the war
And the lizards down by the swollen rivers and
    creeks
And the frogs in the marshes and the magpies in the
    bush
And the children in their bedrooms and Christmas
    coming on
And the bad news keeps coming down the aching
    telegraphic wires
And a mosquito drunk on your blood squashed on a
    wall
Yes in you go Father Jim
And smell her perfume of fading flowers and
    cigarettes
The alluring microcosm of attraction
Like a huge planet's pull on the ichor that flows in
    her veins
Like a murmuring heart in an unfaithful chest the
    clock on the wall
The seconds tick by with a damp pulse
A faint smell of disinfectant
She sits on the bed waiting for you to speak
She sits on the bed with a smile you can't place
She looks at you unfocussed like the eye of a fish
In that moment you realise that she is blind
Blind as a bat
As blind as a post
Eyeless in her Gaza wherever she was from

Why, the woman can see nothing!
Nothing moving under her skies
The dead cry out to her somehow
Who can say how it is for her
She perceives their forms within her fog
She sources their shadows in the chatter
For tears cried in the soul
The dead are lost and don't know where to go
The dead not glorious and under the earth
In you go Father Jim and talk to this woman
Tell her about the Christ on the cross and his agony
Tell her about the whip and the nail and the thorn
    and the hammer
The dust on the way of sorrows
The cheers and the jeers of a crowd anywhere
The cooling breeze that blew across Galilee
She brushes her hair and she says *listen*
With no eyes I had to hear
And when I had heard then I had to listen
To tell apart all the voices that murmur to me
In you go Father rushing into the void of her
    sightless voice
A voice you've heard from the very beginning
A low husky voice like a musical instrument
The elongated vowels and truncated consonants
The voice of a Dakini
The voice of the mother of Lucifer
A voice that echoed of a Shub-Niggurath
The voice of a sister of the poor
A homeless voice a transient voice
The voice of an empress in waiting
Yes the evening as a woman
An evening falling down and never leaving
Stretching all-around the world and squeezing
An evening as deep as a chasm reaching the
    underworld

The woman was a rent in reality where shadows
    oozed forth
She was a hole in a screen that let the darkness in
She was the echo of lives that had in themselves
    become silent
If your brother speaks would you desire to hear him Father?
If your brother cries out from his grave at The Front
He fell right at the beginning
He's been so long away from home
With his medals and shrapnel and his mention in a
    telegram
His hands all full of soil no one to bury him they've all
    been killed
And then from out of her voice came another voice
It was the voice of the priest's brother
Like it was coming from a long way away
Like it was being whispered in your ear
Fragile and tremulous
Reedy and thin like an evaporating mist
James is that you? said the voice
What trick is this? asks the recoiling priest
James it's me it's Mick your only brother
I'm on a field by a beach and I've lost my legs in the fog
And it's winter Jim and I'm so bloody stinking cold
Father Jim you go and say *no*
You say *no that's how it is…where are the angels and the*
    saints?
The medium offers up a harsh cackle and it's hard to
    tell if it's her or dead Mick laughing
Then silence
He's gone says the medium suddenly and matter-of-
    factly
He shouted out in the room
Well you bloody-well bring him back!
He entreated her but the threat was implied
She smiled her blind smile looking out at nothing
    that could be seen

Thunder crackled overhead dividing the warm
   stillness of her room
Were you injured in the war Father?
Her voice soft now full of sympathy
The priest stood momentarily puzzled
Yes I was hit but thank the Lord I survived
Her unfocussed gaze
What happened?
The priest frowned
I was hit I was talking to some boys and we was hit
The medium waits a long time until
And then…
The priest listened to the rain on the roof
And then…
Go on then Father Jim tell her what happened then
Reach into your memory and find the words which
   will not come
And then?
The priest returned to the room as though returning
   from a long trip
He looked at her blindness and her wet hair as she
   sat on her bed
Patiently waiting for his answer time seemed to
   elongate
Father Jim is that the rumbling of thunder over Port
   Kembla?
Or is it some obscene cannon spewing carnage in the
   mud of Flanders?
In a small voice he said *after I was wounded I came back
   here and took my vows*
The medium shook her head gently and a sad smile
   appeared on her face
You are the reason I am in this town tonight Father
What do you mean? asked the priest in a voice almost
   inaudible
What would you want with me?

I can see you and hear you…no one else can…you have
    passed on…
He says: *Are you bloody-well saying that I'm dead?*
You're lost Father and yes, you've been dead for nearly
    three years
These words hung in the room and slowly released
    their meaning
You bloody lying witch he whispered
He turned and left the room
The corridor was empty
The public salon was empty
Crown Street was empty and the gardens were
    empty
There were no ships upon the ocean delivering coal
The steelworks off in the distance was silent and no
    smoke came forth from its chimneys
No horses no bicycles no light in any window
It felt to him as if the world had come into him and
    he himself was not there at all
He cried out but his voice made no sound
The rain falling steadily did not ever touch him
The moon above he knew was not his moon
The hazy stars were not his anymore either
This air he did no longer breathe
No prayer seemed forthcoming
Walking in the sea mist
It swallowed him
And he was gone

ASLEEP BENEATH THE DRIPPING

JASON FISCHER

Cornelius Tesselaar had visited Australia twice before. The first time was three hundred and eighty seven years ago, when he sealed the dreaming dingo-god Karpangga into a deep tomb. The second time was two hundred and thirty years ago, when he sold the land above it to some long since dead functionary.

Now he was on a boat, rolling gently with the waves, many metres above the whole, drowned city. The giant Dutchman was shirtless where the rest of the crew went wrapped in sola-kling, and he did not care as the sun of this savage time tickled at his old leathery flesh.

He had set various instruments around him on the deck. A child's skull, still covered in wisps of blonde hair. A three-thousand-year-old noose from a tar-pit sacrifice, the rope still as strong as steel cable. A mummified foot with a dwarf lime tree grafted directly to the tibia and fibula, with one black fruit that even he dared not pluck.

Central to this occult diorama was the fossil of a perfectly preserved dragonfly, over two feet in length. The stone that encased it was hot enough to sear a normal man's fingertips clean off, and it hummed like a high-voltage cable, cracking and spitting as Cornelius interrogated it.

"It sleeps?"

Crack. Snap.

"Do the waters approach it?"

CRACK. The dragonfly stone shifted a full three inches, and rocked impatiently.

"You will answer me!" Cornelius said.

He placed a jade knife on the fossil, and lightly traced it across the wings of the dragonfly, which gave off a screech like a thousand fingernails on a blackboard; like the grinding of steel on steel; like the warring plates of the earth itself. He lifted the dagger, noting the pale ichor now lining the blade's edge.

All around him the ship's crew studiously ignored this scene. He'd conquered them months ago.

"Is the sandstone holding?"

Snap. Crack. Hum.

"Is there an aquifer nearby, some way for the water to seep into that cavern?"

Crack.

"If you lie to me on this, I will put a lizard in there with you," Cornelius said. "I will have it eat you with geological slowness. I will pass the Blade of Nothri through your skin one dozen times one dozen. Do not test me!"

BANG. The stone hopped a full inch from the deck. When Cornelius held the jade knife towards it, it retreated from him two quivering inches, before laying still.

"Good. It is important to be truthful with our friends, do you not agree?"

The stone lay silent. Cornelius draped a hessian cloth over it with a sigh. He could only press the old sage so far before it fell back into its reveries. He'd had other means of scrying for answers once, but had lost a lot of things to the centuries. Always his great work continued, but supplies were hard to come by in this broken age, even as the people grew low and base, and fell for the old tricks more easily than he'd ever seen.

Rising from the deck, Cornelius stretched up until he stood on tip-toes, stretched towards the sails and the kite-tree. He looked on the ruins of the old city, the skyscrapers hollow-eyed, the top span of the great bridge rising just above the waters now, like the arc of a water serpent. Cornelius Tesselaar looked upon the ruins of old Sydney, but the greatest tragedy for him was knowing that he might live to see these waters fall, would be back to tread the drying earth with even ruder instruments on some distant dawn.

A warden checking in on a troublesome prisoner.

"You idiots are hardly worth saving," he told a passing crew member, who nodded in agreement, running off on some fictitious errand. The enormous Dutchman could not help himself, and laughed at the man's fear, a great, rolling belly laugh that echoed against the ruins of that drowned city.

He'd bound them into his service, this miserable gaggle of cultists. They'd been cannibals, haunting the shrunken islands he would always think of as the Dutch East Indies. Cornelius did not begrudge them the eating of man-flesh—he'd understood hunger himself once. What brought him to hunt them was their master, an ancient Crusader only known as the Knight of Ma'aara.

The Knight had been the first to turn to cannibalism during that ancient siege, and he'd been lured into immortality by Yidhra, that original epicurean of man-flesh. Like most of the hidden things of this time, the Knight of Ma'aara had come to a sad ending long before Cornelius Tesselaar unearthed his lair. Bloated and immobile, the creature relied on his little gang to kidnap his meals, guiding them through the mountains and raft-towns with his Ka, and gifting them with the hunger in return.

The Knight could do little as the big Dutchman carved out his heart, his curses and telepathic assaults failing against a far greater sorcery. When the cult tried to avenge their master, he'd tickled that thousand year old heart with the Blade of Nothri, driving these servants to their knees, howling with pain and fear.

Cornelius marched them out of the mountains, past the raft-towns and putrid slums, and onto his yacht, the *Toby Jangles*. In the final days of the oil age he'd kept wealth all over the world, the gains of a career spanning centuries, but the banks fell when the wars began, and he could rescue only some of his treasure caches before the oceans drowned everything else. He had little to his name now but the boat, and a crew of terrified slaves to run it.

He locked the Knight's heart in a reliquary of his own making, a puzzle box with three outer shells. Sketching a burning symbol onto the box's lid with his thumbnail, and he invited the cultists to take back their master's heart.

They could not approach the box without retching and howling in pain. One made it close enough to bring down a sledge hammer on the flimsy-looking box, but the maul merely bounced away, not even marking it.

"You are mine now, and I own you," Cornelius told the wretched group. "Defy me, and I will tickle your master's heart with my little knife."

He did this at least once a week, regardless of whether they behaved or not. When one cultist approached him with a garrotte, he froze the man in place with a word, and made him watch as he shaved off a thin slice of the Knight's heart with the jade edge.

He made the survivors watch as he slathered the slice of heart with mustard and put it into a sandwich. He ate it with great gusto, the men and women howling as his teeth ground into that ancient meat, finally tearing through it.

"You people are right. This really is delicious," Cornelius said.

He charted a course around the south-east of the new continent, past New Melbourne and all the way over to the southern inlet. Cornelius had read accounts of the old things in the ranges above dead Adelaide, but the waters did not reach their nests, and they slumbered on under the crack and grind of moving plates, the creep of small beasts, and the endless baking heat.

The *Toby Jangles* was incredibly old, with sorcery plugging dozens of leaks, but it was a comfortable home for Cornelius, and a way to continue his never-ending task. The kite-tree was near new, as was the osmotic engine, and while he did not have the speed and reach of a zeppelin, it was enough for him to crisscross the world, sniffing, watching, waiting for monstrosities to stir.

"These people will never know the joys of business class," he told the dragonfly god, his deep voice booming around his private cabin. "Fifteen hours around the globe!"

Crack. Slide. The fossil ground against the table, backing away from him. He tapped the hilt of the jade knife against the creature's thorax.

"Behave yourself."

Snap. Hum.

"I fear this new inland sea of Australia," Cornelius said. "This land dried out a long time ago, and my masters sacrificed greatly to keep the interior miserable and dry."

Crack. Craack.

"You see them, don't you? You remember those soggy old things, splashing about in the centre, scrabbling for power when great Cthulhu first slumbered?"

Skitter. Slide.

"They were forced out. Driven to the centre when the waters fell. They could not think to shed gills for lungs, and so they dug deep into the bedrock, thinking to hide in the aquifers, but they drove them out, my masters! Sent them deeper still, into the mantle itself."

Hum.

"How much we have lost! If only I had a fraction of my masters' power, I could end this menace for good, hide *myself* in a deep hole for an age or two. But no, I must trudge about and keep the lamps lit."

The fossil was still. Squinting at it, Cornelius finally set the knife to his thumb, shedding a thin trickle of blood, a flow that was as much grey as red.

"Drink up," he said, smearing the blood around the fossil's face. "I will not have you retreat into reverie. Give me the answers that I seek, and I will feed you."

Skitter! Snap! Hum! The fossil slid around the table, jerking about a full four inches in each direction.

"You greedy old thing! Extortion! I can give you half the crew, and you're welcome to them."

Bang. BANG! The fossil hopped in place, steam rising from it. Cornelius pressed his palms down, heedless of the searing heat, holding it in place and letting it char the table.

"Fine. I shall give you one seventy-seventh of my soul. A bargain, and you know it."

The stone stilled. Cornelius made the necessary arrangements, and felt the weight of a dozen decades slip from him. He could still see the rich patina of his life, but the memories felt dull now, both the joy and the terror now tasteless to him. He had nothing but apathy for his fifth wife now, a witch who'd enchanted him in Mongolia, and the loss of their righteous feuding saddened him.

"Speak now, you rotten old thief. Tell me of Cro-Moloch, the Dreamer in Ink, the Tiddalik and his brothers. Do they still slumber?"

Slide.

"Does the water reach them?"

Suddenly he had the sensation of being drawn into the slab of stone, the dragonfly seizing him within its grip, and he was down in the waters beneath the yacht, scratching at the silty floor of the ocean, digging through clay and then rock and then reaching the aquifer, the fresh water slowly turning to silt, and then they were beneath all of this, the crushing weight of an entire continent pushing down on them.

Cornelius knew that if the godling could find a way to abandon him here, his essence would moulder in the dark for an eternity, the pressure changing him into a most dangerous diamond. Even as he fought to free himself, he saw what the dragonfly had brought him to see. A great cavern, suspended between surface and magma, and it held every twisted beast, every devil frog and god-snake from his masters' halting records, mile upon mile of coil and fin and fang. Eyes larger than his boat, sheltered beneath nictitating membranes long crusted with stone.

From the ceiling of the cavern, a drip fell, then another. Water fell onto a dry scale, across the suckers of a tentacle, and into the shell of a towering crab thing.

Small drips, much like in the hull of his boat, but try as he might his sorceries could not bind the cracks in the ceiling. It may have been his imagination, but the water seemed to come faster after he tried this.

"Release me now," he commanded the dragonfly. "I must prevent this!"

N'GHA HLIRGH EE EBUNMA GEB KN'A, the creature told him.

"We will die together then, when these things awaken!"

The dragonfly held him tighter, wings flickering. It buzzed and crackled with what passed for laughter.

"Fine. Another seventy-seventh of my soul, and may you choke upon it!"

The dragonfly assented, and they sprang back towards the surface as if a bow string released them, back through aquifer and mantle and ocean and once more into his cabin on the *Toby Jangles*. He sat there in stark panic, his sluggish heart remembering the tremors of youth. He may have almost reached the pulse-rate of a sleeping man, and this pace sickened him.

Crack. Shift.

"You know I may not renege on a deal. I certainly cannot lie."

Cornelius Tesselaar gifted the old sage another fraction of his soul, losing most of the 1980s and part of the Napoleonic campaign. He then drew the Blade of Nothri and sank it deep into the fossil, twisting it around in the stone like he was carving up a bird, chasing the fossil from corner to corner, fending off its feeble attempts to attack his mind.

"Oh, please! I never lied to you," Cornelius scoffed, as he stabbed the greedy old thing one dozen times one dozen. On the one hundred and forty-fourth strike, the stone was merely an empty slab. He then swiftly broke it across his knee.

They brought the *Toby Jangles* through the throat of Augusta, past dozens of new towns where once had been wasteland and lonely highway. More arcologies, slums and greenhouses, and every other inch of the shoreline was a desalination plant or an osmotic power generator. Dredges worked the strait here, clearing the sea bed for ships with bigger bellies than his little boat.

There was a slate in the helm, a temperamental old thing that barely worked. Cornelius called up a chart of the inland sea, noting the towns and cities, the great bulge of ocean over old Lake Eyre, and then the northern strait through the Darwin Delta and back to Asia. He remembered where the dragonfly had taken him, the cavern that held Cro-Moloch and the others, and guided his finger unerringly to a spot on the map.

The very centre of the Inland Sea.

"What is this?" he asked the woman behind the wheel. A label and a dot with a trajectory, moving across the screen. The cultist leaned over nervously, poking at the slate with one finger.

"They have made a great floating city," another cultist gabbled. "They move it wherever they wish!"

"Well, how about that?" Cornelius mused. "Of all the things to do."

He noticed where this floating city was moving, and his eyes narrowed. An entire city, passing over a nest of sleeping gods. A ceiling that he could not seal against leaks, despite his centuries of skill in the sorcerous mysteries. Cornelius Tesselaar had hunted down enough cults to suspect that he was sniffing out another one.

"You must stay upon the boat," Cornelius boomed out. "If you slip down the gangplank or over the rails, I will know. If you seek to sabotage my vessel, I will know."

He held high the box containing their master's heart, and twitched his shirt to reveal the Blade of Nothri on his belt. The remaining cultists stood in a row on deck, hang-headed.

"Cheer up. If you behave, I shall bring back rum. All sailors enjoy it."

The *Toby Jangles* was fastened to a docking cradle, along with other pleasure craft and supply boats. All about them was the majestic city of Eyre, a Venice afloat, driven by building-sized sails, with enough kite-trees and osmotic drives to support a fleet of boats.

He walked down the gangplank and was met by a customs official. Cornelius offered false identity papers, and permitted the man to scan his retinae and swab his cheeks for DNA. He suffered through the pin-prick health exam. Some years back, he'd paid a criminal syndicate a fortune to have his official records updated, to show that he was a man of this century and not a quasi-immortal sorcerer. In his first lifetime his word and mark had sufficed, but trust was thin in this savage, new world.

He asked the way to an entertainment district, and soon he strolled through the marvellous city, admiring the sweeping metalwork, the glass spires, the plazas nestled in dozens of different layers. He'd seen the Hanging Gardens once in an esoteric vision, and felt that this was a tropical equivalent, with rainforest so thick that it formed its own ecosystem here, sending the patter of soft rain throughout the agricultural levels.

The place was a mash of style and themes, but compartment-alised enough for it all to work. He strolled through a replica Roman Forum, through a seaside 'town', past high-end hotels and boutiques. There was a section aping 1980s Amsterdam, and he felt a hollow twinge as that memory escaped him.

"Damned dragonfly," he mumbled.

There was sex and drugs of every stripe, and street-side orgies were permitted in certain parts of the city. Other parts were more staid, and he saw churches of every denomination, schools and universities, residential blocks and parks, even a zoo holding most of the animals that weren't extinct and clever simulacrums of those that were. Cornelius took in all the sights and smells. He ate a steak that was a reasonable facsimile of real flesh, and enjoyed the company of a man, a woman, and a machine that could be many other things. He paid to shoot a prisoner at the daily executions, and looked on the Parliamentary debates from the public gallery.

Always, always he watched the people, both with his eyes and with other hidden senses. Eyre was a wondrous place, but there was still the dark side of humanity here. Criminals preyed on the weak in dark corners, lovers fell to violent passions, and the elite performed their own violence with money and power, but none of this concerned Cornelius. It was no worse than a jungle, or how bacteria and viruses behaved. Nature was ferocious and beautiful.

There was a smell behind the life though, the whiff of rot wherever he turned. He found it in school and brothel, in homes and even the halls of power. The rot was within, a deep cancer set in the heart of every soul on board Eyre. There was a cult here, followers of Shub-Niggurath, and all fell under her feral influence, whether they knew it or not. The children were being taught the dark mathematics in secret. The gossip of neighbours had the weight of curse and hex behind it. The Black Goat of the Woods with a Thousand Young held supreme authority, and every act and transaction was done by her design. Cornelius dug deeper, slowly sifting through whispers and documents, through computer records that were guarded with lines of infernal code.

The group behind this all was a group that called themselves the Elders Twelve, who'd worked in patience on this plan since the landing of the First Fleet. Now, finally, within weeks the worship of the Old Ones would be out in the open, and the Elders would guide the city above those buried monsters, break the bedrock, and wake them with the waters of the Inland Sea. He heard their whispered plans, spied upon their maddening Lodge with a hidden eye. They meant to use this nest of beasts as a weapon, to gain mastery over the earth, and then to finally call up Cthulhu from his sodden house beneath the waves.

This was a cult in the thousands, carefully cultivated. Cornelius was far too late to stop them on his own. It was all he could do to stay hidden from the Elders Twelve, who soon suspected they had an intruder. Soldiers and police officers hunted high and low for him, dread marks set upon their temples and within their eyes. Cornelius watched as even children were deputised into searching for him, their games abandoned, little hands curled into claws.

Even as they began to corner him in the depths of the city-ship, Cornelius Tesselaar laid out the tools of his art around him. The Tree of Lagash, the bog-noose, the Blade of Nothri, and all the rings, vials, and ephemera he had left to him.

He then took the heart of the Knight of Ma'aara, and rolled it into the advancing cultists, even as he dropped the barriers keeping the Knight's children trapped on the *Toby Jangles*. They came pouring through the hallways of Eyre, and when he freed them from his bonds they shed the human skins he'd imprisoned them in. He watched them walk as Komodo dragons, tearing the other cultists in half, ripping through steel and concrete as they fought to reach their master's heart.

The Elders fell into a great panic, attempting to destroy the Knight's heart, but they only enraged his children, who grew in size until they were school buses with teeth, tearing and ripping the floating city apart in their frenzy.

"Stop them!" the head Elder cried. He was the Prime Minister of Australia, the latest of thousands of skins he'd worn over time. "We will grant you great wealth, our secrets, whatever you desire!"

"You have nothing I want," Cornelius scoffed. The ones who'd attacked him lay in pieces, the Blade of Nothri keeping those of Shub-Niggurath at bay. The cultists watched him hungrily, waiting for him to tire, even as they flinched at every noise, the Komodo beasts digging their way towards them.

Cornelius plucked the fruit from the Tree of Lagash, and both root and mummified foot shrivelled into dust. The black rind unravelled on its own, revealing flesh of a violet hue, and it grew, it split, it sprayed out a juice that ate through everything as he cast it across the floor.

As it broke apart, it ate through the hull. It sent out more tendrils, and the new plants grew up through cultist and ship alike, dropping more of the black fruit. The Komodo beasts broke through, shrieking as the wicked juice ate at their flesh, dissolving their master's heart. Cornelius laughed and laughed, even as he drove the Blade of Nothri deep into his own wicked heart.

He awoke with a gasp. The big Dutchman lay on the shoreline, the waves grinding him into the red sands of the interior. His skin was new, already burnt red by the vicious sunlight, his body otherwise unharmed by the destruction of Eyre. Some small fragment of his flesh must have made it loose from the sinking city, enough to wash ashore, to grow a new body.

"More is the pity," he groaned, new vocal chords twingeing from the effort. Death was not an easy thing for him to set aside. It seemed his great work would continue, through this age and perhaps another, until his old masters were finally finished with him.

A tendril brushed up against his feet. A fragment of the Tree of Lagash, killed off by the salt water. Only one other time had someone dared to pluck a fruit from it, and the Sahara desert was the result. He felt relieved that the Inland Sea had contained the damage, even as he cursed his own rotten luck.

Tens of thousands dead to save the world, and he would do it again and again, without hesitation. He would level every shining city if mass murder would keep the greater dark at bay.

Eventually Cornelius Tesselaar found his feet. He stood nude, penniless, without even the *Toby Jangles* to call home.

"I do not like Australia," he said to the blue sky.

SUPERSYMMETRY BLUES

DAVID CONYERS

AMDO, TIBET

"**T**his is how the world ends," shouted the muscular CIA field agent over the drone of the U.S. Marine V-22 Osprey, flying low and fast over the icy tundra of the Tibetan Plateau. The cold air churned fast in the turbulent, propeller-driven winds, chilling exposed skin between gloved hands and shirt cuffs, between collared necks and scarves. Conversation was near impossible.

Only it wasn't just snow, rock, grass and icy-rivers below — which would have been a normal scene in Central Asia — it was a sight far worse. NSA Agent Harrison Peel stared with disbelief at the blood-splattered landscape of butchered cows, elephants, whales, camels, fish, and now octopi. The dead were scattered randomly, like they had just fallen out of the sky in their millions and broken open like rotten pumpkins. Decaying despite the sub-zero temperatures, the corpses wafted a stench the likes of which Peel had not imagined possible for this world to produce.

"This is how it begins."

Peel nodded, stared through his sunglasses at his CIA companion. Both men were dressed in thick leather coats, laced boots, jumpers, beanies and thermals under their shirts and pants. They slung weighty M16A2 rifles and wore flak vests and combat webbing with extra ammo clips and frag grenades. Cables kept them secure as they lent outwards from the lowered loading ramp, allowing them a wide view to study the landscape passing underneath the tiltrotor aircraft. Three hours of non-stop flying since lift-off from the U.S. Marine base hastily erected on this outlying province now that the Chinese Government had collapsed into a state of civil war, and nowhere was free of dead animals.

"It's not just here that is turning weird, buddy," shouted the American. "You wouldn't believe half of what I could tell you."

"I believe you, but what is it you think I can do?" Peel shouted back, even though less than a metre separated them. He remembered the weirdness of the last few months in Peru, and later the South Pacific, and wondered if events then were connected to events now. He had a horrible feeling his instincts were on the mark.

The CIA operative went by the alias of Jordan, the only meaningful name Peel knew him by and the only consistent cover he used. Today he was Colonel Jerimiah Isaacs of MCIA, the Marine Corps Intelligence Activity. But that cover was as false as any sense they could make from the scene witnessed below.

"You have a knack, Peel."

"A knack for what?"

"Interpreting."

Peel looked away, not liking where this conversation was headed. On the horizon, a storm was brewing. Dark clouds were composed not of water vapour, but sand and rock, and probably more dead or dying animals ready to be dumped on this unforgiving landscape.

"I'm not doing it."

"The hell you're not, Peel! You're the only man on the face of the earth I know who has any chance of working out what all this means."

Peel wanted to tell Jordan to go fuck himself, but held his tongue. There was no point arguing, not against the flood of unexplained phenomena gripping the world everywhere. It was inevitable that he would accept this assignment, because there were no more options left.

"You brought me all the way from Washington, DC to fly me around this graveyard? Why?"

"I wanted you understand how big this is. This isn't like Venezuela or Peru, or even Mexico," Jordan listed the various locales of their past operations together. "This has kicked up to a whole new level. Look at that." He pointed to the approaching field of whales, split open to reveal their red meat and white blubber like prime cuts in a butcher's shop. Between the scent of blood and rot, there lingered the salty odour of the ocean.

"What about it?"

"What about it? Can't you see?"

"No, Jordan!" Peel shouted, although he had his suspicions as to what Jordan referred.

"The science boys are telling me there are more dead whales down there than can possibly live in all the oceans, ever!"

Peel wanted to argue. He wanted to go home, watch soccer and drink beer, and forget that the world had problems. But the world was about to fall apart. Hiding away wouldn't save him, or anyone.

"Peel, I need you to compile an intelligence report for good ol' U.S. of A. You have *carte blanche*. Uncle Sam is paying, and you can travel anywhere in the world to document whatever you want—"

"Why?"

"Why? Because if there is a pattern, you'll see it. You'll be able to tell us—me—what's going down here. What's going down everywhere!"

Peel said nothing.

"Okay, you stubborn Aussie bastard, let me show you something worse." He spoke into his headset, instructed the Marine pilot to head to a location called 'Site 18F'. "You're going to like this," he grinned.

The Osprey turned on its axis and flew north, deeper into the tundra and further from the remnants of civilisation. Peel spied snow-capped mountains on the horizon looking uncannily like they had given up their solidity and were ready to crumble into dust and powdery snow. Perhaps they were the source of the dust storms.

Soon the landscape changed, from still and silent dead to the recently resurrected. He wasn't certain what was more bizarre; the scene before him or his ready acceptance of what his eyes witnessed. Here dead monks, yaks, shepherds, camels, sheep, horses and herders ran, rolled, lumbered or crawled depending on the state of their gaping wounds or missing limbs. The smell was worse here, like faecal material had been poured into his nostrils. The screams were like chalk scraped on a blackboard and amplified by a rock-concert sound system. There were hundreds of thousands of living corpses below.

"Jordan. You got it wrong. I don't like this at all."

"What do you see?"

"What I've already seen: enough—you bastard."

"And what is that? Tell me, and we can leave."

"The butchered cows, camels and horses were the same. They were all male."

Jordan grinned. "See. I knew you were the right man for the job." He fired a short burst from M16A2, which took down a couple of the shambling, half-decayed monks. They fell, but they didn't die. Now they crawled, and they kept screaming. "What does it mean?"

"Mate, I have no idea. Not yet."

"See, I knew you'd come 'round."

They took off before the noise and stench and visual parody of life made them do something stupid, like letting go of their straps and falling into the chaos. Peel had thought about ending it all. It was only Jordan's instructions to the pilot that stopped him from performing a stupid act. No words had ever been as sweet to Peel's ears. In response the tiltrotor turned again, rose high into the sky and headed south.

"Are we doing this together?" Peel shouted through short, sharp breaths. The man reflected in Jordan's sunglasses looked pale and gaunt, like he had given up on life and, well, just about everything else too.

"No, Peel." Jordan wiped sweat from his forehead with a shaking hand. "As much as it would be fun to reminisce on old times, I unfortunately have my own date with the end of the world."

"I guess I'll see you on the other side then."

"I guess you will."

CERN, GENEVA, SWITZERLAND

One hundred metres underground, Peel walked the circular concrete tunnel only a few metres in diameter but much, much longer. It seemed to stretch forever, but that was an illusion. Still, twenty-seven kilometres was a hefty hike and like Möbius the tunnel would serve only to return them to where they started should they walk for long enough.

In the centre of the tunnel ran the metal tube of the Large Hadron Collider, the poster child of the prestigious CERN research facility. It seemed to wobble and pulsate, but Peel was certain he was imagining that. He did know that inside the tube, subatomic particles accelerated to near light-speed smashed into each other, annihilating their structure to produce a flurry of tinier particles, micro black holes and energy quanta in hope of recreating the first moments of the Big Bang.

While he walked, Peel sensed a humming in the ground beneath his feet. He hoped he imagined the more distant sounds, similar to the guttural chants of the monks he had left behind in Tibet, but these noises suggested vocalisation from mouths of far more primordial creatures.

The scientist who accompanied Peel had said very little, but she stared often. Dr. Tsukino Chizuko was tall for a Japanese woman, slim, with a fine mouth that never properly closed, and large eyes making her look much younger than the mid-thirties Peel guessed her to be. She walked daintily like a crane, with her hands constantly behind her back and fingers interlaced.

"What is bothering you?" Her gaze barely left his. She rarely blinked.

"What's bothering me?" he replied, wondering if she too heard the near subliminal chanting, but afraid to ask in case she did not. "CERN is the one with the anomaly. What's bothering you?"

Her smile was like a line. Her head turned slightly on her long, thin neck. "We always have anomalies. This is theoretical physics we are talking about, Mr Peel. We're trying to unlock the secrets of how the universe works."

Peel nodded, grinned. "So why is Pi suddenly a problem?"

She twisted her head. Her eyes grew larger. "You know what Pi is?"

"Of course. It's basic mathematics." He looked at her wondering why she was asking such questions. "Pi is the ratio of a circle's circumference to its diameter. It's one of the universe's physical constants."

"A fundamental one at that. So it shouldn't be increasing."

"Increasing?" So that was what all the chatter at CERN was about. He sensed a breeze, but when he looked to Chizuko her hair wasn't moving and neither were her clothes. There was no movement in the air at all. His senses were all out of alignment with reality. "I remember Pi from high school, it's 3.14159, from memory."

"A good estimate. Pi is an irrational number so its decimal places go on forever. Did you know we've calculated Pi to thirteen point three trillion digits?"

"Impressive. But it's changing, you say?"

Flushed now, she rushed her next words. "It shouldn't be changing at all—"

"But it is..." Peel paused to gather his thoughts. "That's why I'm here, Chizuko. I want to understand."

"For your intelligence report?"

"Yes, for my report."

She wouldn't look away. Her eyes stared into his, like she could see what kind of man he was and hadn't yet made up her mind if she liked or detested what she saw. He found her moments of silence unsettling, and so willed her to talk again.

"If it keeps changing won't that affect everything?" he eventually said, to fill in the silence. "I mean everything: geometry, engines, biological processes, relativity, planetary orbits and quantum mechanics. Don't all have some kind of basis in Pi being a constant number?"

"The change is small right now. The margin of error is insignificant for day-to-day activities, but it's getting bigger and the mathematics we are testing it with are becoming nonsensical.

Also, the increase rate is variable, depending on your location. Beyond the Solar System, it's not changing at all. The epicentre seems to be somewhere on the surface of the South Pacific." She saw his interest pique at that last reference. "Is that odd to you?"

He shrugged. He knew recent truths concerning the South Pacific he never wanted to relive ever again, and the rest of the world should know nothing about. So it did not surprise him that Pi had altered the most amongst the weirdly dimensioned ruins he'd encountered in the cold, churning oceans of the Pacific.

"Do you know anything about the square root of two, Mr Peel?"

He turned to her, remembering where he was, that she was real and the subliminal chanting was his imagination. "Yes, again from high school."

"It is another irrational number. It is 1.414213. It *should* be irrational."

The humming, or chanting, Peel was certain he could hear it now. He was certain that it was real. Chizuko didn't seem to notice.

"What do you mean?"

"What I mean, Mr Peel, is that the square root of two is decreasing at the same rate as pi is increasing. What do you make of that?"

Now it was his turn to stare, as he finally understood why she bothered him. Her long moments of reflection; the terror that lurked just beneath the skin, crawling to get free but held under control nonetheless, because to lose one's mind was to lose all options. No one else at CERN had made the connection relating Pi and the square root of two, but she had. Dr Tsukino Chizuko made uncanny connections the same way he did.

She was just like him.

"You want to help me?" he asked.

"Help you to do what, Mr Peel?"

"I've got a sizeable operational budget to compile this report. I've even got a government aircraft at my disposal, to take me anywhere in the world I need to go."

"Are you asking me on a date?"

He nodded. His tongue licked the inside of his teeth, sensing the tension in his jaw. He wished for a moment's peace he hadn't had in years. "Perhaps this is a date, Chizuko; you and me at the end of the world. Do you want to understand why it's going to end the way it is?"

She said nothing. Her mind was processing again, seeking answers, just like he would.

He considered if he was trying to convince her, or himself, that there was any point to what they were doing. "If you do want to team up, I might be able to offer you front row seats."

MAUNA KEA, HAWAII, UNITED STATES OF AMERICA

The air at 4,200 metres was crisp, dry and cool. The winds were harsh, though, blown in from the gathering clouds alive with lightning and the crackle of thunder. Everywhere in the world, the weather was getting wilder. The terrain here was rocky and desolate, like a desert, but gathered up upon a peak. Peel waited for rain, but none came.

From atop Mauna Kea, four kilometres above the ocean and ten kilometres above the ocean floor, Peel could see the vast Pacific stretching out to the horizon in all directions. In contradiction to the skies, the seas were calm like they had transformed into glass.

Peel closed the door to the Mazda sedan he and Chizuko had hired at Kona International Airport. It had been chaotic in the terminal. People rushing about trying to enter the state or get away from it permanently, as if sensing there was something unnatural about being on an island in a vast ocean. Many travellers were arrested for anti-social behaviour, a contradiction to customs who rushed arrivals through with barely a glance at their luggage or histories.

Chizuko had said little on their flight from Europe to continental United States and onwards into the Pacific. Most of their time together was spent digesting the numerous news reports from around the world, trying to make sense of them. It had been her suggestion that they come to Hawaii.

Now at their destination, she glided from the passenger side and smiled at Peel across the roof of the car. He sensed relief now that there were no crowds to bother her.

"This is the Gemini Observatory," Chizuko pointed to the large, metallic, domed building on the peak of the mountain, the distant lightning reflecting as flashes off its shiny walls. She walked with speed towards the complex and Peel followed. "It consists of two 8.19 metre telescopes, this one here and another in Chile. Together they provide almost complete coverage of both the northern and southern skies, the largest and most advanced optical infrared telescopes in the world."

"You think they might bring us answers?"

"They already have. I have a colleague here who can help."

They were quickly welcomed inside, taken into a room lined with computer monitors and server stacks processing the arrays of big data pouring out of the skies. Chizuko introduced Peel to Professor Jasvinder Sharma, an elderly Indian woman with a pronounced mid-western American accent. She wore a traditional sari yet the music she had been listening to when they first entered was David Bowie from his Trent Reznor influenced days; industrial with heavy beats. Sharma was as contradictory as the world outside was becoming.

"Professor Sharma was my lecturer during my University of Arizona days."

"Namaste." The short, plump woman pressed her hands together and gave a slight bow.

"Namaste, Professor." Peel reciprocated the gesture.

"Please call me Jasvinder. Titles are for published papers."

A sharp lightning flash interrupted. The interior lights dimmed and for a moment they were shrouded in darkness. Then the lights flickered on again.

"I'm sorry to drag you all the way to Mauna Kea, Major Peel?"

He raised an eyebrow at the use of his former military title. "You've done your homework."

"You were with the Australian Army. The internet is a wonderful research tool. I'm sure you've done all you can to research me, too."

He nodded, smiling.

"You've found nothing startling, I hope."

"Impressive is the word I'd use," he said, noting that Professor Sharma had published several journal articles on dark matter, galactic super-mergers, and postulations on how the singularities of super-massive black holes could affect the supersymmetry of fundamental particles.

"Come with me. I would have emailed you the files, but they refuse to."

Peel raised an eyebrow. "Refuse to...what?"

"Refuse to, Major, as I said."

Peel and Chizuko followed the professor to a computer console. She offered them chairs. They sat in a half circle around the monitor and watched the video files she was loading. Static lines ran across the screen and occasionally flickered with white noise. "Hopefully we'll get a long enough viewing to see the detail before the servers go down again."

The video played. The scene was of Jupiter, the huge gas giant seen up close with its ochre and earthy-coloured bands, the gigantic red storm-eye prominent, which Peel knew to be large enough to fit the Earth in several times over.

"This image was captured from the *Juno* orbiter. One of the last images we received before it went off line. But the anomaly I'm about to show you was first picked up by an astronaut on the International Space Station, Anatoly Bogdanov."

The bands of clouds and swirling storms moved at a discernible rate, suggesting that the video had been sped up considerably. "What are we looking at?" Peel asked. "What do we have to thank Mr Bogdanov for?"

"There." Chizuko's thin, bony fingers pointed to a moon in orbit around the gas giant. "That's Europa, right? But..."

"Very good, Chizuko," beamed Sharma. "I always said you should have been an astrophysicist, studying the super-large instead of the incredibly small."

Peel gritted his teeth and clenched his fists. The storm outside was gathering in intensity and he couldn't remember when he had last seen the sun. It began to rain, but the rain sounded more like tiny rocks pelleting against the metal dome.

He looked again at the video. He knew some details of the peculiarities of Jupiter from a previous mission in Mexico. Europa was one of the Solar System's largest moons, covered in a thick layer of ice supposedly hidden in an ocean two hundred kilometres deep. It was speculated that the brown crisscross markings on the surface were indicators of microbial life beneath the icy shell.

"What about it?" Peel asked.

"It's leaving the Solar System, isn't it?" Chizuko asked.

"What?" Peel grimaced.

She pointed to the tiny dot. "You can see it in its motion."

"It just took off," said Sharma with a shudder, "broke orbit a week ago. It's accelerating into deep space towards the Pleiades Star Cluster."

"How?" Chizuko said loudly.

"I sense you are shocked, my dear. But you are looking for anomalies and that is why you came to me. I think this is the mother of all anomalies. Europa is way beyond the orbit of Neptune by now. It will be far beyond the Oort Cloud by the week's end if it keeps up its acceleration."

Peel nodded. He didn't want to think about the implications of this development. It was like whoever lived there—and he was certain something did, and had done so for millions, if not billions of years—now they were running. They knew about Pi, the storms, the living dead and the naked singularity phenomena rising in the heart of the South Pacific. A dark, rotten catacomb Peel knew only as R'leyh was the catalyst here. He had been there, and had barely survived. He had seen only a glimpse, and that was enough. But now R'lyeh was rising again. Everyone and everything in the Solar System, it seemed, was afraid of it.

"The energy alone," Chizuko spoke fast, taking shallow breaths with each word. "The energy required to move that fast, to accelerate…iIt's impossible."

Jasvinder Sharma nodded, took Chizuko's hands gently in her own. "I'm sorry, my dear, but there is more."

"And what is that?" Peel asked, trying to keep up with two

scientists who understood cosmology and quantum-ology in far more detail than he ever could.

"Io, the closest of Jupiter's Galilean moons, is disintegrating." Sharma played another video, this one of the orange-yellowish, mountainous satellite pocked with sulfur-spewing volcanoes. Soon the video revealed that the volcanoes were gone and so were the mountains. The surface became smooth, black rock. Sharma sped up the video. Io seemed to be shrinking. "It's giving up its mass. I've done the calculations, Chizuko. At the rate Io is shrinking, converting that mass into pure energy, well, it equals the energy Europa is requiring to accelerate away."

Subconsciously, Peel whispered his thoughts: "One is sacrificed so the other can live."

"What was that?" asked Chizuko, unblinking, staring at him, through him like the layers of his soul were shedding off and folding away into nothingness. Jasvinder stared too, just as lost as her former pupil.

"Nothing!" said Peel.

"Nothing?" Jasvinder asked with a raised eyebrow, mimicking him from earlier outside.

"Nothing," said Peel again, adamantly. "I've got nothing."

CANBERRA, AUSTRALIAN CAPITAL TERRITORY, AUSTRALIA

Peel, in his crisp, new military fatigues, watched from the front passenger seat of the Army Bushmaster. The driver, Sergeant Emerson Ash, crawled through the outer suburbs of Australia's capital. Police cars, fire trucks and ambulances parked everywhere and in random locations had their warning lights flashing. Uniformed first assist personnel and civilians wandered the streets, some to gawk, some just to get away and some to get in the way. Peel knew many would be searching for lost loved ones, for many were missing.

Chizuko in the closest of the back passenger seats was shivering from the cold and had crossed her arms against her body. She couldn't take her eyes off the scene before them.

Every now and then they passed perfect half spheres of earth, rock and tree roots, transplanted as random piles in gardens, bushland, through power lines and in houses.

"What do you make of all this, Major?" asked Ash, carefully navigating stunned men, women and children staggering and shambling on the road ahead.

Peel respected and trusted Ash, and so when the Sergeant called Peel with a problem that he couldn't fix, Peel and Chizuko had flown direct to Australia's capital. Although both men were former Australian Army, they had not met until their post-military careers during a special operations assignment in Afghanistan. They'd worked together many times since, mostly on operations like this one, trying to understand the weird when the weird just couldn't be understood. At least they understood each other.

"I don't know." Peel turned to the scientist in their midst. "Let's ask our scientific expert. Do you have any idea, Chizuko?"

She shook her head.

Peel could guess what she was thinking, though, that these were spheres perfectly cut from the earth; or were they perfect? How much had Pi's corruption affected everything here?

Up ahead a crowd of several hundred civilians had gathered. More ambulances, fire trucks and police cars had gathered in a maelstrom of red and blue flashing lights. Peel's, Ash's and Chizuko's arrival now signalled military involvement.

"I'd suggest handguns, Major. Nothing more. Don't want to scare the civvies more than we already have."

"Sure." Peel returned the Steyr rifle he had been about to take. He checked that he had at least a few spare clips for his Glock 9mm.

The three climbed out of the Bushmaster. Sergeant Ash cleared a path through to whatever it was the crowd had gathered to see with a few authoritative commands. Peel noticed a middle-aged woman with her eyes wide, hand over her mouth. Another man next to her shed tears. Many young children watched with morbid curiosity.

At the epicentre of the crowd, Peel, Ash and Chizuko found

not another perfect half sphere, but a perfectly flat circle. Where there had been a house, several of the rooms and a significant portion of the roof had vanished. Fire officers were checking the interior in search of survivors. A woman in her mid-thirties wearing a dressing gown and slippers, being comforted by two paramedics, asked after her children and husband.

"The cut," Chizuko whispered in Peel's ear, "through the house. It's spherical too."

"Thanks," he whispered back, noticing now what she meant.

They approached the police patrol officers erecting temporary barriers around the circle. Introductions were made.

"We've got Department of Defence clearance. We're here to prepare an assessment of the situation," explained Ash. "What can you tell us?"

"Sir, these strange domes appeared overnight in the suburbs of Watson, Kenny and here in Hackett. We also have reports of more domes in the adjacent Majura Nature Reserve, but since no civilians have disappeared there we're not really investigating that location. Not enough resources."

"And the flat circles, what are they?" asked Chizuko.

The officer looked to Ash and Peel, and both men nodded that she was one of them.

"About equal number, ma'am. In the same places. Perfectly level too, I might add."

"Mind if I have a look?" she asked.

Peel, Ash and Chizuko moved into the circle. Much of the circular ground was smooth, flat whitish material not unlike stone. Peel noticed that the lines met at a perfect right angle.

He crouched down, touched the stone. It was smooth, like glass. He noticed holes in the stone, circular rings with white... plastic? Up close there was a smell, like a drain or sewage.

"Oh, fuck!" he exclaimed as he got to his feet. "You!" he pointed to a fire officer. "Bring that sledgehammer."

The fire officer leapt into action, "Yes sir!"

"Break that concrete for me, will you?" Peel pointed to the smooth, whitish surface.

The tall muscular fireman acted as instructed. One crack, two, three, and then the concrete gave way. A few more solid cracks and a sizable hole opened up.

"Stand back, please."

Peel lent in, looked down into the hole and shone his Maglite. He stared into a bathroom, only it was upside down. Towels, toilet rolls and brushes had fallen on a heap on the ground. A little girl, no more than six or seven was curled up in a corner, holding a teddy bear. Her wide eyes reflected in Peel's probing light.

"We're coming to get you," he told her, "you're safe now." He turned to Ash. "Give me a hand?"

"Certainly."

Peel climbed into the hole, went to the girl. "Are you okay?"

She nodded. The poor girl looked dehydrated, terrified and in a state of shock.

"Are you hurt?"

She shook her head.

"I reckon your mum is waiting for you up there. You want me to lift you up?"

She nodded, put out an arm indicating that he come and get her. She held onto her teddy bear as Peel lifted her up and out of the hole, into Chizuko's arms.

"Gabby?" Peel heard a hysterical woman, possibly the mother in the dressing gown he had seen earlier. "Oh, Gabby, it is you!"

Peel searched the remainder of inverted house. He found a boy of about nine huddled with his father in a bedroom. The boy had broken his leg during the inversion. The father was unconscious with a bloody head wound. Within half an hour they were both lifted to safety, and received medical assistance.

Out of the hole, Peel saw that he was covered in dust. Everything down there had been shaken up pretty badly.

An Australian Federal Police Commander approached Peel asking for details.

"The mounds, they are inversions in the landscape," explained Peel. "The house down there was flipped. I'd suggest you get everyone you can to check all the circular mounds and circles, dig through them and see who else is trapped in there."

"How did you know?" asked the police woman.

Peel looked to the Commander. He shrugged, not willing to explain again his history, as to why he knew so much. Instead he wished to be like everyone else in the world who was blind to these weird phenomena. Ignorance was easier on the soul. "Experience," he said by way of explanation.

Near nightfall, after Peel, Ash and Chizuko assisted in the rescue of trapped residents wherever they could be found, he discovered Chizuko standing motionless across the road from him. There was movement all around them; people attending the wounded, some digging, some directing and many running from one locale to the next, but Peel and Chizuko were motionless. She was taking the time to really look at him, and he found it difficult to hold her stare.

Eventually she came to him, put her arms around his neck and kissed him gently on the lips.

"What was that for?" He found that he liked her kiss, but her stand-offish attitude had confused him.

"I saw what you did today."

He looked away. "It was nothing. You did as much as I did."

"We all helped, sure, but that's not what I meant."

"Then what did you mean?"

"You're the only one. The only one I've met since the world turned strange who I believe might really see a path through this and find a way out to the other side. You *saw* what was wrong here."

She kissed him again. This time, Peel reciprocated.

MATAVERI INTERNATIONAL AIRPORT, ISLA DE PASCUA, CHILE

The rain cascading from the early morning skies drenched Peel and Chizuko. The raging winds forced them to constantly adjust their posture, leaning against the variable gushes. To the southwest, huge dark clouds rumbled and tore through the skies. Waves four or five metres high pounded off the coast. They all originated from the same location: R'lyeh.

"Jordan, this is Peel. Can you hear me?"

"Nn… Fzz… Ch…"

The encrypted satellite phone the CIA operative had provided to Peel just before the two went their separate ways claimed a connection, and it sounded like Jordan's voice on the end of the line, but words were impossible to guess, let alone hear properly.

"Can you reach him?" asked a drenched Chizuko looking like a poodle after a bath. "You've been trying for hours."

The air temperature was over thirty and tropically humid so they weren't cold, but they were both wet enough that they might as well have had buckets of water thrown over their heads. The dampness left her summer skirt clinging to her body, and Peel could see her slim shape. The curve of her breasts and legs reminded Peel that their relationship had not progressed beyond kissing and holding each other, and that he wanted to know her in a far more intimate way.

"No, I guess you're right. I can't reach him. I can't reach anyone anymore."

The line was as good as dead. Peel wondered where in the world, or in time and space Jordan was right now, and if they would ever meet again.

"What were you going to tell him anyway? It's not like we've achieved anything here. Or anywhere else."

"I don't know. Report in I guess. He wanted me to find something, anything that might explain all this."

"He was a friend?"

Peel nodded.

The sky lit. Thunder echoed across the airfield. Within seconds there were further flashes, streaks of lightning clipping the tops of the rocky hills at the centre of the island. The rain kept falling, unperturbed by nature's luminous and warped sideshow.

"I tried my parents earlier, from the airport. Harrison, I couldn't reach them."

Peel nodded, blinked away the raindrops splashing in his eyes. "Do you want to see if we can find them? I mean, really go and find them?"

She looked up, caught his stare and held it, hopeful for the first time since Canberra. "We could do that?"

He looked away. "Why not? We can't fly into that," he pointed to the storm of thick dark clouds alive with tiny distant flashes of lightning, edging noticeably closer to Easter Island with each passing minute. "I know that's the source of all that is wrong, but…"

"But we can't reach it?"

He nodded. Peel didn't like admitting defeat, but that was exactly what he was doing. "There is no way in hell Jamison will fly into that," he said referring to the pilot of their U.S. Army variant Gulfstream IV jetliner that had already taken them to one side of the world and back again. A crazy, deranged side of his personality wished to see what was really occurring nearer the pole of inaccessibility, determined to know one way or another if the alien island of R'lyeh really was rising again.

He remembered a quote from an ancient book he had owned once, long ago, called *The Masked Messenger*.

"In his house at R'lyeh, dead Cthulhu lies dreaming…"

He mouthed those words.

Was the naked singularity that was Cthulhu awake again? It had only been months since Peel and Jordan had thought they'd closed the unstable wormhole that was R'lyeh. But had they? Time was skewed. Space was skewed. Could a gateway to multiple, infinite other dimensions ever really be closed?

He looked out across the ocean. Even if they could make it, who could they report it to, and what could be done to stop it?

He knew the answers to those questions: No-one and nothing.

"Chizuko, we can fly to your home if you want. We've got nowhere else to go and Easter Island really isn't where I wanted to see out the last of my days on planet Earth."

She came up to him, snuggled into him so their wet bodies pressed against each other.

The satellite phone rang. Quickly Peel answered it. "Peel," he introduced himself.

"Harrison." It was Emerson Ash. "We're…late. They've… the…pole."

"The what? You're breaking up. Ash?"

"Sorry, sir?…Breaking up…Where…you?"

Peel tried for a different frequency. Soon the static lessened. "Is that better?"

"Yes, except for the wind."

"I'm sitting out a storm at Easter Island."

They kept their conversation brief because it could cut off at anytime. Ash was now in Antarctica. They discussed Ash's findings down there. They talked briefly on what he should do next.

"You take care down there, Emerson. I'm not sure how we'll go up here. There's something weird going on out here too, but; it's been a pleasure."

"Likewise, sir. It was good to catch up and have that beer. I'll see you on the other side."

Harrison laughed and that was it. Emerson Ash, like Jordan had been cut off from Peel forever.

Lieutenant Rick Jamison stumbled across the runway, struggling against the rain and wind. When he reached Peel and Chizuko he saluted. "Sir," he spoke rapidly. "We have no time. That storm will be on us in half an hour. If you want to get somewhere else, this is your last chance."

"Thank you, Lieutenant. Think you can make it to Okinawa Island?"

"Yes, sir, with the extra fuel tanks, that won't be a problem. I'll make arrangements with MCAS Futenma. But we need to leave now."

"Sure."

The three jogged to the Gulfstream, climbed on board and strapped in. Within two minutes they were taxiing, dripping in their seats. Within fifteen minutes they were in the air. The rain had not relented and the lightning lit up everything. When they were a couple of hundred metres above ground level, Jamison took them east along the southern coast of the triangular island. As they banked, Peel looked down. He had never seen the enigmatic statues of Easter Island, and hoped to see one now. He would never get this chance again.

Then he saw them, the fifteen standing Moai at Ahu Tongariki, stone eyes staring out across the ocean, towards R'lyeh. But there weren't fifteen. There were hundreds. Living, breathing, bellowing Moai.

The aliens were gigantic, semi-humanoid shapes, lumbering like all the bones in their bodies had been broken multiple times, then put back together in a haphazard, messy fashion. Their feet and hands were large, and were composed of neither fingers nor claws nor tentacles, but a combination of the three. Their mouths and eyes were disproportionally huge for their heads, which also supported scaly fins. These amphibious monsters were six or more metres tall. They were coming up out of the ground as if they had been buried there for a very long time, like lungfish, and were now shambling towards the ocean. About half dived in, swam southwest. The other half split open when they reached the water, gushed with biological geysers of their own internal organs, which the survivors fed upon.

The waves came up faster, rushed several hundred metres inland, consuming the monstrous entities, vanishing them from the surface world.

"What is it?" Chizuko asked, as she absentmindedly played with her seatbelt. She was on the wrong side of the aircraft to have witnessed what Peel had seen. The plane was shuddering continuously with the strong winds and violent weather. If she got out of her seat now to come across to Peel's side, she might be thrown across the cabin. "Harrison?"

"You don't want to know."

She forced a smile. "We got away just in time?"

He nodded.

He reached out across the aisle and took her hand, squeezed it tight.

He just hoped they could climb high enough, get out of the storm for smooth flying to what would likely be his last destination on planet Earth.

OKINAWA ISLAND, JAPAN

The southern islands of Japan were devoid of all people. Kettles had boiled out in houses. Irons were left on. Cars idled on the roads. Spot fires burnt in many houses. Road crashes and rolled cars were all too numerous, but no bodies. No birds in the sky. No cats or dogs. Piles of clothes lay everywhere accompanied with watches, mobile phones, wallets, purses, glasses, shoes and jewellery. The semi-tropical islands were left pristine and untouched. There were even the occasional moments of blue sky, and it didn't rain all that often here.

Peel released Jamison and the rest of the crew, sent them on their way to the United States so they could be with their families at the end, if they could reach them in time or reach them at all.

There was no news anymore. The internet, television stations, radio, it was all gone. No one was reporting on the end of the world anymore. When the Gulfstream was little more than a dot in the sky, Chizuko and Peel were left with only silence.

Chizuko cried for hours while they ate in a sushi restaurant where they were the only patrons. They drank Sake and Japanese beer. He lit candles for light and for comfort. They said very little. Peel knew Chizuko's parents had vanished with the rest of the island's inhabitants.

Later they walked down to a beach. She stripped off her dress and underwear and wandered into the ocean.

Peel watched, not sure what to do. He suspected that she would keep swimming, far out into the Pacific Ocean until she drowned. Instead she seemed to frolic, and eventually called him into the water.

He stripped and followed her.

They swam together, embraced, cuddled and kissed often. It began to rain.

"I want to feel real. I want to feel you," she whispered in his ear when they were close. So they made for the surf where they made love in the breaking waters. She cried and so did he.

There was a large ocean villa overlooking the ocean a few hundred metres distant. After their coupling, Chizuko walked towards it. Peel gathered up their clothes and followed her.

The villa was deserted like the rest of Okinawa. Peel hung out their rain-soaked clothes to dry, then followed her as they explored the house. The interior was modern, open with large windows, a spacious kitchen with lots of bench room and a substantial pantry, and a luxury bedroom with a spa and large shower. Peel cooked a meal of rice, chicken and vegetables with a spicy Asian sauce. Chizuko lay on the lounge, still unclothed, as she talked on mundane and normal topics. They had discovered a bubble of stability while the rest of the world decayed and disintegrated around them. They didn't want to spoil it just yet, but eventually the conversation had to turn to the end of the world.

"You regret anything?" she asked while they ate, outside on the balcony.

Peel finished his beer, opened another. "I regret everything."

"Everything?"

He shrugged. "Well, not everything. Not today. I'm glad I had today. It was like Lou Reed said: a 'Perfect Day'."

"Me too. One last perfect day."

Peel looked up, distracted by a shooting star. The skies were empty of clouds. The Milky Way was brilliant, easy to see when the only light to dampen the celestial glow came from the candles in their commandeered villa.

Then, one by one, the stars blinked out of existence, and within a few minutes they too had vanished. The only celestial lights were the quarter moon and a couple of planets.

"What...?"

He felt her fingers slip into his, holding him. "It's dark energy, Harrison. It's accelerating space around us, faster than the speed of light. Much, much faster."

"What, you mean...?"

"I'd say we're being quarantined from the rest of the universe."

He thought of the Europans; wondered if they had gotten away in time.

"I don't know how long this bubble we found will last." She kissed him. "You deserve this. This moment."

"*We* deserve this."

"No, Harrison. You do. I heard about you from Emerson. I know what you've done, in your career. How many lives you have saved. How many terrors you have halted, like in Canberra. You deserve better than this."

"I want you," he said staring into her eyes, finally able to match her intensity. "That would be enough for me."

"You can have me, for as long as it lasts."

He followed her into the bedroom, where they made love over and over again, until exhaustion finally drove them to sleep, because nothing else would.

In the morning Chizuko rolled over in the bed to snuggle into the powerful arms of Harrison Peel, but he was gone.

She searched the house. There was no sign of him. There was no sign that he had ever been there, not even his clothes. He existed only in her memories.

Outside, the weather was turning. The perfect bubble had popped.

She walked out onto the beach, stared at the gathering storm, felt the cold winds blowing in from the southeast on her arms and face. Far away, near the horizon, she saw what she suspected to be icebergs falling out of the sky, like meteorites.

A tsunami, the length of the ocean, was gathering on the horizon. It seemed to be kilometres high.

She thought of Peel as the ocean on the beach receded. She looked down, into the rocks where there had once been seawater hundreds of metres deep. The undersea was crawling, alive, festering with mouths and teeth and spines and claws and tentacles, a thousand or more monsters no human could ever possibly describe or imagine, as real and tangible as anything else in life.

She closed her eyes and felt the sand on her bare feet. She felt the breeze on her bare skin and hugged herself, imagining it was Harrison who held her now.

She hoped these sensations would be her last memories before the tsunami hit.

In the morning, Harrison rolled over in the bed to snuggle into the tender embrace of Tsukino Chizuko, but she was gone.

He searched the house. There was no sign of her. There was no sign that she had ever been there, not even her clothes on the drying rack. She existed only in his memories. He didn't know where the idea came from, but he felt certain they had slipped into different time streams. Hers was now an alternative version of the Earth to this one, and never again would their paths meet. Supersymmetry blues, indeed.

He dressed. Found his gun and the field kit he had taken with him from the Gulfstream before its departure from the island. The world outside seemed calm, normal. The blue skies hid if the stars were still gone when space around the Solar System had accelerated apart, separating them from the rest of the universe by billions of light years in a single evening.

The universe had protected itself from the naked singularity that was Cthulhu in R'lyeh, but in doing so had abandoned humanity to face the consequences of his return alone.

Peel walked out onto the beach. Although the world was serene, it had changed significantly. The sand now stretched for tens of kilometres before it reached the ocean, which he could see easily enough because the Earth was flatter than it had been yesterday. Much flatter. Beyond the sands the sea seemed to stretch on for hundreds of thousands of kilometres. R'lyeh was further away now than the Moon had been yesterday.

Returning to the villa, Peel found the previous occupants' car. He drove out, saw that the neighbouring house, which had only been a few dozen metres away the night before, was now a half dozen kilometres up the road.

"Fucking Cthulhu," he growled into the silent skies.

No one answered because he was alone. He always had been alone, so nothing had changed there.

He got behind the wheel and drove.

AFTERWORD
I'M LOOKING RIGHT AT *YOU*, H. P. LOVECRAFT

JACK DANN

Creative minds are uneven, and the best of fabrics have their dull spots.

H. P. Lovecraft, *Supernatural Horror in Literature*

Those bulbous eyes; the tight, condescending and pugnacious downturn of the mouth…and there you are, Mr Lovecraft, sitting atop my desk and staring blindly and perhaps malignantly at me. I'm looking (of course) at the World Fantasy Award Janeen Webb and I received for our Australian anthology *Dreaming Down-Under* in 1999. The award is a bust of H. P. Lovecraft created by the late, great artist and cartoonist Gahan Wilson. It is a brilliant caricature of one of the most influential creators of a body of work and a shared universe that has become known as 'Weird Fiction': a particular combination of science fiction and existential horror…horror that emphasises our utter helplessness and hopelessness in the face of a vast and pitiless universe. (And, yes, tentacles, gothic castles, and ichor can often be found!)

Lovecraft has influenced popular culture every bit as much as another 'genre' author: Philip K. Dick. You might not have read H. P. Lovecraft or even the many writers who have contributed to his shared universe (well, *you* have, of course, because you've just read this book!), but you have probably been affected by his worldview nevertheless…you've seen his influence in films as diverse as *Aliens, Dagon, Color Out of Space,* and *Ghostbusters;* directors such as John Carpenter, Stuart Gordon, Dan O'Bannon, Ridley Scott, and Guillermo del Toro (*Pan's Labyrinth*); television shows such as *Rod Serling's Night Gallery, Buffy the Vampire Slayer, Angel,* and the "Coon and Friends" trilogy of the animated series *South Park*; artists such as Jean 'Moebius' Giraud and H. R. Giger; rock bands such as *Metallica, Gunship,* and *Lovecraft*; games such as *Dungeons & Dragons* and Chaosium's *Call of Cthulhu*; and writers as diverse as Stephen King, Jorge Luis Borges, Robert Bloch, Michel Houellebecq, Fritz Leiber, Clive Barker, Ramsey Campbell, William S. Burroughs, Neil Gaiman, and Mike Mignola, the creator of *Hellboy.*

This specifically Australian volume (and its companion tomes) and the chilling and sometimes confronting stories contained herein are part of a continuing literary zeitgeist that adapts to changes in the general culture(s) and keeps reinventing itself (look up the term 'New Weird')…and these new stories from Down-Under are proof of that. Although it may be difficult to *define* a particular story as Lovecraftian, readers seem to know one when they see it. Whether it be gothic landscapes populated with slimy, tentacled, godlike creatures or subtle, contemporary tales of forbidden knowledge and the protagonist's subsequent and inevitable descent into insanity, Lovecraft and his philosophy of cosmic indifference (Cosmicism) is ever-present.

But there is an even darker side to this influential icon of the Weird, which brings me back to my desk and that sculpted bust with the bulbous eyes.

Right next to H. P. is another World Fantasy Award, this one dated 2017. It is a sculpture of a leafless and twisted tree sitting atop a polished wooden base; the thick metal branches seem to be supporting the disk of a full moon. It is the creation of artist Vincent Villafranca, who won a competition to redesign the award, which was sponsored by the World Fantasy Awards Administration. It is a beautiful conception…and a tangible response to a fundamental aesthetic conundrum: can you—should you—separate the artist from their art?

So, let's deal with the rather larger—in fact, enormous—pachyderm that is also sitting on my now metaphorical desk. Why did the WFA Administration decide to replace its award statue of Lovecraft (nicknamed the 'Howard') with a more generic (and inclusive!) representation of the collective genre of fantasy?

Because although Lovecraft is a venerated icon of pop culture, his important and influential legacy is immutably tainted. Lovecraft was an avowed and unregenerate racist, xenophobe, and anti-Semite.

One of the catalysts for rethinking how we approach, embrace, and deal with our genre past was a blog post by the Nigerian-American author Nnedi Okorafor, the first black person to win the World Fantasy Award for her novel *Who Fears Death* (2011).

She wrote:

> A friend of mine wanted to see my World Fantasy Award statuette. When he saw it, he was taken aback. He looked like he'd seen an ugly ghost.
>
> "That's a bust of LOVECRAFT!" he said.
>
> "Yeah, so?" I said. I had a bad feeling.
>
> Then he showed me a nice little poem that Mr. Lovecraft wrote about our people:
>
> *On the Creation of Niggers* (1912)
> by H. P. Lovecraft
>
> When, long ago, the gods created Earth
> In Jove's fair image Man was shaped at birth.
> The beasts for lesser parts were next designed;
> Yet were they too remote from humankind.
> To fill the gap, and join the rest to Man,
> Th'Olympian host conceiv'd a clever plan.
> A beast they wrought, in semi-human figure,
> Filled it with vice, and called the thing a Nigger.

Okorafor wanted to create a public discussion about the issue: "I want to face the history of this leg of literature rather than put it aside or bury it. If this is how some of the great minds of speculative fiction felt, then let's deal with that…as opposed to never mention it or explain it away."

She well and truly succeeded. That blog created a firestorm… and a lot of soul-searching.

And a new World Fantasy Award statue.[1]

And we're still left with the question of can we—should we—separate the artist from the art?

We can't erase the past, nor should we. In the social media flame-war that ensued after Okorafor's post and the decision to replace the 'Howard', emotions ran high. The Lovecraft biographer S. T. Joshi returned his World Fantasy Awards and wrote: "I was deeply disappointed with the decision of the World Fantasy Convention to discard the bust of H. P. Lovecraft as the emblem of the World Fantasy Award. The decision seems to me a craven yielding to the worst sort of political correctness and an explicit acceptance of the crude, ignorant, and tendentious slanders against Lovecraft propagated by a small but noisy band of agitators."

He made his case (in part) as follows:

"The World Fantasy Award is a purely literary award. It is awarded purely for literary excellence in the field of weird fiction. It commemorated Lovecraft because (a) it was created for the First World Fantasy Convention in 1975, held in Providence, R.I., which was essentially a Lovecraft convention, and (b) it acknowledges Lovecraft's literary greatness, both intrinsically and in terms of his influence. That is all that the award 'means.' The award says nothing about Lovecraft as a person (just as other awards in this and related fields say nothing about the person or character of the figures they are named for). The changing of the award is an implicit rejection of Lovecraft's literary status. It suggests that Lovecraft's racism is so heinous a character flaw that it negates the entirety of his literary achievement."

But Lovecraft's racism (and anti-Semitism) *was* a heinous character flaw. It was over the top even for the prejudices that existed at the

---

1 It should also be noted that author Daniel José Older separately initiated a year-long campaign and a petition to remove Lovecraft's association with the World Fantasy Award.

time. Although he married a Jew, he rationalised it by saying that she "no longer belonged to these mongrels."

Well, I'm one of those mongrels. I'm a Jew…at least I'm a cultural Jew.

Does that mean I should burn my H. P. Lovecraft library? Or send back my World Fantasy Awards?

I think Laura Miller got it right in an article she wrote for *Salon* in 2014 entitled 'It's Okay to Admit That H. P. Lovecraft Was a Racist': "Of all the people currently expressing their reservations about Lovecraft and the WFA trophy, I've yet to find one who's telling others to stop reading him. In fact, most of these critics continue to enjoy his work for its imaginative scope, gothic sensibility, and any number of other reasons. *The World Fantasy Award, however, is another matter. It's an expression of the values of a community, not a reader's private choice.*" (Italics mine)

I believe that H. P. Lovecraft was a very disturbed human being, filled with hatred and self-loathing; and it might well be that, as Laura Miller has suggested, "the power of his fiction derives from the hot mess of its creator's psyche. Like Poe, Lovecraft speaks to a gnarled, doomy and phobic corner of human nature that all of us visit from time to time."

In a blog post entitled 'Disturbed by Lovecraft, Whose Racism and Hate Weren't Merely a Product of His Times', Jason Sanford wrote: "Lovecraft's influence on dark fantasy and horror isn't going to disappear merely because people are aware of the troubling aspects of his life and writing. No, Lovecraft's legacy is secure because of all the authors and creators who took his ideas and ran with them."

And I would add that these authors—the authors in this *Cthulhu Deep Down Under* series—are part of that continuously reinvigorated zeitgeist that is expanding and reinterpreting the darkly powerful genre of Weird Fiction.

Oh, by the way: I'm not sending back the awards!

Postscript: As I write this, I am reminded that after employees staged a protest walk-out, Woody Allen's publisher axed his memoir *Apropos of Nothing*. The book was to go on sale next month. Whatever horror Allen might be as a person, I would have liked to be the one to decide whether or not to read his book.

Yeah, I think it's time to start separating the artist from the art.

BIOGRAPHIES
(IN ORDER OF APPEARANCE)

STEVE PROPOSCH, CHRISTOPHER SEQUEIRA & BRYCE STEVENS are the award-winning and multiple award-nominated co-editors and creators of the *Cthulhu Deep Down Under* concept. Their decision to collaborate on a rolling series of anthologies under the group moniker 'Horror Australis' reflects their belief that the most exciting opportunities for southern equatorial genre fiction lie ahead. Works by the members of this team in collaboration include the commissioning and editing of award-nominated material for *Cthulhu Land of the Long White Cloud,* and for *War of the Worlds: Battleground Australia* (Clan Destine Press), and the co-editing of both *Terror Australis: The Australian Horror and Fantasy Magazine* and *Bloodsongs* magazine. Their biggest project, *Caped Fear,* is due for release shortly after this present tome and will feature contributors of the greatest international renown in genre fiction.

STEVE SANTIAGO became a fan of all things weird at an early age and that attraction has never stopped. He graduated with a BA in Graphic Design and has over 20 years of experience working as a full-time graphic designer in California. The past few years he has been able to devote most of his time to illustrating and photoshopping covers and interior art for anthologies, magazines, ezines, CD covers, board game art and concept art for a Lovecraftian film. As a freelancer, Steve has created art/designs for clients from as far away as Australia, Germany, Hungary, U.K., and the Netherlands—www.illustrator-steve.com.

MICHAEL CUNLIFFE is a British artist and illustrator specialising in the dark and surreal. He lives with his family in North East England and spends his days making nightmares out of pixels and paint. You can find him online by searching for DreamsofEgo.

CAT RAMBO lives, writes, and teaches somewhere in the Pacific Northwest. Her 200+ fiction publications include stories in *Asimov's Science Fiction Magazine*, *Clarkesworld Magazine*, and *The Magazine of Fantasy and Science Fiction*. She is an Endeavour, Nebula, and World Fantasy Award nominee. Her most recent works include novel *Hearts of Tabat* (WordFire Press), story collections *Neither Here Nor There* (Hydra House Books) and Altered America (Plunkett Press), and novelette *Carpe Glitter* (Meerkat Press). Forthcoming works include the final novel of the Tabat Quartet, *Exiles of Tabat* (Wordfire Press) and the first of a space opera series, *You Sexy Thing* (Tor MacMillan). She is a two-term President of the Science Fiction & Fantasy Writers of America and continues to volunteer with the organization. Her Rambo Academy for Wayward Writers has provided inspiration and impetus for new fantasy and science fiction writers for over a decade.

ALF SIMPSON is a writer and editor currently living in Adelaide. When he's not removing words from manuscripts, he writes for an online magazine called *Breach*, where he specialises in stories about plant-monsters and extremely deep oceans. His piece 'Sub-Urban' won the 2018 Aurealis Award for best horror short story. Another of his stories, 'The Endless Below', was shortlisted for the same award in 2017.

CAT SPARKS is a multi-award-winning Australian author, editor and artist. Career highlights include a PhD in science fiction and climate fiction, five years as Fiction Editor of *Cosmos Magazine*, running Agog! Press, working as an archaeological dig photographer in Jordan, studying with Margaret Atwood, 78 published short stories, two collections – *The Bride Price* (2013) and *Dark Harvest* (2020) and a far future novel, *Lotus Blue*. She directed two speculative fiction festivals for WritingNSW and is a regular panellist & speaker at speculative fiction and other literary events.

STEVE PROPOSCH is publisher and editor of *Trouble* magazine (www.troublemag.com). Previously he has edited the seminal street press magazine *Large* and has had fiction, poetry and non-fiction published in various books, magazines and literary journals. Most recently his short story 'The Knowing Stone' appearing in the *Goldfields* (Accidental Publishing, 2019) anthology, released as part of the Bendigo Writers Festival. In collaboration with co-editors Bryce Stevens and Christopher Sequeira he has edited the three volume *Cthulhu Deep Down Under* anthology series and *Cthulhu Land of the Long White Cloud* (IFWG), as well as *War of the Worlds Battleground Australia* (Clan Destine Press) and *Caped Fear* (IFWG) featuring high profile internationally recognised authors.

ALAN BAXTER is a multi-award-winning British-Australian author of horror, supernatural thrillers, dark fantasy, and crime. He's also a martial arts expert, a whisky-soaked swear monkey, and dog lover. He lives on the beautiful south coast of NSW, Australia, where he lives with his wife, son, hound, and a bearded dragon called Fifi. He is the author of *The Alex Caine Series*, *Devouring Dark*, and *Hidden City*, novellas including *Manifest Recall* and *The Book Club*, and more than 80 short stories and two collected volumes; *Crow Shine* and *Served Cold*. With US bestselling author, David Wood he has co-authored the short horror novel, *Dark Rite*, action thrillers in *The Jake Crowley Adventures*, and *The Sam Aston Investigations*. Alan has been a seven-time finalist in the Aurealis Awards, a six-time finalist in the Australian Shadows Awards (three wins) and a seven-time finalist in the Ditmar Awards. www.warriorscribe.com. Twitter @AlanBaxter

JULIE DITRICH is a writer, editor and comics creator, and has a BA in Professional Writing (University of Canberra). In 2021, Julie became the first credited Australian woman comic book writer on *The Phantom* with the release of *The Adventure of the Dragon's Leg* through Frew Publications. Her past comics credits include *ElfQuest: WaveDancers* (co-writer), the *Dart* miniseries (co-writer), as well as 'Djiniri' in *SuperAustralians* (writer) for

Black House Comics and IFWG Publishing. Her short story credits include "The Adventure of the Walk-Out Wardrobe" in *Sherlock Holmes and Doctor Was Not* (IFWG Publishing).

Website: www.julieditrich.com

ACKNOWLEDGEMENT: I wish to thank Dr Christian Kenfield, Trauma Surgeon and Chair of the Trauma Committee (Vic), Royal Australasian College of Surgeons; Michelle Wassall from Michelle Wassall Fine Art Conservation; Carol Falconer; as well as Pateenah and Quentin Hordern for their generosity and time in helping me research "The Depiction".

STEVEN PAULSEN is an award-winning writer and editor. His bestselling dark fantasy children's book, *The Stray Cat*—illustrated by the Hugo and Oscar Award winning artist Shaun Tan—has seen print in English and foreign language editions. His short stories have appeared in *Terror Australis, Strange Fruit, Fantastic Worlds, The Cthulhu Cycle,* and *Dreaming Down-Under.* The best of his weird tales appear in *Shadows on the Wall* (IFWG Publishing Australia), which won best Collected Work for the Australian Horror Writers Association 2018.

He has also written extensively on genre fiction and conducted interviews for *Bloodsongs; Eidolon, Aurealis; Interzone; The Encyclopedia of Fantasy, Fantasy Annual; The St James Guide to Horror, Ghost and Gothic Writers; The Melbourne University Press Encyclopaedia of Australian Science Fiction and Fantasy; The Best of the Scream Factory* and *Other Spacetimes: Interviews with Speculative Fiction Writers,* and is a two-time winner of the William Atheling Jr. Award for literary criticism. www.stevenpaulsen.com.

MAURICE XANTHOS Like 'most other potential writers' Xanthos was influenced by Lovecraft stories and those promoted by August Derleth. The bulk of his "success" came from publication in *Terror Australis,* and for a short time after that with *EOD* and *Bloodsongs.* Other works include "Silence of the Trams", which you should be able to find on the internet, with *Spinetinglers,* and a co-authorship with Steven Paulsen, called "Severing Ties."

STEVE KILBEY was born in England in 1954. He migrated to Australia in 1957 and lived in Wollongong (where his story is set) until he was nine. In 1981 his band The Church broke through to international acclaim and have since sold well over one and half million records worldwide. He is a songwriter, singer and bass guitarist as well as a writer with a number of books out there alongside many articles and even more blogs. A fan of Lovecraft and all weird fiction (and fact), a big fan of Houdini, too, and his book *Magician Among the Spirits*. Kilbey believes we are all only the tiniest change of a channel (brought on by drug, dream, trauma, hypnosis, meditation, yoga, etc) away from a thousand other realities. some more real even than this reality (which is really unstable). He lives alone in Sydney with his one bonsai plant which doesn't even have a name.

JASON FISCHER Jason Fischer is a writer who lives near Adelaide, South Australia. He has won the Colin Thiele Literature Scholarship, an Aurealis Award and the Writers of the Future Contest. In Jason's jack-of-all-trades writing career he has worked on comics, apps, television, short stories, novellas and novels. Jason also facilitates writing workshops, is an enthusiastic mentor, and loves anything to do with the written or spoken word. He also has a passion for godawful puns, and is known to sing karaoke until the small hours.

DAVID CONYERS David Conyers is a science fiction author and editor living in Adelaide, South Australia. He completed a degree in engineering from the University of Melbourne, and today works as a tender writer in the construction industry.

David has published over fifty science fiction and horror short stories, won several awards for his writing, and edited five anthologies including one of the first fiction collections to explore the concepts of exoplanets, *Extreme Planets*. For over a decade he was the Arts and General Editor and reviewer for *Albedo One* magazine where he interviewed many top science fiction writers including Iain M. Banks, Greg Egan and Will McIntosh.

His extensive portfolio of Cthulhu Mythos fiction included his popular Harrison Peel espionage versus the Elder Gods series, and for more than a decade was a prolific contributor to the Call of Cthulhu tabletop role-playing game.

Today David writes contemporary thriller fiction novels under a pseudonym. www.david-conyers.com.

JACK DANN has written or edited over seventy-five books, including the international bestseller *The Memory Cathedral*, *The Rebel*, *The Silent*, and *The Man Who Melted*. He has won many awards including the Nebula Award, the World Fantasy Award, the Aurealis Award, and the Shirley Jackson Award.

He is the co-editor, with Janeen Webb, of *Dreaming Down-Under*, which won the World Fantasy Award, and the editor of the sequel *Dreaming Again*, and *Dreaming in the Dark*, which won the World Fantasy Award in 2017. Dr. Dann is an Adjunct Senior Research Fellow in the School of Communication and Arts at the University of Queensland. His latest novel is *Shadows in the Stone*. Kim Stanley Robinson called it "such a complete world that Italian history no longer seems comprehensible without his cosmic battle of spiritual entities behind and within every historical actor and event." Forthcoming is a Centipede Press *Masters of Science Fiction* volume.

J. (JOHANNES AKA JAN) SCHERPENHUIZEN is an academic, writer of fiction, artist, editor and publisher. His comics, illustrations and prose pieces have appeared in Australia and the United States. As well as collaborating with other talents, he has also acted as both writer and illustrator, notably on the gritty horror graphic novel *The Time of the Wolves*. As an editor and manuscript appraiser he discovered a number of professional authors who have credited him with playing a significant role in helping to establish their careers. Jan's recent work includes contributing illustrations and a short story to the well-received *Sherlock Holmes: The Australian Casebook*, and illustrations for the hit graphic novel *SuperAustralians*. His short story 'The Island in the Swamp' was published in *Cthulhu Deep Down Under Volume 2*. Discover more about Jan's activities as a manuscript assessor and writing mentor, etc. at www.janscreactive.com. His illustrations can be viewed at www.jscherpenhuizenillustrator.com.